GUARDIAN PROTOCOL

A CYRUS JENNINGS FBI THRILLER
BOOK 4

ALEX PARMAN

waking moments bathed in the blue glow of a bank of monitors moved past the window. Then passed back the other way. Back and forth. Pacing. Impatiently. At least Misty had finally developed the good sense to wait until the meeting adjourned rather than draw attention to herself by busting in late. Again.

She was slowly learning.

Once the SAC released them, Cyrus pushed through the herd.

In the hall, she snagged his shirt sleeve then tugged him toward a corner. "I have a problem."

"No argument here." His grin faded at her scowl. "What's going on?"

"You know the secure chat system I use to talk to my... friends?"

The first time he'd met Misty, she'd used that system to request a dossier on a bad dude. For all their detail, the resulting docs could've been pulled right off the Bureau's servers. Hard to forget.

"The thought of you using it keeps me up nights."

"My watch got pinged by one of my VMs this morning."

Virtual Machines. She spun them up to cover her tracks when she delved into vigilantism, deleting each when she was finished with her work so no one could track her Internet or computing history. Cyrus sent vibrations of hope to the universe that she wasn't back to her old games.

"Your watch?"

"I have a trigger set up so incoming messages ping my watch with an alert."

"So you can log into your secure chat to get the message."

"Exactly. This morning at five-thirty, I got the alert. I logged in from the refuge—"

The *refuge*. Her bat cave.

"Skip to the message, Misty."

"My sister is missing."

Cyrus's mouth gaped. "Your... sister?"

"A friend of hers reached out. Said he hasn't heard from her since last week. Anastasia told him if she ever went dark for more than five days, he should send me a message."

"Okay, rewind further." He cast glances over each shoulder for prying ears. "You have a fucking sister?"

"Yes. Long story."

"Well, I imagine so. But we'll come back to all that because you look like you've seen a specter."

"She's an investigative reporter. Was working on something long form. I can't reach her, Cyrus."

He folded his arms across his chest, thankful he'd left his suit jacket hanging on the chair in his office. "Okay. What else did this friend know? When was the last time you talked to...?"

"Anastasia. Anna. About a year ago."

That made him feel a little better about not knowing Misty had a sister.

"So, you're estranged?"

4

"That's kind of personal."

"If you want my help, that sentiment isn't gonna fly."

Misty sighed. "We aren't estranged. You're missing a lot of background, but I don't think any of that is relevant."

"You never know what ends up being relevant. Haven't you learned that by now? Tell me what you know."

"My sister and I had this back door communication plan set up in case our past came back to haunt us. Do you really want to know more than that?"

Sometimes it was hard to discern between what he did and did not want to know, especially where Misty was concerned.

"Did Anastasia's friend report her missing? Call the police?"

Misty shook her head. "She told him to come directly to me."

"Does this friend have a name?"

"I don't ask for peoples' IDs when I'm on the chat."

"Your sister ever mention this friend?"

"No. But like I said, we haven't talked since my grandfather died a year ago."

Through the window, he saw the SAC was still in the conference room. Cyrus considered Misty for a few beats then turned toward the door. "Wait here."

"Whoa!" she snagged his shirtsleeve. "What are you doing?"

"Talking to Blake."

Her ginger curls bounced as she twisted her head. "No. No way. This is my family. My problem."

Cyrus stopped and wheeled on her. "Your family, yes. But your problem is my problem. Why did you come to me if you didn't want help?"

A moment of silence passed. She chewed her lower lip.

"I'm an FBI agent. We investigate kidnappings."

"It isn't going to work, Cyrus. He won't help."

"Why not?"

"She's a reporter. The story she was working on involved Sam Lockhart's new enterprise."

Cyrus clenched his teeth.

Lockhart. The One Who Got Away.

An army of lawyers had leveraged the prick's political connections and carefully manufactured plausible deniability. The SOB had strolled out of the prosecutor's office wearing a grin that made the front cover of the local rag.

The grin was branded onto Cyrus's brain. And the loss was branded on his personnel file. Blake wouldn't want to touch this.

"Dammit."

Misty patted his shoulder. "That's what I mean. He isn't going to help."

Like she'd read his mind. He swore sometimes she could.

But despite losing Lockhart, Cyrus had collected

CHAPTER 1

Well, aren't you just full of vim and vigor this morning?

Cyrus Jennings heard his mama's voice in his head as clear as he heard the Special Agent in Charge droning on at the front of the conference room. Monday morning briefing was always three parts over-worked agents bitching about interagency obstructions and one part SAC lecture about resilience or persis-tence or the toxic positivity meme of the day. Business as usual. So while Mama's intrusion into his thoughts surprised him a little, her sarcasm was on point. Glancing around the room, Cyrus saw little vim and even less vigor from his peers.

He couldn't blame them. They were playing catchup on every front. Despite the best technical tools and more task forces than you could shake a stick at, the bad guys—from cartels and militias to lone wolf serial killers—always stayed one step ahead.

"Jennings?" SAC Sean Blake repeated with an obviously fake cough.

Cyrus shuffled a stack of papers and stifled the urge to glance at the empty seat beside him.

"With the help of Misty Daniels"—who couldn't be bothered to show up on time—"we arrested Carmen Dawson on Friday for the hack of RMF Distribution." A recent ransomware attack targeting the truck-tracking system of the food service company had brought Denver and Boulder restaurants to a screeching halt. The hacker had demanded twenty-five million from the company in exchange for control of their system. "We believe he acted alone, and my team is putting together the package to send to the US Attorney. Except for a few months' rent and seventy-five thousand the dipshit spent on a Corvette, the money is frozen and will be recovered."

Blake nodded his approval. "Pass my congratulations to Miss Daniels. We'll make a real fed of her yet."

Keep dreaming.

Even with—or maybe because of—the military service in her rearview, Misty Daniels was not one to march in step with anyone else, especially a class of green Bureau recruits. She would be out of there the moment the court order expired.

As the remaining department heads ran through their updates, a flash of movement in the hallway caught his attention. Auburn curls and the pale, vampiric complexion of a woman who spent all her some capital of his own. His approach was at times problematic, but he got the job done, and his relationship with Sean Blake was on steadier footing than with Denver's prior SAC.

On the other side of the door, the boss tapped his pencil a few times on the edge of the table then continued his scribblings on a legal pad. Blake was old school like that.

Maybe Cyrus could use that.

"Screw it. Wait here." He turned toward the door.

"Seriously?"

Without turning, he said, "Don't take it the wrong way, but I'm your boss. I carry the badge. I'll call for you when I need you."

Ten minutes later, he needed her.

Blake sat back in his chair then crossed one leg over the other when Misty swung the door open. Although he gestured toward the chair opposite Cyrus, he didn't wait for her to sit.

"Your boss is trying to trade favors with me."

"What kind of favors?"

Cyrus froze.

"The kind that interest me. Let that suffice for now. What's the deal with your sister?"

As Cyrus quietly released the breath he was holding, Misty caught Blake up, omitting the piece about her secure communication channel. Smart. If Blake even suspected she was up to her old tricks, it wouldn't wash.

7

"Any drug history?"

"Nope. Cleaner than a new penny. Never touched the stuff, and for good reason."

"What's that?"

"Family problems. Can we leave it at that?"

Cyrus's interest piqued.

"For now, I'll take your word for it. Let me explain my hesitancy." Blake leaned forward until they were at eye level. "I don't like Sam Lockhart. Can't stand the sound of his name. I don't know him personally, but I've read Cyrus's file on the Sutton fiasco, and this PR campaign he's running like some kind of Hollywood starlet on Late Night annoys me on principle. But as much as I trust my agents, the conflict of interest is enough for me to send the two of you packing. I like that even less."

"I understand." Misty pushed back from the table then stood.

Blake pointed at the chair. "I wasn't finished, Daniels."

Misty cast a glance in Cyrus's direction then plopped back down. She wasn't hard to read. Had the chastising come from him, she'd have scowled, but she knew better than to screw with the SAC unless she wanted a return to trip to the judge who'd ordered her into service.

"As I was saying, I usually wouldn't touch this with a machete duct taped to a ten-foot pole, but Cyrus made an interesting point."

"What was that, sir?"

"You're going to do this one way or another. Go off on your own, and you'll get into trouble. Would you say he paints an accurate portrait?"

The nodes in Misty's jaw bulged. "Respectfully, sir, that's absolutely the case."

"Right. And if I ordered you to stand down and let the locals handle missing persons cases until we determined it was a kidnapping, you'd just ignore me, judge-be-damned."

To her credit, she mulled that one over.

To her discredit, she answered. "She's my sister, sir. We don't talk much because there's a history. But it's not a problem between us. It's a family thing."

Cyrus's curiosity threatened to blow his brains out through his ears.

Blake nodded. "I run a clean shop. I can't have agents—nor their court-ordered analysts—going rogue. Your work on the RMF Distribution case bought you some latitude, so I'm willing to sanction this, provided you agree to my terms. Here's how this is going to work. Neither of you goes near Sam Lockhart. You so much as order a pizza from a distant cousin of his you didn't know worked at Domino's, and I'll yank you so fast your neck will throb. Do you understand?"

Misty nodded.

Cyrus didn't bother.

"Good. Since your sister's a reporter, I'd start with her editor. Go have a chat. But remember—despite your contributions to the Dora Lassiter case, you are not a field agent. You're a contractor. Cyrus wears the badge. He takes the lead. You march behind him in lockstep."

"Sounds good, sir. There is one problem."

"I'm unsurprised. Shoot."

"Her friend says she was returning to Lockhart Public Security's compound the day she disappeared."

Blake scratched his chin. "Tell you what. I'll look up the compound on my maps app. If it's not on a private road, I'll make some calls, get you traffic cam access."

"Thank you, sir." She rose.

"Misty?"

"Yes, sir?"

He raised a finger. "No hacking. Stay out of Lockhart's servers. Cyrus, report to me every twenty-fours."

When the door's latch engaged behind them, Misty sighed. "That was... more than I expected."

Cyrus stopped halfway up the corridor. "You have a fucking sister?"

CHAPTER 2

Sam Lockhart suspected Alex Riddle was the kind who sweated profusely when he got off on a tangent. Riddle wore the big-toothed grin that had millions of Twitch and YouTube viewers tuning in. It was a love based on mutual vitriol for the political Left and, although Lockhart knew the political parties were just panderers who rile up their bases over stupid social issues, he'd need to press on both sides. So Riddle served Sam's purposes, for now.

Lockhart returned the smile as Riddle continued his incessant prattling.

"The way I hear it, gun crime is down in all three states where your guys have shown up. Shown up and *saved the day,* I might add. Congressmen and senators on the Hill are touting your company as the private-sector solution to problems the government can't solve. The head of the Senate is even calling you," Riddle raised a sheet of paper, a prop used for a dramatic pause, "the kind of patriot the country needs if the United States is going to take the load off the deficit and national debt. How would you respond to that?"

And the softballs kept coming.

"He got the patriot part right, but I steer away from the politics of it all, Alex. Lockhart Public Security isn't here to score political points. We aren't interested in tribal culture, and we don't want to make enemies on either side of the aisle. The violence is out of control, but this great country was founded on principles like the Second Amendment. Now, I know that isn't the kind of thing the Left likes to hear, and again, I'm not trying to make enemies of anyone. But America has a serious gun violence problem. So we have to ask ourselves, how do we support the Constitution while keeping our children safe?"

Riddle's grin widened. "Enter LPS, right?"

"Enter LPS. But we're not cowboys. Above all, Lockhart Public Security supports our governments, federal and local, in their role to protect our citizens. In areas where elected representatives have chosen a regulatory approach—"

Riddle interrupted. "By limiting citizens' Second Amendment rights."

"Suffice it to say, LPS won't operate in places where it's illegal for civilians to carry guns. While we hope our track record will convince more state legislatures to take up civil debate about how LPS can help keep our citizens safe, we'll work in areas where we're welcomed, where citizens are free to defend themselves, their families, and their communities. And we'll bring our training and predictive modeling used to isolate potential hot spots with us."

"Say more about this modeling."

"I'm happy to. Using publicly available data from sources like social media, we'll identify potential threats and share what we find with local law enforcement. Our search algorithms are top-notch, designed to work with our revolutionary AI model to root out potential criminals before they act. We all know how slow government responses can be."

"Yes, we do!" Riddle agreed with too much enthusiasm. "If our history has shown anything, it's that waiting around for the government to do what's right is like expecting a bear to stay away from meat spitted over your campfire."

Sam wasn't sure his attempt to pander to his base came off. After all, the prick went to Harvard back when he used his real name. He wondered how many people in his Patriotism-and-Preparedness crowd knew that little tidbit.

"That's why we'll offer our services to companies, churches, and private schools we've identified as potential targets."

"Only private schools?"

"We aren't out for government money. But we're happy to consult with local law enforcement and, as I said before, share intelligence divined from our modeling."

"Oh," Riddle wagged a finger, "but that's not what happened at Lincoln High in Missouri, was it?"

"It's true. Lincoln was a public school. We identified a potential threat, shared it with the local cops, then sent a couple of our finest to monitor the situation. I wanted to see if the police showed. They didn't. But we got lucky. Right place, right time."

"You're being modest, Mister Lockhart. What you did was spot a manifesto on social media, send one of your guys out to watch the school on your own dime, then took the culprit down the second the rifle came off his back."

The last thing Lockhart needed was for this talking head to paint a picture of some renegade, some superior rich-guy-vigilante taking the law into his own hands for the Left to lambaste.

"After reporting it to the local PD, Alex. We hope local governments will see that as an example of how private and public sector organizations can combine their resources to thwart violent crime before it happens. In a perfect world, the shooter would've survived, but a few hundred young people did."

"Of course!" Riddle barked. "It's not like you go around looking for people to whack. Everyone knows better."

Not everyone, dipshit. He needed to redirect before the nut job got off on another tirade.

"The proof is in the numbers. Since our work became public, shootings are down by ninety percent in those states."

"And what about the argument on the Left, that it's the government's job to enforce the laws, to control who gets guns and limit the discharging of weapons in public spaces to the police trained to handle them?"

"Again, the proof is in the numbers. In 2022 alone, the FBI reported fifty-six police officer-involved accidental deaths, though the way the bureau collects its information, the number is probably much higher. In the events handled by Lockhart Public Security, despite crowds of people in all three locations, no civilians were harmed—only the shooters. My people are military veterans well-trained in the use of firearms, and they recertify on our range monthly. They are licensed to carry weapons in every state where we operate, whether required or not."

Alex Riddle took the cue. "Since you brought up your soldiers, let's talk a little about that. Seems to me your company is taking another load off the government's hands."

Lockhart waved his hands in from of him. "We're not trying to take over for the federal government, but we love our veterans, and we value their service to our country. That's why we hire vets where we can."

"Say more. Talk about Colorado Springs."

As if he wasn't going to.

"LPS bought two facilities in Colorado to house our

base of operations. We provide medical and mental health counseling to all the vets we bring aboard to ensure they're field ready. And we leverage the specialty training they received in the Army, Navy, Air Force, Marines, and National Guard. Administrators, chaplains, even the doctors who run the hospital facilities are all ex-military."

"So, you're not just selling security, you're actually employing veterans who've returned from the battle-field." He didn't wait for a reply. "Tell me, Mister Lockhart, how many homeless veterans have you taken off the streets?"

"I don't have the exact number with me, Alex."

Riddle raised another sheet of paper. "According to data your company provided, fifty-four vets have been pulled off the streets and out of tent cities. And we all know where those tent cities are. You're serving our boys. Giving them a hand up instead of handouts. You should be proud."

"I only hope we can continue to expand the family," Lockhart said.

"Forgive me for bringing it up, but I heard one of that *family* passed recently. Suicide is a scourge on our country too, isn't it?"

Bastard. Lockhart could only blame himself. Interview with an ego, and you can forget about burying topics you want to avoid.

"Yes." He twisted his head slowly from side to side. "A sad day for us all. But that soldier—our brother—

stands as an example. Sometimes the mental wounds are much deeper than the physical, and we hope to learn from what happened so the rest of our LPS family thrives. We provide trauma counseling to anyone serving Lockhart Public Security."

Alex flashed his poisonous smile again. "And they don't have to wait in line at the VA. That's the best we can hope for our American heroes. Thanks for coming to speak with us, Sam."

One of Riddle's guys pulled the mic off Sam's collar then Alex offered his hand. "That was pure gold, Mister Lockhart."

Back to "Mister Lockhart." Sam could've punched him in the throat for dropping that fucking hellfire missile about the suicide.

"I hope you guys change the way the government does business. Come back in a few months and follow up with us, would you?"

"Of course." He grasped the hand. His phone buzzed. He checked the display.

Tom Rhymer.

He thumbed the green circle. "What's the latest on the reporter?"

"Nothing new to report. The guys are still outside her apartment building and the paper."

"Any murmurings at the facility?"

"It's quiet. I was with her at all times. Any new orders? Want us to check the apartment?"

"Are the lights still out?"

"Roger."

"Don't do anything stupid. We're at a pivotal place, and I don't need controversy. Watch and listen."

"And if she appears?"

"Same orders. Offer comfort for silence."

"And if she refuses?"

"Same fucking orders, Tom. Did I stutter?" Silence ensued, and Sam gathered his wits. "If she refuses, return to LPS, and let the guys from Tactical have a talk with her."

"Yes, sir."

"Tom, cut the sir shit."

"Roger that."

"Find her. Lock it down."

He ended the call without waiting for a reply.

CHAPTER 3

The Post's lobby was a sprawling, open space with high ceilings and marble floors. Photographs and artwork displaying the newspaper's history adorned the walls, and a giant newsstand where visitors could buy newspapers and magazines stood to one side.

Cyrus and Misty lingered with their arms folded across their chests, eyeing black and white posters on one wall while they waited.

"Why didn't you tell me you had a sister?"

"Guess it just didn't come up."

"That or you don't trust me enough to tell me about your family."

Misty's head snapped up. "All I know about *your* family is that your parents are alive, crossing the country in an RV, and that you don't talk to them often. Why are you up my ass?"

"Cool your jets. It's relevant now, considering why we're here."

"Fair enough. What would you like to know?"

Cyrus interpreted this as more of a deflection than a query. But Misty had apparently forgotten what Cyrus did for a living. Or maybe she overestimated her ability to avoid answering.

"Where did the two of you grow up?"

"West Virginia."

This time, it was his head that came around.

She matched his gaze. "What? You surprised?"

"Shit yes. Where's the accent?"

Her response came in a mountain drawl. "What, would you expect me to talk more like the-yiss?"

"No, that sounds like where I'm from. How long did it take you to kill the accent?"

"How long did it take you, Cyrus?"

His left eyebrow climbed toward the sky. "We're not talking about me right now."

"Fine. We grew up in West Virginia. She's two years younger, but our school friends called us the twins because, despite our age differences, we both had wide-set eyes and slightly upturned noses. A high school teacher once told her that, if our hair hadn't been different colors, she wouldn't have been able to tell us apart. Our mother died in childbirth with her. Our dad... is a cop."

"Is? So he's still alive?"

"Unfortunately."

He blinked once. Twice. A third time.

Misty pivoted. "Anna's the curious type. Been that way since she could talk. You know how kids ask, *Why? Why? Why?*"

"Sure."

"Well, let's just say she never stopped at *why*. She's always been precocious. Always pressing. Looking for context."

"And she's a reporter. Sounds like the right line of work."

"Yeah, no shit. Despite my begging her to stay out of it."

"When's the last time you talked to her?" He might have already asked that one, but maybe she'd give a different answer.

Misty hesitated, her gaze drifting to a snapshot of a former editor of the *Post*. The mutterings of the crowd in the giant lobby swelled in his ears while Cyrus waited for a response.

She strolled toward the reception counter. "I already told you. About a year ago. This really bothers you, doesn't it?"

You're treating her like a suspect. Maybe she had a reason for holding out. Don't be a dick

He followed. "Well, I thought we were..."

She stopped then faced him. "What? Like family?"

"Well—"

"Agent Jennings?" They turned to find a tall, White guy in beige slacks with a matching tie drawn up tight. His bald dome reflected the overhead lighting. He offered a thick hand. Cyrus shook it. "I'm Will Bresnan. Sorry for all the bother, but we've had... issues. Come on up."

The FBI investigated threats against newspapers with regularity, and Cyrus could imagine the challenges.

In the elevators, Misty lingered behind the two men, and Cyrus broke the uncomfortable silence. "Worked here long?"

"A few years." Something in his sideways smile didn't quite come off, like maybe it'd been more than a few years, but it wasn't like newspaper editors grew on trees in a world gone digital.

The doors slid open to the sound of a bell. After Bresnan stepped off, he gestured down the hall. "This way."

They strolled along a row of cubicles filled with older men wearing wrinkled ties and younger women in designer t-shirts and slacks until they reached Bresnan's office. He ushered them inside then closed the door behind them. As he circled the cluttered desk, he offered the chairs across from his.

Once he eased into his seat with a sigh, he said, "How can I help the bureau?"

Cyrus hadn't been specific when he'd called ahead. He'd always taught his students to provide the least information possible to people they planned to question.

"We're looking into the possible kidnapping of one of your reporters."

That was misleading, but the bureau didn't handle simple missing persons cases unless there was a federal interest, like a politician's disappearance. The editor might know that. Probably would.

Bresnan's eyes flared. "One of mine? I'm not missing anybody."

Cyrus and Misty shared a look.

"Who're you looking for, exactly?"

"Anastasia Clark."

Upon hearing Misty answer, Cyrus recalled that Misty's given name had been Joanna Reeves.

Where had 'Clark' come from? If Clark was her married name, the spouse would be raising hell...unless they were responsible for it? Or simply a name change?

The possibilities were myriad, so he shoved the thought away.

"Oh." Bresnan dropped a palm down on his desk. "Her."

It was a tribute to Misty's patience she didn't respond to the unmistakable way he'd said it, like Anastasia was a troublesome child.

Cyrus didn't give her long to consider a response. "You don't sound concerned."

"Why would I be? I fired her three days ago."

That pulled Misty's trigger. "Fired her? Why?"

Will eyed her up and down. "Is that relevant?"

"You're damn—"

Cyrus raised two fingers, cutting her off.

"It might be."

The editor's tone changed. "I fired her for her tendency to disappear for days on end while leaving me out of the loop."

"So, it's habitual?"

He waved a hand. "To say the least. Anna does what Anna wants. I sent her off to do a puff piece on Lockhart Public Security. A couple-thousand words, tops. But she's like a dog with a bone, always looking for a conspiracy."

"Why a puff piece?"

"A favor for a friend. We served overseas. Told me what Lockhart was trying to do and, since he works at LPS, he makes a good source. If the guy can help vets and quell the mass killings, it's worth talking about."

"You really think one outfit can stop gun violence?"

"No. That's why I said quell. This country has more guns than people. Domestic violence, gang shootings. Good luck. But if you make a disgruntled former employee think twice, show a political nutjob with bad intentions a show of force somewhere he'd planned to make trouble, I say go for it."

Cyrus gaze shifted to a frame on a bookshelf over one of Bresnan's shoulders.

Misty must've noticed because she interpreted what she saw there. "Silver Star. So, you saw combat."

He nodded. "Iraq. Came to work here when I got out."

"Thank you for your service," Cyrus said. "So, when was the last time you saw your reporter?"

"As I said, she's not my reporter anymore. Although it wasn't ideal, I had to do it over voice mail." He flashed both palms. "I know, it doesn't sound very nice. But when you can't get someone to pick up the phone for three days in a row, someone who has a tendency to go dark when they feel like it..."

Misty sounded off. "Wasn't she up for a Pulitzer a while back? Something about bank fraud? Why would you fire someone like that when she could be chasing leads?"

Bresnan's face tensed like he'd squint at her, but the expression melted.

"She didn't win the Pulitzer. Maybe that would've bought her a bit more latitude, but honestly? I'd have probably fired her anyway. It's a real shame. She's a good reporter, but she doesn't know when to let go. Our industry is in the shitter. News printed on paper is worthless when you can read whatever you want on your phone... for free. We can't have people who go off on tangents and drop three articles per month when we have a website to fill. It's not personal, just business. I'm sure someone with her talents will land somewhere they can afford her approach."

Cyrus interjected before Misty could get on a roll.

"So, you never actually said when you last spoke to her?"

"Tuesday, week before last."

"And you fired her by voice mail, when?" Misty snapped. It seemed she'd picked up his tactic about asking questions twice to see if the interviewee expanded on their answers or lied.

Cyrus drew a slow breath of the stale air through his nostrils.

"Like I said. Friday." As if she was dense, he added, "Three days ago."

Cyrus slapped his legs with both palms then rose. "Well, I think that'll do for now. Thanks for your help."

"Happy to oblige." He stood. "You know, now that you've told me about Anna, we did have a related problem here a couple weeks ago."

Misty turned. "Problem?"

"Well, it was a family thing, so I didn't know if I should get into it."

That straightened Misty's spine. Her lips whitened, but she didn't speak.

Cyrus pressed. "What kind of family thing?"

"Her father showed up in the lobby. I think they were estranged. Later, I realized that, even though her last name is Clark, his wasn't. But I knew Anna had never been married. Kind of interesting, right? I still wonder what's up with that." He waved a hand. "But inquisitive minds are a dime-a-dozen in this business. I'm no different."

Aw, shucks. Cyrus took a deep breath.

Misty's face was an ivory sheet. "What happened?"

"One of the receptionists in the front lobby called up. I told her I hadn't heard from Anna. The guy started barking. Accusing her of lying. I went down to the lobby, and he got in my face. Of course, when you've seen combat, that kind of thing doesn't faze you. I told him to leave before I had to call security. He slapped a card down on the desk and ordered us to give it to his daughter." Will reached into a drawer behind his desk then flicked a business card clasped between two fingers toward Cyrus. "Imagine my surprise when I saw the badge emblazoned there."

"Why is that a surprise?" Cyrus asked.

"Because the prick smelled like liquor. His eyes were red. He had that psycho look. You know the one."

"I do."

"It only occurs to me now, because we've spoken, that this might be a good lead for you to follow. Now I'm kind of worried."

Misty clenched her fists then snatched the card from the editor's hand.

Cyrus nodded as Misty pocketed it. "Thanks for the info. We'll look into it."

"Would you mind keeping me in the loop? It sucks I had to let her go, but like I said, it wasn't personal. I actually like her. I hope nothing bad has happened."

Cyrus shook his offered hand. "I'm sure she'll turn

up." He wasn't sure of anything. "We'll see ourselves out."

Misty fell in behind him as he beelined for the elevators. "You ever heard that much bullshit in your life?"

Cyrus didn't answer until they were secure in the metal box. "What part of *Cyrus takes the lead* didn't you understand? Were you *trying* to put him on the defensive?"

"I'm trying to find my sister." She raised both hands, much like Bresnan had in his office. "My bad, chief. I get it. You're the one with the badge." Her arms dropped.

Her passive-aggressive lamenting spoke volumes. Not just about how emotions were getting the better of the usually stoic Misty Daniels, but how not having a badge made her less-than.

He needed her to focus. "Tell me how Bresnan is full of shit."

Misty leaned against the metal rail inside the elevator. "His reporter disappears after her alcoholic father shows up raising hell, and it isn't the first thing he mentions? He doesn't call anyone? Instead, he fucking fires her?" The elevator bell rang, the doors parted, and Misty turned her body to squeeze out before they opened fully. She marched across the lobby. "Let's go to my place. I wanna view that traffic cam footage Blake promised us in my own space. Maybe do some digging."

Cyrus deliberated. He'd scheduled lunch with Marsha, but that'd been before he found out Misty's sister was missing. Hell, that she even had a sister. He had the distinct impression the digging she wanted to do went beyond tracking her sister's movements. It was about her father, the cop she'd just described as an alcoholic who'd shown up in a rage, looking for his daughter.

He sent a text and canceled the lunch but promised to drag Misty to the apartment that night for the dinner they'd scheduled with her. Cyrus needed to keep her in sight.

CHAPTER 4

Server fans sucked energy from the racks towering on the right-hand-side of her work area. Cyrus scanned the blades' blinking lights from top-to-bottom, recalling Misty frying most of her infrastructure when the feds raided her earlier that year. The cage, named for the back wall of wired mesh from which countless monitors hung, towered over long metal desktops.

"You replaced all your servers."

"I did." She slid into a chair then rolled it across the smooth concrete toward one of three keyboards.

"Looks pretty expensive. Tell me you aren't moonlighting again while you're working for the bureau."

She adopted a formal tone and her shoulders jostled as she spoke. "I need side hustles to maintain the standard of living to which I've become accustomed."

"I wondered how you footed the new ride."

Cyrus had gaped when he'd seen her pull up in a late-model S-class two weeks earlier.

She ignored him. "The solar keeps the electricity bill low enough to keep the power company off my back, but I still have to pay the difference."

"Wouldn't be a problem if you were running fewer servers."

She cast him a wary gander. "I've left room for growth, but thanks for the infrastructural assessment, fed-boy."

"How big is this freaking operation?"

She spun the chair, leveled her gaze. "Cyrus, if you'd care to recall, the work I do here isn't illegal. I'm a security consultant. I test network infrastructure for gaps, and I'm paid well to do it. I automate everything, setup alerts, then spend the vast majority of my time at the bureau, even if I show up late for a meeting or two. Meetings I'm not required to attend, for all Blake's snarky shit."

"The reminder helps. It was a trying time." A time he'd shown up with the alphabet soup of law enforcement to raid her refuge because he hadn't known it was the target until the armored van's doors opened.

She spun the chair back toward the table then smashed a space bar. A monitor flickered to life. "Trust is a two-way street."

"Speaking of which, how old is your sister? Could we be friends? Is she into Star Wars?"

Misty chuckled. "She's two years younger. Smart

as a whip. Tough. Imagine me without the military background, if you can. That's Jolene."

"Jolene?"

She shook her head as if to clear cobwebs. "Anastasia."

Cyrus mused. Misty's birthname had been Joanna Reeves.

Joanna. Jolene. Maybe her parents weren't creative types. But outside of Russia, Anastasia wasn't common. Made sense Jolene Reeves would choose that one if she wanted to cover her tracks. But cover them from who? A drunk dad?

Misty broke his daydream. "SAC got us the traffic cam footage. Tell you what, Blake is no joke. How do you think he gets the locals to play ball?"

"By swinging his—"

"Dick around?" Misty asked.

"*Weight.* I was going to say *weight.*"

She barked laughter. "Sure you were. C'mon man, I was in the Army."

"What, exactly, did you do in the army?"

She raised her hand from a mouse then swung around again. "You mean you don't know?"

"How would I?"

Her head tilted the slightest bit. "You trying to convince me you didn't pull my background when the judge dropped me in your lap?"

"It was me who worked out the deal with the SAC so you could be dropped into my lap, Misty."

She pushed out her bottom lip. "Yeah. True. But you're evading the question."

"I'm not. I didn't investigate you. Hell, Byron sent you. Can you imagine a better reference?"

The death of his previous analyst carved many hollows in his chest and, while Cyrus wouldn't dream of invoking his name in vein, what he'd said was true. Byron Hawkins had been a man of character, and his word was gold.

"Besides, I saw how you comported yourself the day we met. You reeked of spook. Would I have found anything in your file?"

She'd gotten the drop on him at a ghost town west of Denver, thrown a sack over his head, shoved earplugs into his hands, then drove him in his own F-150 to the place where he now stood.

Oh, the good old days.

She was staring at him.

"But you had to be curious. You're a fed."

"And you're my partner."

"If I was your partner, I'd be wearing a badge instead of walking behind you."

There it was again, and it was time to shut the shit down. "I taught at Quantico. You'd be following my lead even *if* you had a badge."

"The ego lives!" Misty chuckled then spun back toward the desk. She spoke while she typed, and it reminded Cyrus of the way Byron split his brain in the same way. "Let's not be contentious. I have good reasons for not discussing my past. But I'll satiate your curiosity a little.

"You, no doubt, intuited my slip when I mentioned Jolene. So, yes, she changed her name, too." A video window popped up. Misty rolled to the next station, and her fingers shredded keys. "And she had good reason." Text streamed down the second monitor's screen.

"That your hacker chat?"

"Yeah. I'm pulling a deck."

A deck was a profile on a person or entity of interest. What the feds might call a dossier.

This was work the bureau wouldn't approve, but Cyrus decided to reach for a little context before going postal.

"A deck on what?"

"The new Lockhart place."

"You're not hacking the Lockhart place. We're looking for your sister."

Her reply came in a disinterested tone. "I'm not hacking anything. Just getting some background."

He detected subterfuge. Upon hearing her father had shown up at the *Post*, Misty had come as close to boiling over as he'd ever seen. So why was she pulling decks and bringing up traffic cams?

She returned to the video on the first screen as the text flooded the second then smacked the space bar.

Cyrus dropped into a chair beside her. Misty dragged a progress bar beneath the video of the street view. A high wall on the right was split by a gate house one might see at a military base, where soldiers and sailors would check IDs before allowing entry. The gate slid open. Soon a car zipped by. She paused, wound it back.

"Nope."

"You know her car?"

She nodded, then scrolled. More vehicles. A pedestrian walking out of the gate waving at the guard over one shoulder. The sun rose, and the two lanes of asphalt merged from black to gray.

Cyrus checked the time stamp then brought up a third station.

"I assume my credentials are still good."

"You assume correctly, *partner*."

Ignoring the sarcastic emphasis on the last word, he brought up Google Maps then zoomed in to street view. "Why would Colorado Springs have a camera on this side street?"

"Good question." Time fast-forwarded on the screen. The sky darkened, and lights outside the gate sprung to life, painting a white halo on the asphalt. A Subaru wagon pulled out and Misty slapped the space bar to pause the video. "That's her car."

"You sure?" He rolled closer then leaned in.

"Yeah, I can't see her face, but see the bumper there?"

He leaned even closer as she wound the video back

a few frames. "It's still dented. She got into a fender bender a couple years ago. It's her car."

"You'd make a fine detective."

"Not on my bucket list."

He checked the time stamp. "So, she was on campus, like your sister's friend told you. But until seven? I could see her doing interviews or something, but that seems late."

"Anna's an investigative reporter. She's one of those people who lights up a room, radiates charisma. Wouldn't surprise me if she had Lockhart himself eating out of her hand. Besides, if he's trying to get the message out about his new Public Security outfit, he might give her unfettered access. Bresnan said he served with someone at LPS, and he was doing a favor by running the piece. That might buy her more access."

"Doubtful," Cyrus grumbled.

"And why is that?"

"Because guys like Sam Lockhart don't do anything on the level. She might have gotten access, but he'd only let her see what he wanted her to see."

"I think your attitude toward him is coloring your—"

"Of course it is." He forced a smile.

Misty didn't mirror it, as he'd hoped. "So, we know she left the compound on Tuesday of last week. Her friend hasn't heard from her since. But she left in one piece."

Cyrus scrunched his forehead in doubt.

Misty swiveled her chair. "What?"

"You're assuming she's the one driving."

Her shoulders sank. "Shit. You're right. Maybe hope is coloring *my* outlook."

More like desperation.

"Who could blame you?" He squeezed her wrist. "We're gonna find her."

"Thanks." The second monitor flashed. She shooed him back from the table. "Move. Deck's back."

"It scares me how much faster you are than the Bureau."

"Ha. But you're forgetting, we're the *real* good guys."

"Fuck off."

She laughed as she clicked on the .tar archive. Files littered the screen. "Here we go."

After a minute or two of her sifting through files and arranging them in an order only a brainiac would understand, Cyrus rose. "I'm gonna grab something from the fridge. You want anything?"

"Water. Sparkling."

"Got it."

When he returned with the drinks, she tapped the air in front of the screen. "Okay. A new highway extension diverted traffic from this area. Lockhart bought out an old hospital and a neighboring hotel. There's a newer hospital two exits up. He walled in both buildings, maybe so any former soldiers seeking treatment there could park their families in the hotel? That's an interesting setup. Google Earth shows a couple other structures. I assume those are new."

"Quite the investment."

"Yeah. Which is the interesting piece." She brought up a document. "He formed an LLC for Lockhart Public Security, but the properties were bought by a different outfit."

"Who?"

"Hmm. I can't tell. This is weird." She cocked her chin. "Ah! Shell company." She tapped an arrow key, to scroll from document to document, from left to right. "Hmm, two shell companies. Three. Might take a bit to find the top of the pyramid. Someone's covering tracks."

Speaking of time. Cyrus checked his watch.

"You coming for dinner tonight?"

"My sister is missing."

"Yeah, and you gotta eat."

"And Marsha wants to measure me some more to make sure I'm not going to get you killed."

"That's a shitty thing to say. Marsha likes you."

She stopped her scrolling. "Okay, that *was* shitty. Sorry, I was focused. I like her, too. I don't usually like people."

"It's all good. I get it. Let's just hope it's like Bresnan said and Anastasia might be laying low somewhere."

"Bresnan. My gut's on fire with that fucking guy."

He hadn't scoped any subterfuge from the editor. But maybe Cyrus had lost his edge.

Maybe Misty was paranoid.

"Dinner's in two hours."

"I'll come, Cy. Just shut up. Go play the PS5 or something. Give me an hour."

He snickered. "A little *Call of Duty* never killed anyone."

"Ha, with your reaction times? Probably kills you plenty."

He took exception silently.

Cyrus was at the bottom of the COD kill list and the top of the deaths list when Misty called out twenty minutes later.

"Got it!"

He slid the controller onto the small coffee table then strolled into the cage area. "Got what?"

"Well, a general feeling about the enterprise. Look."

Cyrus pulled up a chair.

"The owner of record on the incorporation forms—the LLCs—is Robert Singh. I looked him up, and he owns a few convenience stores in the Denver area. No way this guy funded the purchase of these buildings."

"Okay, that's interesting. Why LLCs?"

"You can pull out money and spend it like it's your own. Less red tape. A little more tax liability, but you can make up for it by writing off the expenses. Costs are higher in real estate. I mean, whoever is behind him —probably Lockhart—bought an antiquated hospital and a hotel. Every dollar they spend to refurbish it is tax deductible. While you were getting your ass kicked and cursing in there, I watched a clip of a Lockhart video. If he's to be believed, this place is only hiring vets. As I suspected, he provides health care, probably out of that hospital, so his employees won't need insurance. Which is convenient."

"But the hospital can't possibly be in use yet, can it?"

"I doubt it. Considering the size, it's probably doubling as office space. He can hire them as contractors. They'll be taxed using 1099s. Hell, it looks like Lockhart was trying to ramp up without people seeing it. Using LLCs and hiring contractors creates a veil no one can see through until tax time next year. Lockhart knows what he's trying to do will invite investigations, so when he bought it up and walled it in, he wanted to keep it on the downlow. The quieter, the better. Now that his guys have thwarted some shootings, he's doing interviews. Phase two, if you will. The media will see this rich guy claiming to address the gun violence problem, doing the government's job, and they'll do everything they can to find possible click bait on him."

Cyrus summed it up for his own mind. "So, hire the vets as contractors, handle their health care internally, and get the business ramped up before anyone has fuel to nay say."

Misty swiveled in her chair to face him. "Exactly. And it sounds like a sweet deal for the vets."

Cyrus huffed. "Yeah, it does." Admitting it was like biting down on aluminum foil with a mouth full of fillings, but truth was truth.

"Now, I just need to find out who put down the money."

"No, you don't."

She cocked both eyebrows. "You don't think that's relevant?"

"The SAC limited our latitude. You're a walking conflict of interest because the missing reporter is your sister. And I have it out for Lockhart. He knows it. Even if you found something foul, you'd put me at the center of his lawyers' defense strategy."

"Enlighten me, oh former instructor at Quantico."

"Are you going to keep shoving my words back in my face?"

"From time to time, yes. It's in my nature to shine a light on hypocrisy. My sister was a reporter for the same reason. Oh, God, I just said *was*."

In light of that little revelation, Cyrus let the contention melt, returning focus to the Lockhart topic. "His attorneys would proclaim I'm a fed with a grudge out to manufacture evidence against the guy he wrongfully blames for previous crimes. Crimes I investigated. Just because he's rich."

She nodded. "I get it. But Pierce is in prison for kidnapping, not for the murder of Gabrielle Sutton."

"I don't think I need to convince you to focus on your sister. It was fine to dig, but if nothing points you toward a fiasco Anastasia uncovered, something that made Lockhart want to silence her—and I wouldn't put it past that prick—then we have to stay on track."

Misty swiveled the chair to face front again, gazing blankly at something above her monitors. "I'm with you, but I'm going to dig anyway. Like you said, maybe she found something. You must understand, when Anna gets locked on, the world around her vanishes."

"Sounds familiar."

"She really is a dog with a bone. If Lockhart was up to no good and she discovered that, the editor's puff piece would be toast."

"Why did you two change your names? Did it have something to do with your father?"

Misty didn't flinch or turn to face him. "Why do you want to know?"

"Do we really have to do that?" When she didn't answer, he sighed. "Fine, I'll play, since you're pretending it isn't obvious."

She swung around again, a playful smile creasing her lips, then dipped her chin.

He read her expression for what it was. A challenge.

"Is there anyone from her past who might be holding a grudge?"

Misty frowned.

Cyrus stood, pushing the chair back with his legs. "That's what I thought." He flicked a handful of fingers toward himself. "Out with it."

"Our father is a cop. We're... estranged."

"Why do I think *estranged* doesn't cover it?"

"Because you're a nosy bastard."

"Or a dog with a bone."

She tapped her nose while jabbing the air between them with the index finger of her other hand.

"It doesn't take an intuitive savant to divine why you don't like to talk about your past or even that you have a sister. But if we're going to find her, we have to check all avenues. So, drop the LLC shit for now and let's hash this out."

"Fine." She twirled toward a keyboard, smacked the space bar, then rattled the keys with her fingertips. "Here's the first thing I checked when I sat down, which you missed because you were appraising my new servers and questioning my ethics. Anastasia disappeared Tuesday." A router login screen appeared. The user ID field and password auto-filled. "On Tuesday evening after she left, my father was watching Hulu until he passed out."

Cyrus made a mental note of her description.

"On Wednesday, he was back online by 11 PM, which is around the time he usually leaves his favorite watering hole." She stood, turned, then clutched her hips. "Satisfied?"

"So, your father is so bad you've hacked his router to monitor his activities."

"I also have a weatherproof camera in the woods by his house trained on his front-fucking-door, if you want to know. And it's connected to the same router. He's technologically illiterate. He'll never see it." Misty groaned. "Now, Cyrus, let it fucking go before you irritate me."

"Looks like I've already accomplished that. But you've given your father an alibi. Maybe someday you'll want to talk about it. If so, I'm here. If not... I'm still here."

Her shoulders dropped then her tense expression melted. "We still going to your place for dinner?"

If Misty Daniels was anything, it was adaptive.

CHAPTER 5

A violin hummed two notes then the rest of the section responded inside Ethan Pierce's earbuds as he measured the slight downhill on the putting green. The choir entered, building the slow creep toward release in Mozart's Lacrimosa. When the percussion entered, he swept his putter gently from right to left.

The golf ball rolled down the decline, turned left to follow a low line, then dropped into the cup with a satisfying clatter. One of the prison guards who'd waited lest he broke Pierce's concentration strolled across the green, snatched the ball out of the cup with one hand, then handed Ethan a cell phone.

The guard's nickname was Bubba. The former Alabama nose tackle's wife wasn't working, and his son attended a posh private school. It followed that any murderer who'd cut a deal with the government to be moved to the minimum security prison wasn't allowed within ten feet of Pierce unless they wanted to experience Bubba's baton, and it went without saying Ethan had private shower time reserved.

Pierce took the phone, gave the walking tower a curt nod to let him know he could fuck off, then turned to face the three-story private prison he called home.

There were no fences here. No barbed wire. Minimum security was an understatement, but the feds didn't seem to have problems with the way Lockhart ran the place. After all, he was a stickler for the rules since following them allowed his suckling of millions from the government teat. Quite the irony, compared to what rules he was willing to skirt in his private businesses.

Pierce pressed the speaker button since he couldn't figure out how to connect the damn thing to his earbuds. "This is Ethan."

"Mister Pierce, it's Tim."

Since he'd been convicted and sent to the clink, Tim was his lone contact with the outside world. A rare trusted confidante with the facilities and connections to make wheels turn when Ethan wanted them spun.

"Hi, Tim. What's up?"

The way his assistant hesitated was a tell—this wasn't a good-news call.

"Spit it out, Tim."

"Tiffany Brooks is out in the open."

Ethan clenched his teeth. Brooks. A lurid memory

flashed through his mind of the moments just before Cyrus Fucking Jennings ripped her from his grasp.

"What do you mean by out in the open?"

"Saw her on Fox. She was holding a sign with a small band of protestors at Live Oak Church in Hope Mills, Texas."

"Protesting? I liked her better when she didn't care."

"Understood, boss."

"Is that all you've got?"

"No, I did some digging before I called. Looks like she held onto the townhouse in Denver. Neighbors saw her moving back in. Well, there was no moving truck, but she was sighted going inside."

Ethan preferred it when she was in hiding with the hillbilly mafia in Georgia. "So, she's still paying the mortgage despite leaving her job."

"That's how it seems."

"Any idea who's footing the bill for our little protester?"

"No idea, boss. For all I know, the president is helping."

Of course. Tiffany Brooks's father had been tight with the current occupant of the oval back when they were in the Georgia state house together. She was practically family. Not the kind of trouble he wanted when Lockhart was still deploying his LPS forces across the South.

"Should I put someone on her?" Tim asked.

"Damn right, you should. But don't get caught looking. Put one of Lockhart Tactical's guys on it. No LPS soldiers."

"Understood. Can't have people digging into that with the media hubbub."

"Right. How about the reporter? What's her name?"

"Anastasia Clark. Nothing new from LPS on her."

"Do they have her?"

"That would add up."

Ethan stirred that around in his brain before responding. "How do you figure?"

"Because Sam Lockhart is staying mum. He knows I speak for you, and he isn't telling me shit... sir."

Ethan nodded, though no one could see it. "You think he's keeping me in the dark so I have plausible deniability in case shit goes south? Or has he screwed up and killed her?"

"I'd bet on the former. At least, that's my guess. They aren't answering my questions about this Chet Parsons character, either. Something is off there."

"Remind me. Parsons?"

"Their IT manager. Committed suicide. I mentioned it—"

"Right. Got it. You think it wasn't a suicide?"

"My gut stirs sometimes, sir. That's all."

Ethan fired up the brain blender for that one. Lockhart would be covering his bases. Showing the public what he wanted them to see—the answer to mass killings in the US of A. But killing his own people could shine a light he didn't need, and say what you would about Lockhart, he wasn't stupid. If he were, he wouldn't be part of Pierce's exclusive circle. Probably just the suicide of a distraught ex-soldier. PTSD was nasty business.

"Any news from the insiders?"

"Nothing new. They're spreading money across the campaigns, sixty-percent democrat because of the Barney initiative."

The Barney Initiative. Purple states. Ethan chuckled.

"Last thing," Pierce said. "Did we handle the social media on the Texas guy?"

"In process."

"Process? Fuck process, Tim. Get the shit done. What's the holdup?"

"4Chan is being a pain in the ass."

"Then *pay them more money*, Tim. Everyone has a price. Jesus. The media's going to have a field day on this guy. What the hell are people doing? Call Lockhart. Tell him to move his ass on it."

"Right when I hang up, sir. Any other orders?"

"Let Sam handle the reporter." He'd already forgotten her name again. He would've sworn living in a prison was dumbing him down. He didn't feel... sharp. He made a mental note to call his lawyer about the appeal. "Ignore the suicide, too. We'll trust Sam until he gives us a reason to doubt him. But if you get wind of anything off-putting, you'll let me know."

"Goes without saying sir. I'll call with an update tomorrow."

Ethan clicked off, nodded toward Bubba, then held out the cell phone. He dropped his putter on the green then headed down the hill toward the main complex. It was almost chow time, and he'd do his thinking over a meal.

CHAPTER 6

Misty had to do a double-take when she spotted it hanging on the wall. There, nestled between framed photographs of Marsha's son and one of her receiving an award from the governor, was a professional shot of her with Cyrus standing in a grove of trees adorned with autumn leaves, their smiles genuinely reaching their eyes.

He seemed so... domesticated.

She didn't know if this new turn was adorable or disgusting, but it wasn't like she'd lived a Brady Bunch childhood. Her father was a drunk. Her mother died in childbirth with Jolene—Anastasia, she reminded herself—when Misty was two. One thing she did know, Marsha was a real looker. The pair could have done sugarless gum ads.

Yup. Gross and beautiful.

But even musings over the framed photos couldn't keep her mind from regressing to the Lockhart research. If Anna had stumbled onto something nefarious, she'd done it from the inside. Misty lacked the data to draw any conclusions. LPS was keeping the inner workings of their funding far too quiet. But if the editor could be believed, her sister had been inside to do a puff piece on Lockhart Public Security when she disappeared.

If she wasn't just laying low somewhere—something Misty had certainly taught her younger sibling how to do—why would Lockhart have her taken? If her father was at home, who else might sweep up a reporter?

A killer? A rapist? Both possible.

Misty was just contemplating how she could dig up Anastasia's articles and look for people who might be holding grudges when Cyrus chimed in.

He mimed holding a microphone and tapped his knee twice. "Earth to Misty. Earth to Misty Daniels. Come in, M—"

"Oh, shut it."

"Dog with a bone?" he asked.

Misty couldn't suppress her smile. "Something like that."

Marsha clapped her hands then rubbed them together from her spot next to Cyrus on the plushy white sofa. "Ooh, intrigue. Spill it all. I love a good mystery. What's your latest?"

Misty eyed her. "He hasn't told you yet? I'd have thought with Lockhart in the mix..."

Marsha's expression went slack, and she twisted her head toward her new live-in partner. "Sam Lockhart?"

Cyrus's nose twitched. "Would've been nice if you'd let me bring that up, Daniels."

Misty shrugged.

"Would've been nice if you led with it, too. Don't blame her for your secrecy."

"Hey, who's side are you on?"

Marsha's eyes narrowed. "I thought you said this Blake guy was a stickler. Even I wouldn't let you anywhere near a case involving Sam Lockhart."

Cyrus agreed with a hardy nod. "Which is why we're not investigating Lockhart."

Marsha slumped into the sofa. "Hm. Maybe you should be."

"What?" Misty and Cyrus said in perfect sync.

Marsha gave a little laugh. "I heard whisperings today that a guy who ended up on my table recently worked there. I did a little reading about this new company, but I wasn't about to bring it up to my man."

Her man. She probably thinks that's cute.

Cy perked up. "Why'd this guy end up on your table?"

"Suicide. Messy one, too. Planted a Desert Eagle under his chin and blew his face off."

Misty and Cyrus shared a look.

Marsha continued. "He came in last Monday night. I checked his blood for drugs, the usual. Nothing strange."

"Except for half his head being in chunks," Misty muttered.

Marsha gave an uncharacteristic wince. "Well, yeah. Other than that."

Cyrus scratched the back of his head. "Did you say Monday? That might not be a coincidence."

Misty took up his slack. "Anna drove out of LPS Tuesday. You might be right, but we might both be paranoid. We do have overactive guts."

"Well, mine's stirring."

"Mine too."

"You two are like twins." When Misty saw how Marsha was so easy with her chuckles, she got why Cyrus had moved down the breezeway—other than lowering his rent bill. His girlfriend scanned Misty then looked at Cyrus. "Well, maybe not twins." She laughed again.

Although her delivery had been near perfect, neither of the twins laughed. Misty frowned. "Shit. I wonder if there's something to the timeline. If the suicide was Anastasia's triggering event to... what? Disappear?"

Cyrus redirected. "So, I learned today that Misty has a sister."

Marsha slapped both hands on her knees then

scooted forward on the sofa. "Sister? Why didn't we know this?"

Even the 'we' was kind of gross, but Misty didn't know why. "We have an interesting history. And I thought we were going to leave it for now."

He patted the air with both palms. "My bad. You want a drink to quell that tension?"

Keeping her sister a secret from him had really bothered him. With all they'd been through, she knew she could trust Cyrus. Hell, he'd saved her from years of lockup. Were her protective instincts when it came to Anastasia clouding her judgment? God knew that had gotten her in trouble before.

But sitting around talking about it wasn't going to lead them to Anna. She conjured an even, soft tone. "Let's get her back. Then we'll talk about all of it. The three of us. Fair enough?"

Marsha nodded, and the soft, understanding expression she wore put Misty at ease.

I'd have moved in, too. He'd be crazy not to keep his eyes trained on this one.

"Of course, and Cyrus isn't going to bother you anymore until then. *Are you*, Cy?" She pinched his leg.

He gently swiped her hand away. "No." He leveled his gaze on Misty's. "I'm not ever going to bring it up again." He crossed his chest with one finger. "Scout's honor."

"You got the salute wrong," Misty replied.

"Eat a frog."

"Bite me."

The tension melted out of the room. Well, outside her mind, anyway.

CHAPTER 7

As he prodded an agent's case report for the semblance of a conclusion, a bottom line to draw the elements into a coherent finding, Cyrus mused about training at Quantico. They could turn out agents who understood the Federal Rules of Criminal Procedure that allowed them to investigate crime with an eye for how the courts operated, but they couldn't teach them how to write coherently.

At the peak of his frustration, Misty strolled into his office like she owned the place. Maybe his open-door policy was a problem, but other Cyber team members knocked to announce their arrivals.

Anyone else might've viewed her lack of simple decorum in a negative light. It might've implied she lacked manners, that she found little value in social conventions. And they wouldn't have been far from the mark.

But there were reasons Misty Daniels, AKA Joanna Reeves, was the lone agent he invited to his favorite café for breakfast on Wednesdays and included in dinners with his girlfriend.

He'd only been running the outfit for a few weeks by the time he introduced her to the team, and it wasn't long before shots were fired. Subtle emails hinting at the value of boundaries. Team members sounded off about sharing space with someone who'd never been to Quantico, who came and went as she pleased, and who seemed to lack discipline. Little comments about a certain off-the-books invader who thought her practices were above scrutiny.

Then he'd heard about how she broke into a conversation between two of the basement-dwellers, showed them the error of their approach to a technical problem, and changed the course of the team in one fell swoop.

Now they begged her to check their work before they sent reports to Cyrus. He figured the agent who'd sent over the diatribe filled with technical jargon and no conclusion that morning had bypassed her because she'd been on a dedicated quest to save her sister.

No system was perfect.

Blake probably frowned on their connection, but Cyrus refused a partner assignment from his first SAC when he was banished to Denver, and beyond a brief, deadly pairing with his former protégé, he still hadn't relented on the topic.

All that said, Blake was probably glad Misty was watching Cyrus's back, even if it was from a monitor in the basement. Good leaders make concessions in exchange for results.

In true Misty fashion, she jumped right in. "Turn on your TV. True News."

He snatched his remote, flicked on the tube, then tuned into the proper channel.

A reporter in a cheap tie stood in front of the columns, arches, and pediments of the state's capitol building in Denver.

Cyrus raised the printed report then offered it to Misty so she could review it while he watched. Her gaze skimmed a couple lines before she reached for the red pen sitting in a cup on his desk.

The reporter spun his practiced dialogue. "Chaos ensued when Democratic Senator Fitz Banner's statements to the press about a gun control bill he planned to introduce were interrupted by gunfire on the capitol steps. A lone gunman charged from the crowd and opened fire, but Senator Banner ducked away just in time to save his own life. As the unidentified gunman ran up the stairs, an employee of Lockhart Public Security drew his weapon and thwarted the gunman's attack with a single shot to the head.

"Just moments ago, Senator Banner made a statement from a secure room inside the state capitol."

Banner was bald and round, wearing a blue suit with a blue tie and a US flag lapel pin. His forehead was covered in sweat. "If it weren't for Lockhart, I'd be dead. Although I don't know how I feel about private companies doing law enforcement's work, I have to tell the truth. Where our security failed, Lockhart's guy didn't."

A reporter chimed in. "Was he working for you, Senator?"

Banner shook his head. "No. As I understand it, he was there with my Republican colleague, Jason Miller. But I plan to shake the man's hand when I get a chance."

The camera returned to a live shot of the reporter standing on the capitol's steps. "Lockhart Public Security has been under scrutiny after another shooting in front of a small-town church in Texas two weeks ago. Although he'd previously been unavailable for comment, Reverend Rodney Hinson of Live Oak Church in Hope Mills, Texas, broke his silence earlier today when authorities revealed White nationalist documentation was found in thwarted shooter Michael Bray's apartment. We asked him what he thought about Lockhart Public Security, who stopped Bray in his tracks as he bore down on their place of worship."

The scene switched to the steps of the church, where a broad-shouldered Black man stood wearing a reflective purple shirt with a tie pulled up tight to his neck.

"What do I think about them? We'd be dead without their service. They were there when the police failed to act on numerous racial threats toward our church. Although we mourn the loss of life of a man who was so obviously disturbed, there's no doubt in my mind Lockhart Public Security's agent saved many of my parishioners' lives." Hinson raised a hand in the air like the preacher in Cyrus's childhood Baptist church might have when channeling a message from the Man Upstairs. "Until the United States of America figures out how to protect the people of this nation from the scourge that is assault weapons, we need citizens who will stand up for what's right and protect the meek."

"Scourge that is assault weapons. Protect the meek. That was a nice, clean soundbite." Cyrus said.

Misty dropped the report onto his desk, flicked the pen across it without putting the lid back on, then nodded. "He had two weeks to practice."

The reverend's clip ended, and the reporter picked up the narrative. "But not everybody agrees that private companies should take matters into their own hands."

Another cutaway. The same reporter shoving his mic toward a blonde with pretty, angular features fronting a crowd of protesters outside Live Oak. The stem of a sign was propped on one shoulder, but the way the shot framed her face obscured its printed message.

At the sight of her, Cyrus dropped his elbow onto his desk then rubbed the wrinkles on his forehead with his fingertips.

Tiffany Brooks.

Cyrus hadn't seen her since she emerged from hiding in northeastern Georgia to testify while Ethan Pierce stood trial for her kidnapping and sexual assault.

"Is that—" Misty blurted.

"Yes."

When a microphone was shoved into Tiffany's face, she smiled and lowered the sign.

"What are you protesting?" the reporter asked.

"Many things," Tiffany yelled over the chanting crowd. "Michael Bray was a known threat who'd been reported for domestic abuse, assault, and myriad lesser crimes since he left the service. The police failed to keep watch. The VA failed to get him psychiatric services. He is the worst example of men who served their countries honorably only to get lost in the shuffle of post-service life until they get swept up in cause of White supremacy and driven toward violence. And why does that happen? Because no one cares about them, and extremists fake compassion to take advantage of them." The reporter drew the mic away to ask another question, but Tiffany pulled it back. "Most of all, I want to say private companies have no business doing law enforcement's job!"

Misty's mouth slanted to one side. "Speaking of practiced."

"Yeah, but it's funny how a smooth delivery coupled with the right tone can hide her slant, ain't it?"

Misty chuckled. "Yeah. She's pro."

The reporter asked, "Who should protect everyday Americans in the interim?"

Cyrus sat back in his chair. Anyone else might have stuttered or hesitated, but not Tiffany Brooks.

"How about the FBI? How about the ATF? The federal government doesn't lack the tools and resources to monitor these killers. I'm not out here railing solely on the locals. The federal government needs to get involved, and that includes Congress."

Despite his sentiment about how she could sway minds with her smooth delivery, Cyrus found he wasn't immune. But it wasn't about being susceptible to bias. She'd just prompted his brain to consider the bigger picture, and his inner-investigator was seeing new angles.

Specifically Texas.

Misty reached for the remote then pressed mute. "I see that look, Cy." If she'd been a superhero, her laser focus would've scorched the flesh on one side of his face.

"It's nothing."

"It was you who reminded me earlier today that we're looking for my sister. We can't mess with Lockhart until we have proof he's involved in her disappearance."

Cyrus stood, paced, then shoved his hands into his pockets. "But that's it. Hope Mills happened two weeks ago, before Anastasia disappeared. What if your sister dug up dirt about something in Texas?"

"Is that your gut talking? Do you have a theory? Or are you looking for an excuse to dig into Lockhart despite ordering me to stay clear of him?"

Cyrus let his shoulders drop, his focus on the news coverage. Misty knew the answer to her question, and he had to admit she knew him better than he sometimes liked. Especially when his hackles were up, and she had to call him back to earth.

Misty nodded in a knowing way. "Good. Then you won't mind that I did a little more digging and learned that Ethan Pierce's wife is at the top of the LLC pyramid."

"What?"

"Yup. Pierce is funding LPS."

Curses filled Cyrus's mind, but he pushed the revelation to one side. Marsha was always telling him to live in the moment. "So, you dug despite my insistence you focus on your sister."

"Don't try to pretend that's what you care about right now."

Without answering, he reached for his phone, brought up his contacts, then scrolled until he found the one he needed. The phone rang, then a soft voice answered in a cultivated, slow southern drawl.

"Well, Agent Cyrus Jennings. It's been ages."

They'd established the lifeline for a couple of reasons. First, to ensure Tiffany was protected until federal marshals could take custody of her from what she called the Hillbilly Mafia. Second, because the prick billionaire he'd saved her from had a long reach, and his conviction didn't promise long-term protection after the feds evacuated her safe house.

But he supposed the main reason they'd stayed in touch was that people bonded over trauma.

"Hey, Tiff. I see the phoenix has risen from the ashes."

"Where?"

"On TV, at the church. Which is why I called. You still in Hope Mills?"

"It just so happens I am. Why do you ask?"

"I was thinking I'd pay a visit. Maybe we can have lunch."

"Why Cyrus, that's the best damned news I've heard all day. Let me know when you fly in. I'll send a car."

She hung up.

When Cyrus turned, Misty was shaking her head with her arms folded across her belly.

"What?"

She snatched the report she'd marked up, turned, then spoke over her shoulders as she walked toward the door. "I'll get him to clean this up while you're gone, and I'll pull the Texas shooter's social media. But I'm not going with you to sell this to the SAC. And I'm sure as shit not going to Hope Mills."

Cyrus grinned.

CHAPTER 8

Cyrus's F-150 rumbled off the dirt road and into the warehouse district along the river. He followed narrow, winding alleyways until he came to the door with a security keypad. The Tuesday afternoon sun reflected off the keys, and he had to shade them with one hand to punch in his code.

He strolled up the dim hallway lit only by red emergency lights then typed another code Misty had created for him to enter the cage area. When he approached, she was trained on the center monitor as her fingers performed their epic dance on the keys.

"That was fast. You talk to the SAC?"

"Not yet. I wanted to see what you found first."

"You're in for a ride. Sit."

He pulled up the chair most molded to his backside then plopped down. Leaning back, he interlocked his fingers to rest them over his abs. The server rack hummed. How much did Misty pull down each month in her corporate security work?

And did she ever sleep?

A profile popped up on the monitor. The picture framed on the left displayed a brooding young White guy with a five o'clock shadow. The neatly formatted text on the right scrolled separately from the image. The layout was better than the FBI's.

Why didn't that surprise him?

The dossier wasn't one of Misty's unethical intel drops, but she'd probably constructed it from one. Cyrus couldn't blame her for relying on the hackers who got info for her, especially since they had an unrivaled ability to crawl across the sludge pile that was social media to gather and collate intel.

While he waited for her to continue, the words Tiffany Brooks had uttered to the reporter in Hope Mills echoed in his mind. She professed the FBI, ATF, and Congress needed to get their acts together. While he agreed to a point, Cyrus laid most of the intelligence failures at the feet of Congress. Those bastards pulled the purse strings, and their constant posturing for the cameras combined with the incessant bickering used to convince their political bases they had the country's best interests at heart came at a steep price to the agencies that fell under the bloated Department of Homeland Security's purview.

Although the government's reach into cyberspace was expansive, and despite them thwarting terror attacks the public would never know about, their most powerful data-collection asset—the NSA—wasn't mandated to operate domestically. Not out in the open, anyway. He found it ironic that the secretive domestic data collection could only be protected by keeping it out of other agencies' hands.

Thanks, W.

Despite the Department of Homeland Security mandating the alphabet soup of federal law enforcement combined forces, the National Security Agency wasn't known for playing nice with others.

With the items on screen arranged the way she wanted them, Misty ran him through it. "This is Michael Bray. Texas shooter." She brought up Facebook. "Check it out."

Cyrus didn't bother looking because he knew where she was going. "He's not there."

She nodded. "Same for X, Insta, everywhere. Even 4chan is wiped. But my guys have... back doors to the company servers. All of them. When these SM giants pull down profiles in situations like this, they keep backups for when law enforcement comes knocking with warrants. Both Michael Bray's and Donny Worth's profiles have been removed from the backups."

Cyrus sat up straighter. "You're shitting me."

"I wouldn't shit my favorite turd. Seriously, Cy. They wiped it all."

"What are they going to do when the feds come knocking?"

"The Michael Bray fiasco was two weeks ago. They've probably already come knocking."

"That doesn't invalidate my question."

"True. They can't destroy evidence without obstruction charges coming into the mix, so I suspect they're backing them up somewhere else. Somewhere my friends don't know about. They might even be locking up printed copies, since they're not required to hand over anything digital. As long as the feds get the material included in the warrant, the format doesn't matter. The companies can do what they want. What does that tell you?"

"That the social media companies have conspired to hide shooter data from their platforms?"

"Conspiracy theories abound, but I think you're looking at it from the wrong direction. Try again."

Who's the teacher now, Agent Jennings?

Cyrus mulled. Stewed. "Hmm."

If X, Facebook, Insta—all of them—were hiding the profiles...

He decided he needed more info. "What about 4chan?"

Misty snapped her fingers. "You're on the right track." She spun her chair to face him. "I logged in myself to get a real-time look at the shooter from the Denver Capitol. Donnie Worth had been wiped from the standard platforms, but 4chan still had posts. Standard anti-government rhetoric though not a lot of racist banter. But when I clicked the arrow to load the next post, the profile vanished. Which explains why I found nothing, anywhere, on the shooter from Hope Mills."

"Because that happened two weeks ago, and they had time to get rid of it."

"Exactly. They've moved the backups of these shooters but not anyone else's. What's that tell you?"

"Someone is pulling strings. Covering trails. The feds, the Texas AG, and his counterpart in Denver aren't going to say a lot about an ongoing investigation, anyway, so someone is trying to shut down the media's access. The less they can divine about the shooters, the more they have to focus on the events."

"Which focuses them on Lockhart Public Security, where one person is delivering the message. Think about Tiffany Brooks's carefully manicured responses. If Sam is the only one who can talk with any authority, he's the front page. It's his own practiced narrative that takes root."

"Fucking Lockhart."

"I don't think it's *just* him. Rewind your mind."

Cyrus pinched his lips together. There was a time for teaching, but he had a special agent in charge to convince he should go to Hope Mills, and he could provide no justification. Especially when Blake would shoot down anything aimed at Sam Lockhart.

"Help me along."

"Think about the Sutton conspiracy. Jake Ramon worked for Lockhart. He killed his own charge with a hypodermic. Ethan Pierce is suspected to have been at the center of all that but was never convicted of it. Do you see where I'm going?"

Cyrus conjured the patience to go with her flow.

Ethan Pierce, billionaire, had contracted Jake Ramon from Lockhart. Pierce and Ramon would've kept their work together separate from Sam to lend him plausible deniability. Hell, it'd kept him out of prison. Ramon had conveniently ended up aerated by an AR-15 courtesy of Cyrus's friend and fellow FBI agent, Byron Hawkins, which left no one to roll over and testify against Pierce in the conspiracy to kill Gabby Sutton.

Before trial, they'd traced Pierce's political contributions—the ones they could find—and had been surprised to learn he'd been spreading money across the country to both parties. Cyrus suspected Pierce of having the chair of the Democratic National Committee murdered, too, but cause of death was ruled a suicide.

An alarm klaxon rang in his head about the suicide of the guy working at LPS, but he forced it away to keep on track.

Tiffany Brooks had been swindled by Pierce and convinced he'd been trying to get Gabby elected. She'd planned to testify about the billionaire's wider scheme to rebuild America in his own image by funding candidates who would do his bidding and pitting those who wouldn't against better choices. But Pierce's lawyers had stifled her ability to testify with objections, arguing her fantastical conspiracies had nothing to do with the kidnapping, were prejudicial, and would lead to any verdict against their client being overturned on appeal.

Although many Americans liked to believe courts were impartial by nature, judges shared the self-serving egos possessed by all human beings, and they didn't like having their decisions overturned. Cyrus had seen enough valuable evidence excluded from trials on this account.

He slid puzzle pieces around in his mind. Lockhart was trying to push the narrative that private companies could put an end to the mass killings. Most frustrating of all, he was proving it.

If Misty was right, and he was hiring the vets as contractors to keep the media from having something to dig into and report about, it wasn't much of a leap that he'd shroud the pasts of the shooters if there was something about them he didn't want people to know.

The idea set Cyrus's mind ablaze, but a moment's deliberation tamped it down. Sam Lockhart was a prick, but he wasn't stupid. Pulling strings of the social media giants could lead to leaks. All he needed was some social justice warrior from a tech company leaking details about how he was hiding information about the shooters his men had taken down.

Sam Lockhart ran private prisons and a defense contracting firm, and those enterprises were connected to government. He had to bid for them. If some do-gooder popped off in the media about nefarious happenings at LPS, it wasn't just his new enterprise that would be at risk, it'd be the whole kit and caboodle. Every company carrying his name would be scrutinized.

He'd need someone with serious pull in social media sectors, who made his living puppeteering politicians and media outlets, alike. Someone with the capital to keep people quiet.

"Ethan Pierce."

Misty snapped her fingers again. "Exactly! That fucker is still pulling the strings. And since his new home is a Lockhart Enterprises prison..."

"Yeah, he has full access to the outside world. That's an interesting conjecture, but I'm not sure it will get me to Texas. What do you have for me to take to the SAC?"

"Texas is your problem. I want to find Anna."

"So do I, and the answer might be in Hope Mills."

"Based on what?"

A good question. Cyrus realized his gut was trumping his brain, again. But Anastasia Clark wasn't the only dog with a bone when shit hit fans. He had an ace in the hole in Texas named Tiffany Brooks. She'd been there for at least two weeks, and the former pharma rep knew how to shake hands. To dig.

"Based on pure conjecture. If Ethan Pierce is shutting down social media, they're hiding something about the shooters. What other explanation could there be? Why would he bother?"

"Okay, I'll grant that. The absence of the data on their servers feeds your theory, and I don't have an alternate explanation. They're hiding something. But is that good enough for Blake?"

"Until we have other trails to follow, I might as well find out."

CHAPTER 9

"You are not going to Texas." Blake waved Cyrus toward the door. "No way. DC is already muttering in my ear about this missing person's shit."

"How did they know?"

"Don't be dense."

"Oh, right. You told them."

Blake's hands got busy. "Anastasia Clark almost won a Pulitzer. Did you know she recently turned down an MSNBC contributor contract? Could you imagine if she'd gone on the air with Nicole Wallace or Joe Scarborough then vanished? If I'd known her ticket was that hot, I wouldn't have sent you to the *Post* in the first place. I'm surprised her editor hasn't spread the word. Imagine the attention his paper would get."

Misty's earlier suspicions about William Bresnan sent warning bells off in Cyrus's head while the SAC plowed forward.

"Her peers will put on a full-court press when word gets out she's missing. And wait until you see how the airwaves vibrate when they learn she was working on a piece about LPS! Anastasia Clark is one of *them*. So, if that shit... no *when* that shit inevitably hits the fan, how do you think the director, who I assure you is already up to his eyeballs in the politics of this Lockhart crap, will react when he finds out I didn't tell anyone?"

"I get it."

"Yeah, If anyone should understand, it's you. Never let your boss find out what you're doing from somebody else. And in a situation like this? Sheeeit. You know DC is pushing early retirement, right? Do you want to be on that list? I don't. Although sometimes you make me contemplate it."

Cyrus chuckled. "Hey, I think I've been a very good boy."

"Agreed." The SAC's energy diminished. "Your stock went up when you took down Dora Lassiter's compound. People are talking like you came out of your funk. Hell, you should be the one sitting in my chair. So, why spend all that capital on this?"

"Because Misty's sister is missing, and she's already feeling trapped beneath the weight of a court order that's planting her here for five years."

"You're an empath, Cyrus. I mean that as a compliment. But this is more than a colleague with problems.

I know she's more than some pet project to you. Everyone does."

"She's one of the most talented people I've met at the bureau."

"Bullshit. She's like family. A connection to the analyst you lost in that fucking train wreck across the street. I don't need a master's in psychology to assess that one, Cy."

Cyrus scrunched up his nose. "Yes, she's fucking family."

"Well, excuse me if it sounds harsh, but she's not bureau. She's an outside analyst. And while I'm willing to grant some leeway because of who you are and how you get results, people are watching Hope Mills, and I can't risk riling shit up with Lockhart right now."

"Can't? Or won't?"

The SAC slid his arms onto his desk. "Feeling contentious today, Cy? Well, I don't give a shit. Find the sister, leave Lockhart alone, and stay the fuck out of Texas."

Their gazes locked. Blake didn't blink.

Cyrus used the duration of the standoff to order his attack, then let loose. "Someone has wiped the data about both shooters from social media, their servers, and their backup servers."

Blake covered his eyes with one hand. "God, how I long for a smooth day in this place." He ran his palm down his face. "Maybe early retirement wouldn't be so bad. I could pick up a gig as a Walmart greeter."

Cyrus ignored him. "So, I've been asking myself what media master could wield that particular stick. Bully tech giants into hiding information from the media."

"Or pay the kind of money it would take to keep it quiet."

Cyrus cocked one thumb and shot Blake with a fingertip. "Bang."

"Lockhart wouldn't risk it. Too dicey. So let me guess." Blake's eyelids lowered to half-mast. "You're bringing Ethan Pierce into it." Cyrus cocked his finger again, but Blake showed him the longest one on his right hand. "What's wrong, Cyrus? Wasn't putting him in prison enough?"

"If you need supporting evidence, Ethan Pierce's wife funded the purchase of LPS's compound."

A long silence passed before the SAC finally leaned back in his chair.

"Fucking Misty Daniels. Still working her network, right? Is she ever going to play inside the lines?"

"It's her sister. She's drawing new lines."

"Not the right answer."

"I was going to ask to go to Hope Mills before I found out about the social media. She... we gathered data in support of the trip, that's all."

"I noticed how you switched that pronoun to make it appear like a team effort. Don't want to let her take the rap herself, huh? Why does this contractor really mean so much to you? I know you're not boning her."

"Refer to my previous answer. She's the best at what she does. Better than anyone we have. Better than Byron was."

"Tell me the truth, Cyrus. The whole thing, or the answer is fucking no. I need to know what's going on in my shop."

Cyrus huffed through his nose. "Okay, set aside how I respect her toughness, her thoroughness, her hyperdrive speed on a network, and I'm left with this sense she's been on her own for a long fucking time. Like no one has ever helped her with anything. She's got her shields charged to full—"

"How many science fiction metaphors should I wait through before—"

"Fine! It's because I'm the only person left who she trusts, and I'm not going to let anyone fuck her over."

Blake snapped his fingers, pointed at Cyrus, then popped out of his chair. "Finally, you're talking." He walked to the window, reminding Cyrus of how his former boss, Mona Davies, used to peer through it when Cyrus pissed her off. "Despite your successes, she compromises you. I just wonder if you see that."

"I taught at Quantico. I'm not a rookie. I know how the bureau works."

"Which is the only reason she sees the light of day. I know you'll reel her in. We can drop it, for now." He turned and stepped closer to Cyrus. "I'll admit it gets my hackles up that the social media on the shooters has been wiped. It looks like Pierce, especially if his wife bought up the LPS compound."

Cyrus thought Blake might take another jab at just *how* Cyrus acquired that intel, but he was grateful the SAC went another direction.

"It's almost obvious. There was a time you'd have just gone off on your own, but you've stayed on the straight and narrow since that fiasco in the mountains, and your team is closing cases. So, I'm going to give you a little latitude." He pulled the door open. "I'd like to see Lockhart burn for Sutton as much as you. Since we can't always get what we want, maybe we can both get what we need."

"What do you need?"

"Well, for one, I need Misty Daniels to stop hacking private companies. She's going to get us both retired."

"Okay, I'll work on that."

"Sure. And she'll just go behind you. She learned from the best."

"That's an interesting way to compliment someone."

"Let me put it this way, Cyrus. Next time she does anything that teeters on illegal, I'm going to send her back to the judge. And *Her Honor* is *not* going to like hearing what I have to say. Is that clear enough for you?"

"Like a cloudless spring day."

"Good. I assume you have someone on the ground in Texas so you're not going in blind."

"Tiffany Brooks."

The SAC cupped his forehead, but he also chuckled. "Perfect."

"She's been there for two weeks. She'll have greased some wheels. Maybe if I keep the trip short, I can slide in and out undetected. Poke around."

Blake folded his arms across his torso. "You can't be that naive. Lockhart's guy put a bullet in a White supremacist hell bent on shooting up a Black church. LPS—and probably Pierce's guys—are going to be watching that town like Wall Street investors hungry for a tech firm to buy up and sell off for parts."

"Like hawks," Cyrus agreed. "Doesn't scare me. We'll be... subtle."

"Ha! Tiffany Brooks. Subtle. That's the funniest thing you've said in weeks. I watch the news, Cy."

Sean Blake mulled in silence for a full minute, and Cyrus let him while thanking his lucky stars his newest SAC wasn't as impermeable as Mona Davies had been.

"Now, brass tacks. Just so you know what story to tell when Lockhart gets you dragged up to Capitol Hill, I'm officially forbidding you to go to Texas on the company dime. If you pay for your own ticket and rush down there, I barely even know you. As far as I know, you and Daniels are running around Denver knocking doors in search of Anastasia Clark." He jiggled the doorknob and eyed the loose rattle with suspicion. "While you're gone, that better be exactly what Misty is doing."

"That sounds like a solid plan, boss man."

"Sometimes I rue the day I met her."

Cyrus stood then made for the door. "Well, it could be worse."

"How's that?"

"You could've said you rued the day you met me."

"Jury's out, asshole."

Cyrus laughed. As he shuffled up the hallway toward the elevators, he suppressed his urge to whistle a happy tune.

Tiffany picked up on the first ring.

"Well, if it isn't the cutest fed upon whom I ever laid eyes."

"Why are you buttering my roll?"

"Can't a gal show a little affection for one of her few friends in this backstabbing, vitriolic world?" Her voice dropped into a mutter. "Hell, you might be my last friend."

He softened. "I consider that an honor. So, it's final. You're not going back to pedaling drugs?"

"Nah, politics is in my blood."

"Yeah, generations of it."

"Plus, I love owning these broflakes on the TV." It came out TEE-vee.

"Try not to let that one slip out in Texas. I can only save your life so many times before my luck runs out, you know."

"You still coming?"

"Tomorrow." He texted her the details for the flight he'd booked prior to meeting with Blake.

"I'll be waiting at the airport."

"Don't hang up yet."

"What's up?"

"In the interest of a fostering a new sharing agreement, I'm going to drop the four-one-one on you."

"Cy, stop trying so hard."

"Fine. You want to share intel?"

"With you? Of course, I do."

"Good. Ethan Pierce's money is all over this Lockhart thing. He used a shell LLC in his wife's name to buy the compound in Colorado Springs. He's funding Lockhart."

"I can't act but so surprised. It explains how Sam got up and running under the radar. Cash cuts timelines everywhere except government. Now I know why he's being so aggressive."

"Why is that?"

"Because he's using someone else's money. Not that Ethan wouldn't insist Lockhart throw in a few of his own dimes, but money is to Pierce what leaves are to oaks in summer, and Lockhart's happy to throw it around. Speaking of which, I think I'll file a civil suit for the pain and suffering after the basement episode."

"I'm surprised you waited this long." Cyrus chuckled.

"The idea of his cash in my pocket makes me feel dirty. But I'd love spreading it around to every cause he despises."

"Could be lucrative. But seriously, why didn't you sue his ass into oblivion?"

"Your memory is slipping. I told you when I was in the mountains. It was too soon, I didn't need a higher profile, and I didn't want to end up dead before I testified."

"You could still end up dead."

"Not if he doesn't have any money left to pay someone to kill me."

"No jury is going to award you that much."

Tiffany clammed up for about twenty seconds, and Cyrus had just started to think the call had dropped. But his screen showed it was still active, so he let her ruminate.

"I hate it when you're right. But we can't run around in fear for our lives when we're trying to make the world a better place, can we?"

"I sure can't. Danger comes with the job."

"Fucking-A, Agent Jennings. So, Pierce and Lock-hart are in cahoots, still pursuing their political agendas. Anything else?"

"I'm just happy to be working with you again."

"Me too, Cyrus. I mean that. But I'd just as soon

not put you in a situation where you have to come barging in to save me this time."

"I should've shot him."

"I remember asking you to. But if you'd done it, things would be different."

Which could've meant a million things, and Tiffany didn't elaborate.

"I texted you my flight info."

"I'll be ready with a big hug for you. Kiss, kiss."

She clicked off.

Cyrus to flipped through his contacts to call Marsha and tell her he loved her. Oh, and that he was flying out to Texas in the morning.

Marsha went quiet.

"What is it?"

"You mind if I go out-of-bounds for a minute?"

"Go for it."

"What's Tiffany Brooks's interest in all this?"

"I've been asking myself the same question. She's a lefty."

"Yeah but be more specific."

He found it wasn't easy to do on the fly. Tiffany Brooks had grown up in Georgia, the daughter of a popular politician whose best friend and colleague in the state house now occupied the Oval Office. Southern Democrats were gun owners as much as their counterparts, they just didn't spout off about them in front of the cameras because their base wouldn't cheer.

Hell, Tiffany probably carried a couple in her purse.

So, her interest wasn't just about guns.

He took a few seconds to order his words. "The shootings are out of control. That's what she would say. But people like Sam Lockhart and Ethan Pierce boil her blood. They stand for everything she'd die to defeat. Lobbying, in particular. I think Gabrielle Sutton's death emphasized that. It was all about getting Pierce's guy—Gabby's opponent—into office when Pierce figured out he couldn't buy her. Sutton's campaign manager once said Tiffany was thrilled to hand out fliers and perform mediocre tasks to get her friend elected. No ego. She's a true believer."

"In other words, you think her family's political bearing has finally broken through and she really wants to change things."

"Did you just imply I'm long-winded?"

"Lucky for you, I haven't tired of your voice yet."

"In that case, let me add Tiffany seethes with hatred that Sam Lockhart breathes the same air as her since he skated out of a conviction for her friend's death."

"Which is understandable, right? The perp who got away?"

Cyrus grinned. "You're cute when you try to talk cop."

The soft music of her laughter resonated between

his ears. "I think I understand you two. Tiffany's someone you don't feel you're using as an asset because the friendship is real, right? I certainly understand why she'd want you for a friend, aside from being the hero who rescued her from Ethan Pierce."

"Because I'm a fed who can feed her intel?"

"Because you're a rare breed, Cyrus Jennings. People feel that, feel safe with you."

His face warmed.

"Want to know the best news of all?"

"What's that?"

"The women also know someone like you would never screw around on his lady, and that means I don't have anything to worry about. Which is particularly good because I'm an M.E., and I know right where to cut a motherfucker so he bleeds out fastest."

Cyrus chortled. "Thanks for the clarity."

"Just keep yourself out of the political crossfire. After the media coverage of your testimony against Pierce, your boss wouldn't like to see you on the front page again. You don't look your best in black and white, anyway."

"I like how you cut through the bullshit."

"And I admire how you manage to befriend such worthy women instead of just using them as tools."

Cyrus decided her sentiments were something to live up to, and he typed the words into a notepad on his phone for later reference.

"But Cy?"

"Yes, love?"

"I'd also like you to get Tiffany Brooks over for dinner so I can see for myself." She laughed, same music.

"I'll get her schedule."

CHAPTER 10

Misty sipped her coffee then shot an email off to a fellow analyst who'd reached out for help tracing a hack. It'd been simple, but she didn't let on. Who ever said she couldn't play nice?

Cyrus had called the night before to let her know his trip was happening and to warn her the SAC was pissed they'd hacked the servers of the social media outfits. She'd asked him how the SAC knew, but he hadn't needed to answer. He'd used the information Misty collected to justify his trip to Texas. It would've been nice if he found a way to work around it, was all. Blake didn't trust her, and use of her private sources instead of bureau data probably hadn't earned her any favors.

So be it. As much as it burned her to admit it, Cyrus had seen something in her and, not only had he kept her out of prison, but he assigned her valuable work. When he sent her into the field to interview a soldier at a national guard armory, she'd figured out the source of guns discovered in a mountain compound filled with preppers who wanted to form a new nation. The SAC had appreciated that bit of work, and Misty had started seeing her new role as an opportunity to dish out justice to assholes who deserved it. Definitely her cup of tea.

Although Blake had congratulated her on the investigative work, she still wondered if an outsider could ever earn his trust. Be more than a tool.

A hammer the SAC probably wanted to shove into his toolbox and forget about. Considering Cyrus's warning about Blake's disposition toward her, it was a good morning to work remotely.

But with Cyrus on a flight to Texas and the cases in Cyber progressing without her, she found herself tapping one foot incessantly. The cage was too quiet, giving a memory that surfaced that morning too much room to breathe in her brain—Joanna and Jolene at the house in West Virginia, emptying their backpacks to fill them with clothes, their father unconscious on the floor of Jolene's bedroom.

Anastasia, she reminded herself. Always Anastasia.

She caught a memory of her younger sister's face, an image of her laughing as they ran along Greenbriar River in the rain. Misty couldn't recall what had happened that day. The memory was foggy. But the images magnified her sense Anastasia was in danger. If she didn't find a trail to follow as the cool quietness of her tech lab bore down, she'd go crazy. Especially when Cyrus was out of pocket. It'd been a long time since she'd felt so alone, and she was surprised to find herself wishing he was there, breathing down her neck in the way that usually annoyed her to no end.

When the judge had suspended her sentence and ordered Misty to serve five years with the FBI or in prison, her mind had conjured Cyrus's badge. How it contrasted the symbol of oppression her father's silver shield had been.

A new thought took center stage.

Cyrus had been so quick to jump on the plane that they hadn't sat down to strategize. Had that been intentional? Had he warned her about Blake knowing she'd stay in her little lab? To keep her out of the SAC's danger zone? Was that motherfucker handling her?

You're looking for excuses to fuel your determination.

The internal warning wasn't far off the mark. When she dropped her discipline long enough to let her aggressive nature out to play, ideas came. Flurries of them. Then she was able to settle back down and focus. But it sometimes fed her left-shoulder demon, got her bearing down so hard she couldn't come out of it for hours.

I don't have time for that shit.

She drummed her fingers on the table and squeezed her eyes closed. In her military days, she'd done this—forced herself into the here and now, painted her consciousness with a black sheet to remove distractions, suspended reality so she could play a role to keep from getting shot... or beheaded.

The dinner from the previous night swept into her mind when she opened her eyes. The framed portrait of Marsha and Cy. Then, just Marsha.

Misty's heart thumped. She snatched up her cell then dialed.

"Well, this is a pleasant surprise."

Misty conjured her friendliest tone. "Hey, there. You busy?"

"The dead never rest." Coroner humor. "Okay, I didn't think that one through. What's up?"

"At dinner, you told us about a guy who'd worked for LPS who committed suicide. Do you remember his name off the top of your head?"

"Chet something. Hold on." Misty tapped her fingers on the desktop until Marsha spoke again a minute later. "Chet Parsons. Want his address?"

"Well, sure."

Marsha rattled it off, and Misty tapped it into her phone.

"Thanks, Marsha. Oh, and would you mind keeping this between us for now?"

"Keep what between us?"

"Thanks."

"You got it. Any word on Anna?"

That she'd remembered her sister's name said something about Marsha that Misty liked.

"Nothing new. I'm digging."

"Well, If you need a break, stop by for a glass of wine tonight. We don't get any one-on-one time with Cyrus sucking the air out of the room."

Misty laughed. "I'll see how things go."

"No pressure. Talk to you later."

Misty slapped her space bar then ran a low-tech web search for Chet Parsons. An obituary announced he'd served in Afghanistan, like Misty, but at another base. God knew there'd been enough of them. Among his many awards was a purple heart. She found a line at the end that would keep her from having to hack into LPS's servers, which would keep her from pissing Blake off.

Chet loved his job as an IT Security Manager for Lockhart Public Security.

There it was. One of those little rays of sunlight sifting through the darkness to reveal a path when she needed one most.

The plan forming in her head was insane. Cy would lose his filter. The SAC might take her back to the judge and be done with her. But the case of her sister's disappearance wasn't going to be solved in Hope Mills, Texas. Maybe Cyrus would dig up some dirt on Lockhart, and maybe he wouldn't. But sitting idle in Denver was pointless when Jolene—Anna, always Anna—might be in peril.

She checked every source she knew for job postings at Lockhart, but found nothing. Zilch. Nada.

New tack.

Since Lockhart had been on a PR run lately, and since the federal and local governments were watching, there'd be plenty of media coverage. If LPS hadn't filled the IT management position in the wake of Chet Parson's death, she had an angle. A way in. While she could try to hack personnel records, the SAC would *definitely* drop her off at the courthouse for it. But sitting around wasn't helping her sister.

Misty filled her screen with news articles, checked the accompanying photos. For an hour, she dug. Then she found a video of Lockhart giving an interview on the Alex Riddle podcast. About twenty minutes in, the camera panned, and Misty spied a figure standing in the wings, cast in the backstage shadows. She zoomed the view, homed in on the broad-shouldered man in a suit.

Then she grinned.

Now she needed a number. After a half hour of nothing, she went to the secure chat and asked for an info dump. It came fifteen minutes later, which told her the intel network was growing. It was time to contribute some untraceable cash to the effort, and she made a mental note to do it when her work was finished.

The dossier on Tasker White included a cell number. She just hoped he hadn't changed it.

It rang three times, and she started to think he wouldn't pick up an unknown number. But the fourth ring was interrupted, and his voice burst through the speaker.

"This is Tasker."

"Hey, dickhead. It's Daniels."

"Bagheera? No shit! Where the hell you been?"

"Everywhere. Nowhere. How about you?"

"You wouldn't believe me if I told you."

"Ooh, the suspense."

"You been watching the news?"

"Here and there."

"Seen anything about Lockhart Public Security?"

"I don't live in a cave." Noting the dark surroundings and sparse furnishings surrounding her, that wasn't exactly true. "Wow. You're with that outfit?"

They went back and forth for a few minutes. Tasker claimed to love the new gig. Misty said it sounded like a pretty good setup for the vets, probably better than the VA and returning to the war zones as a mercenary. Tasker White agreed, telling her they'd set up a nice place in Colorado Springs. Then he told her he'd need to run, but they should catch up.

"Hey, did you say Colorado Springs?"

"Yeah. Why?"

"Dude, I'm in Denver. Are you guys hiring?"

A long silence ensued, and Misty wondered if she'd pulled the trigger too fast. But Tasker adopted an even, deliberate tone. "What kind of work are you looking for?"

"I got a degree in Cyber Security at Georgetown after I left the service, remember?" They'd only touched base a couple times since they'd made their exodus from Afghanistan, but it'd come up.

"Shit, I forgot about that." Another few seconds of silence on the line. "Tell you what, I'll talk to the boss, myself. We had an unfortunate loss recently, and I think you might be a good replacement. But he works fast, and he doesn't bullshit around. That's why I like him. If I can get you in for a tour, how fast can you be here?"

"By the time you hang up."

He laughed. "Perfect. I'll wait for the right time to drop it on him. Get him in the right mood. Might take a day or two, might be today. You sure you're up for that kind of speed?"

"Ever known me to be any other way? I'm at your disposal. Need the work."

"Which is lucky for us. The interim guy is a pain in the ass, and I fear he's learning on the job. We need to get someone in here before he breaks the whole system. I'll hit you back."

Her phone beeped as the call ended.

CHAPTER 11

Something about sitting in a metal tube zipping across the sky made time stutter like wheels on a rusty axle. Cyrus drew a deep breath when he cleared the exit ramp and entered the terminal.

Tiffany Brooks proved good for the hug she'd promised, and she actually squeezed. Although he'd sat in the second row the day she testified against Ethan Pierce, she had vacated the premise with her own security team immediately after testifying. They'd talked several times on the phone, but this was their first in-person conversation since the night he'd pulled her out of Pierce's basement.

So, it was something of a reunion.

Brooks squeezed his shoulders. "So good to see an old friend." They'd known each other for just under a year, but he wasn't going to point it out. Like airplanes, bonds forged in intense situations elongated time.

When she whisked him out the sliding doors at the airport, a limo was waiting. The driver opened the back door, and Cyrus peered inside at the leather seats on either side of the passenger compartment.

"What the hell is all this?" Cyrus studied her, noting her turtleneck and jeans seemed out of place against the backdrop of the formal furnishings.

If a curious photographer got a picture of a fed exiting a limousine at the church shooting scene, Blake would be less than pleased. Especially when the tall, lean, and inarguably beautiful Tiffany Brooks stepped out with him. Her protest interview there had been plastered on the national news. Not the kind of trouble Cyrus needed.

She read him like a children's fairy tale. "Get over it, Cy. We're going to the hotel first, and we can grab a cab from there. Just thought you'd like to ride in style for once."

"Hotel? I'm not staying over."

"Oh." She twisted her hands and tugged at one of her fingers. "Well, that's fine. We'll park a few blocks from the church and walk."

He scanned the limo a second time. "Who's paying your expenses, Tiffany?"

"I'm afraid that's confidential. Now, you want me to call you a cab or you want to get in the fucking limo?"

Tiffany had pulled out the stops. He remembered what she'd said about his being her lone remaining friend and, although he wasn't sure he believed that, embarrassment over his lack of gratitude decided him. "Ladies first."

"Always a gentleman." She slid in and scooted, then Cyrus dropped into the seat across from her.

The driver sped them across town in fifteen minutes. Two weeks after the shooting, the crime scene tape had been removed, but reporters still lined the sidewalk, which told Cyrus they were on to Lockhart like birds of prey to carrion.

Tiffany read him again. "Vultures everywhere. Here. The Denver Capitol. The school in Missouri. It's like they're waiting for follow-up attacks. They'll interview anybody. Glad you wore jeans."

"Yeah. But not everyone is keeping it low-key." He pointed toward a couple of feds wearing windbreakers on the sidewalk, separated from the media crews. A closer look revealed a familiar woman with dark hair pulled back into a bun, the way she'd worn it during the joint task force in the Rockies. Shauna Edenborough was chatting with one of her colleagues, golden ATF logos stamped on the backs of their windbreakers.

He coaxed Tiffany to walk with him.

"Fancy meeting you here," Cyrus said after they'd approached. Shauna turned, scanned the pair, then recognition dawned.

"Agent Jennings." She shook his hand. "Good to see you. What's the bureau got going on down here?"

"Nothing official. This is how I spend my vacations."

Edenborough smiled. "Right." She offered Tiffany a hand. "Miss Brooks."

"I guess my news interview precedes me," Tiffany replied. "I don't know if I'll get used to that."

Cyrus's bullshit meter sounded off. Tiffany had funding, and funds came with objectives. She had every intention of garnering attention and, notoriety was a long family tradition.

Edenborough introduced them to her coworker. "This is Eddie Gunn. Asshole I work with."

Eddie flashed a smile and grasped their hands, but he didn't respond. Cyrus had to respect that.

"So, are you two on vacation *together*?" Edenborough asked. She winked at Cyrus.

Tiffany hooked her arm inside his. "Absolutely. Why, we'll be checking into my hotel room when we're finished here, and I doubt we'll come out again for days."

Recalling his discussion with Marsha the night before, Cyrus found himself at ease. A surprising, accompanying thought reared up.

It's time to process the divorce papers.

Although they'd been separated for years, Cyrus had never cut ties with his long-distance, super runner ex-wife. Although they remained friends, they hadn't talked in ages because she galivanted around the world to train and race. He made a mental note to pull the trigger.

He cleared his throat and trained his attention on Edenborough. "Why are you guys lingering? Shooting was two weeks ago."

"We're trying to trace the purchase of the guns. The serials were filed down. But our bosses like to tie up loose ends. We want to follow the White supremacy angle, see if the weapon came from some connection in a local community, but the local sheriff isn't being very cooperative."

"Makes sense. No one's going to claim responsibility for selling weapons with no serial numbers, even less to a White nationalist psycho. Go figure."

"We've exasperated local pawn shop owners, but we don't have anything yet."

"Dead ends suck," Tiffany said.

Edenborough chuckled. "Reach a lot of those in your line of work?"

"You'd be surprised."

A car door slammed, and Edenborough shared a look with her partner. "Here we go again."

A portly guy in a brown and tan uniform pulled his hat onto his rotund head. He made a beeline for the group, waving off reporters as he passed.

"Play dumb," Edenborough said.

"Comes naturally," Cyrus replied.

There was no mistaking the sheriff's up-and-down

gander of Cyrus. Disdain. The fucker was spoiling for it.

"Friend of yours, Edenborough?"

Shauna wore a mask of stoicism. "What's it to you, sheriff? It's a free country. Public sidewalk."

The sheriff cleared his throat. "Who are you?"

Cyrus deliberated then reached for his cred pack. "FBI." The contentious vibe between the local and the ATF agent aided in his decision not to share his name. Blake didn't want the attention. Cy shoved the pack back into his pocket.

"Thought you guys cleared out." Without waiting for an answer, he returned his focus to the ATF folks. "Thought you would have too by now."

"Why? Because you had someone call our boss?"

"I didn't call anyone."

"Right. Look, sheriff. We're here to do a job, and we're going to do it."

"Not if you get in my way, you aren't."

Cyrus gave the sheriff an up-and-down of his own. "Who the hell are you?"

The local cop stepped forward, but not quite close enough to threaten. "I'm Sheriff Newsome. And you're standing in my county."

"And no one else is going to piss in it, right? Why don't you go bust a meth head or something? The real cops are trying to work."

"That why I saw you walk up with a liberal operative?" The sheriff dipped his chin. "Miss Brooks."

She didn't reply.

It hit Cyrus that the sheriff knew Tiffany's name. From news coverage?

Newsome thrust a thumb over one shoulder. "I'm willing to bet those reporters would find that real interesting. The feds. A democratic operative. That could get noisy."

Blake's face flashed in Cyrus's mind. He'd already gone too far with his aggressive inquiry, and this wasn't his SAC's idea of low key. But before he could respond, Tiffany rang in.

"Who says I'm an operative of any kind?"

"Because you were on the TV with a bunch of lib protestors."

"I hope you do better police work than that."

"I notice the FBI guy still hasn't said why he's here."

"Sure. You win, sheriff. I'm here on vacation, and I heard Miss Edenborough, who I worked a case with earlier this year, was in town. So, I thought I'd come over and say hi. Tiffany is an old friend, and that's all there is to it."

"Right. You usually take your badge on vacation?"

Cyrus could no longer resist. "Yeah, I go all-out on the rest and relaxation, and I've found it's useful when local law enforcement shows up to rouse me. They sometimes have a way of doing that to folks who look like me."

The sheriff's nose twitched. "Ah, the race card.

Look, y'all. It's been two weeks. My department is investigating, and I don't appreciate you all sticking around. With your manpower, you've had all the time you need. Now, I'm not one to cause trouble—"

"The hell you aren't," Tiffany replied. "What do you think you're doing right now?"

The sheriff clutched his hips. "And you, little missy, have no authority here at all." It came out as 't-all.' "You'd do better to let the people with badges hash this out."

When Tiffany turned her gaze toward him, Cyrus gave her a subtle head shake. She fumed but kept her peace.

Edenborough took up the slack. "We got your message, sheriff. If it's of any consequence to you, we're packing up tonight and will be on the first flight out tomorrow. Anything else?"

The sheriff nodded, his smug expression showing how pleased he was with himself. "Well, that'll be just fine." The fucker pinched the brim of his hat. "Have a nice day." He shot Tiffany a final sneer. "Y'all."

Shauna waited until he was out of earshot. "Asshole."

Tiffany nodded. "Agreed."

Edenborough took a step toward Cyrus and spoke in a low voice. "In the interest of sharing..." She looked over Cyrus's shoulder, obviously checking the proximity of the reporters. "We have a line on a guy who was friends with Mike Bray. The dead guy. The sheriff has deputies following us around, and my boss doesn't want a lot of hassle. I smell politics, but we can't get near anyone without Newsome showing up and reminding people they don't have to answer our questions without an attorney. There's something dirty at work. But we might be able to help each other out. That asshole has been watching us like we're the shooters. As you've just seen, he interrogates us on the regular, as if we answer to him. Constantly asking where we are on our investigation."

Tiffany nodded. "He holds elected office. The shooting happened on his watch. Even though it was thwarted, he didn't stop it, and that won't play well if he doesn't get in front of it. From what my contacts tell me, he had warnings about the shooter prior to the event. His next opponent is going to find out," she raised a hand to one side of her mouth, "because I'm going to tell whoever that is." She dropped the hand. "He probably wants you out of the way so he can harass the locals himself and find out where those guns came from."

Edenborough tilted her head to one side. "You ever think about going into law enforcement?"

Cyrus chuckled. "I think she'd stand out."

"The fuck is that supposed to mean, Cy?" She punched his shoulder.

Edenborough scanned her again. "Yeah, I see what you mean."

"Are you sexually harassing a private citizen, Agent Edenborough?"

"No, but if you'd like to have coffee sometime..."

The four burst out laughing, including Tiffany.

Edenborough leaned toward the group. "The first time Sheriff Newsome came over to ask us why we were still here, I tried to be polite about it. But he's persistent as Tom at Jerry's mouse hole. So, I showed him my badge as a reminder to go fuck himself. Next thing you know, my boss's boss is getting calls from a congresswoman. My supervisor's not the kind to give a shit, usually. But look around. The media's still here. Newsome could walk right up to them and talk about how the feds are obstructing *his* investigation, and how we're coming up empty."

"And because it's so high profile, your boss is telling you to keep quiet."

"He's telling us to fly back tomorrow. Like he suddenly wants to let the locals deal with it."

Cyrus tilted his chin toward the ground. "This sounds entirely too familiar." He looked up. "How can I help?"

"We've been wanting to talk to the friend, the shooter's neighbor, but the sheriff tails us. Maybe we could try a little bait and switch then you could let us know what you find out."

"This sounds like fun," Tiffany said, but her tone didn't convey the sentiment very well.

"It could be. If Cyrus were to knock on some doors, we could lead the sheriff off on a goose chase."

"I want in on that action," Tiffany said.

"No badge. You're not law enforcement."

"Fuck your badge, sonny boy. I'm your ride, and I want Lockhart's ass on a platter. I think I've earned it."

An image of Tiffany in Ethan Price's basement served as a reminder she had.

"Fine."

Edenborough flashed a thumbs-up. "Just let us know if you find anything on the weapons, and you can use whatever you like for the bureau's investigation."

"There is no bureau investigation." He winked at her. "But I don't like that asshole, and I'm happy to help."

Edenborough smiled, and Cyrus found it disarming. "Who ever said there was no inter-agency cooperation?"

CHAPTER 12

Perched behind his oak desk with his third-in-command lounging in the chair across from him, Sam Lockhart listened as the CEO of Country Bank prattled on over the speaker. If Sam played his cards right, he'd land an instrumental client to get the cash flow moving in the right direction. Although he and Ethan had planned the new enterprise for years before pulling the trigger, and despite Pierce's deep well of liquid assets, no one wanted to be in the red forever. Especially when tax time came, LPS's records became public, and media scrutiny kicked into overdrive.

The CEO cleared his throat. "I'll be straight with you Sam. I'm dealing with a bunch of small-time security contractors in each state where we operate. Do you know how many states that is, Sam?"

"Including single branches in Hawaii and Alaska, Fifty."

"Right. Every state in the union. Ever since we started our investment firms, we've been blowing up. And while paperwork is part of banking, paying thirty-five security firms at varying rates is inefficient. My accounting firm is making too much money. The board brought me on to slim things down. To trim the fat, as we like to say in Arkansas."

Sam decided not to mention they said that everywhere.

"This is where I think we can help each other. But I also need reassurances."

"Name them."

"All these hippie liberals in Chicago, New York, and LA love their gun control laws, and I know you've been avoiding those places to stay away from the red tape. While I'm willing to take you on in the states where you can operate, I need assurances you can expand so I can ditch the little guys. Are your guys ready to get licensed in California? Illinois?"

"I'll tell you, Randy, that's exactly what we plan to do. All the stuff you've been seeing on TV is just the beginning. Red states are easy, so that's where we've started. I can barely manage the switchboard with all the companies calling us in those areas. Our call centers are lit up. But we're also planning some PR in the other places you mentioned. As a matter of fact, I'll let you in on a little secret. You ready for this?"

"Sure."

"Watch your cable news channel of choice on

Tuesday at one. We have a little surprise brewing that'll turn the tide in our favor."

"Fair enough. You lock in those cities, promise me a fair rate, and show me you can roll out trained personnel to protect all our branches over the next twelve months, and I'll buy the executive package."

"Music to my ears, Randy."

"I'll call you later in the week."

"Looking forward to it."

Sam tapped the speaker button to hang up.

"Holy shit, boss," Tasker said, leaning forward in his chair. "That's big."

"It could put us in the black a year ahead of schedule. And if a smaller outfit like his buys in, imagine what the big boys can do when the PR tide turns."

"That's what you call a small outfit? I can barely fathom it."

Lockhart eased into his chair. "Speaking of which, we're all set in Chicago, right?"

Tasker nodded. "Last time I talked to the XO, he said as much. Sounded confident."

"Good. I can't wait to watch the talking heads explode on Fox and CNN. You heard from Rhymer?"

Tasker shook his head. "Told me he was taking care of something for you and would be off-site for a bit."

That was as Sam and Tom had discussed on the phone after the Alex Riddle interview. Fucking reporter. He hated being in containment mode.

"That's fine. Anything else?"

"As a matter of fact, I think I've found a replacement for Chet."

Chet. The former IT Security Manager.

"Who's the candidate?"

"A chick I served with in Afghanistan. She got a degree in Cyber Security after she separated. We haven't been in touch for a while, but I can vouch with confidence. She's living in Denver."

"Was she part of your team in special forces?"

"I'll put it to you this way, boss, but we have to keep it between us."

Sam nodded. "Okay."

"On paper, she was a sniper. Fucking good one, too. But after sundown, she paired up with another guy on our team and did things they don't log. Like a fucking ninja. We called her Bagheera."

The name rang a bell. Lockhart rifled through his brain shelves then nodded. "Like the black panther from Jungle Book."

Tasker smiled. "Damn, I'm impressed."

"I had a kid, remember?"

Tasker frowned. "Right."

"So, she's an operative, but she'd be better for IT?"

"Unless you're planning on expanding into corporate espionage or something."

Sam chuckled. "I think we'll keep it on the up and up. But who knows, maybe she could go to work for Tactical." Lockhart Tactical was his military contractor. If it hadn't been for the Gabby

Sutton fiasco and Jake Ramon's employment by that wing of his enterprise, LPS would probably have dangled from that branch on the org-chart. But Pierce had wanted a clean start, and Sam couldn't blame him.

"I don't think she'd want that job. She left the service because she didn't believe in the mission anymore."

"Is she an attitude case?"

"Would I bring her to you if she was?" Tasker leaned in and set his elbows on his knees. "She's disciplined. Attentive to detail. I've seen her stay awake for over forty-eight hours at a time. I think she's a good fit. Besides, Justin isn't a network security guy, and I want to get him back in his own wheelhouse before he sets the server room on fire."

"If you think she's family, pull the trigger. I've heard Justin Watson is chewing the XO's ear off about getting him out of the interim position so he can get back to the email stuff. What's it called?"

"Active Directory. Exchange servers."

"Right. He's burning the candle at both ends, and Xavier is tired of listening to his shit. Seems the two of you are of one mind on this, and that's good enough for me. Let Xavier know then get this lady in for a tour ASAP."

"How's today grab you?"

Sam admired Tasker for a long moment. "That's why you're my third, Tasker. You always manage to surprise me. Get it done." He pressed the button on his phone. "Janie, who's next?"

His assistant's voice rang out of the speaker with perfect clarity. "The CFO from Ticket Nation is waiting on the line. The concert promoter."

"Perfect."

CHAPTER 13

The guy answering the door wore a flannel shirt with one tail tucked and a pair of dirty jeans. Construction, Cyrus guessed. His swift glances at Tiffany's form-fitting turtleneck didn't go unnoticed.

Tiffany unleashed her southern drawl with complete conviction. "Hey there. I'm Tiff. This is Cy. We've been going around the neighborhood asking folks about the shooting at that church across town. We understand the shooter lived in this neighborhood."

Smart. She didn't let on that this was the only door they'd knocked, that they knew he was a friend of Michael Bray's. Best to keep him from getting defensive. How he answered would determine their angle of approach.

The guy's forehead formed waves. "Y'all media types?"

"Oh, Lord no. Not the kind you're thinking about.

We write for *Second Amendment Truth*. You know, to shine the light on liberal hypocrisy surrounding gun rights." The speed of her response was a credit to her quick wit, but Cyrus also made a mental note about her ability to lie when it suited her purpose. The untruth also said something about the bias flowing through her bloodstream.

If the guy saw Tiffany on the news, they'd be fried. But if Cyrus had learned anything on the job, it was that peoples' attention spans had been emaciated ever since Apple dropped the iPhone. Then social media pervaded society, and all bets were off.

"Oh!" His features lit up. "Well, in that case, I'm Rayford Clemmons, and it's your lucky day."

"How's that?" Tiffany asked.

"Because me and Mikey went to high school together. Were really close until recently. Matter of fact, I came home for lunch to feed his dog."

"His dog's still at his house?" Tiffany asked. "They didn't take it to the pound?"

"Naw. When I heard about the shooting, I high-tailed it up the street. The cops beat me to it, and I was afraid they'd shoot her—they do that when they're clearing a scene, you know. Shoot the dogs."

Tiffany nodded. "Atrocious."

Cyrus didn't read this response as a lie. But he'd also never seen her with a dog.

"Sure is. But Bessie was chained up in the back, and I arrived in time to *explain* to them that he'd been watching her for me. That I wanted to take her home." He beamed with pride about his own lie. "Even if they didn't shoot her, I couldn't have her sitting alone for days at his place. Of course, that beast would probably chew through steel. She's a pittie, you see. Sweet as can be, but you wouldn't want to stray into her territory by mistake. Cops would've shot her."

Cy nodded. "Love those dogs."

"Yeah," Rayford replied, "They get a bad rap."

"Sure do!" Tiffany's exuberance was a bit elevated for Cyrus's taste, but Clemmons didn't seem to notice.

"So, what did you want to know about Mikey?"

Tiffany eyed the wicker chairs and a swinging bench on the porch. "Mind if we sit?"

"Not at all."

Cyrus took the swing.

Rayford sat with his legs splayed wide open. "Shoot." He frowned a moment later. "Okay, maybe not the best wording, considering the circumstances."

"Probably not," Tiffany agreed with the kind of smile that could drain a guy's wallet in any hotel bar in America. "We heard rumors Michael was in with some bad dudes. Know anything about that?"

The Texan scoffed. "More media trash. It's not true. Why would he risk falling in with a bad crowd if he wanted to work for Sam Lockhart? Say what you will about military contractors, but I'd be willing to bet that Lockhart guy wouldn't shine to hiring a crazy."

Cyrus's heart jumped into his throat. "Wait," he blurted. "He worked for Lockhart?"

"Not quite. Mikey went up there because one of his service buddies said they was hirin' and stuff. Spent two weeks in a hotel. But he come back empty-handed. We hung out for a Longhorns game when he got back. I'm not afraid to tell you, he was pretty pissed about it, too. Said they'd wasted his time. That his former commanding officer'd turned out to be a real asshole. But when the cops said Mikey had been spending time with the Truth Tellers, well, I knew something was off. Mikey's a good man. Loved his country and respected the law. He ain't the type to fall in with them nutjobs. Heard they found pamphlets, papers about the KKK and the like. Sounds fishy to me." He shot Cyrus a poorly conceived nod of brotherhood. "We avoided them guys in high school. Don't believe for a second they sucked him in, no matter how pissed he was at this Lockhart place."

Cyrus's mind raced with the new information, and he tried to tie strings together on his mental vision board.

Tiffany chewed her lip for a few seconds before taking up his slack. "So, he wasn't the racist type?"

"Well, it all depends on how you define the word." He cut his eyes toward Cyrus. "Maybe you'd say different, but no. Mikey ain't racist. Not many folks 'round here are like that, really. Might not acquaint with people of color, but we ain't gonna go out and burn crosses in your yards, either."

Cyrus needed to meditate, and Cyrus didn't meditate.

"But these guys are full-on white supremacists, these 'Truth Tellers.' Whatever happened in Colorado, I could tell he was mad about it, but he'd never turn away from common sense like that. He'd been the gentle giant type before Iraq, and I still saw some of it in him after. And when he got back from LPS, well, I admit he turned like bad spinach. Just not *that* bad."

"Did he tell you what happened in Colorado?"

"Not much." Then he smacked one knee. "Well, he did say he expected too much from the XO."

Tiffany nodded her understanding. "Military titles. Executive officer. Second-in-command."

Her knowledge continued to surprise Cyrus.

Rayford slipped right back into his stream. "Lockhart folks wanted him to do counseling or something, and Mikey said he was willing, but then they bowed out."

A car door slammed, and Cyrus leaned forward to get a view around some high shrubs. A sheriff's cruiser shone in the afternoon sun, and none other than Sheriff Newsome strolled across the street toward the sidewalk leading up to the house.

Shit.

Cyrus and Tiffany stood. Newsome flashed them a shit-eating grin before turning his attention to Rayford.

"Heya, Ray. Talking to the feds, are ya?"

The flannel-wearing younger man's shoulders tensed. "Feds? They aren't feds."

The sheriff thrust a finger toward Cyrus. "That one is."

"But you all said..." Rayford backed away. "Well, that ain't right! Ain't right at all!"

This fucking guy.

The sheriff went for a simpatico expression. "You probably want them off your property, don't you Ray?"

Rayford nodded without losing his sneer. "I sure as hell do! Bunch of lying—"

"You two come with me," Newsome ordered.

Cyrus looked over his shoulder before mounting the stairs. "We're going to find out what happened and make someone pay for it. That's the truth."

Rayford's screen door slammed when the trio reached the sidewalk.

Cyrus's mind went into overdrive as he considered the rotund local. A light bulb flashed. Something Edenborough had said about phone calls to her boss. Congresspeople getting involved on the sheriff's behalf. As they strolled, Cyrus looked up and down the street to ensure the minor ruckus hadn't stirred up any onlookers before unclenching his teeth to speak.

"What's it like being Lockhart's puppet, Sheriff?"

Newsome wheeled, and one clawed hand rose from his side, like he planned on getting a handful of something.

Cyrus thought about Blake. The likelihood he'd be disavowed if he pushed. But this prick was pressing buttons, and it was time to test the waters. Cyrus stepped forward. "I dare you to put your hands on me."

Newsome reached for the cuffs on the back of his belt then let them dangle from his grasp. "I'll run you in for resisting. How will your bosses in DC feel about that?"

"Resisting arrest? That's a reach. What's the offense you're arresting me for?"

"I think Ray would agree you were trespassing."

Cyrus lowered his voice to a whisper. "By the time those cuffs graze my skin, you'll be flat on your back. I'm a federal officer on a federal investigation, and you're a podunk cop with a bad attitude. If anything, you're interfering with a federal investigation and, while the ATF might've bowed to your bullshit, I'm not the ATF."

"Thought you were on vacation."

"I lied. And you're not that naive. Or maybe you are."

True to form, Tiffany stood straighter. "You really want to think about your next move, Sheriff. You're not the only one with political connections, and I'll have him out in an hour."

"You talk big, but I'll bet you're just some small fry from nowhere."

Tiffany flashed her teeth, but it was the kind of psychopathic smile that negated beauty. She spat words through her teeth. "Then why don't you slap those cuffs on *me* and find out."

Cy's mind took a right turn. If the sheriff called her bluff, Blake would have his badge, whether by early retirement or an outright firing. The SAC's bosses would be the final deciders. But it wasn't just Blake who he worried about.

What kind of a hypocrite am I? I told Misty to focus on her sister's disappearance. That we would play by the book so Blake could sell what we were doing.

Yet, there he was. Standing on a residential street in Texas investigating a shooting under the guise that Anastasia Clark might have discovered something about Lockhart and the shooter and gotten herself into trouble. But she could've been anywhere. Her editor had been clear about how the reporter went dark sometimes. Even if she had linked LPS to the shooter, Michael Bray never worked there. He'd left Misty on her own so he could chase his inner demons. Follow his gut down a dead-end road to find dirt on a guy who'd already gotten away with his crimes.

At the very least, they had nothing to go on in the case of the vanished reporter, and he wasn't going to find the answer hundreds of miles from where Anastasia had last been seen.

He waved one hand. "That's enough. Let's go, Tiffany."

The sheriff snatched her arm. "I didn't say she could go anywhere."

If Newsome hadn't been clutching her with his gun hand, Cyrus wouldn't have dreamed of reaching for his cell phone, but he did. He tapped the screen. Time for one final bluff.

"The hell are you doing?"

"Calling the FBI Field office in Austin. When I tell them how you've been obstructing federal investigations, they're going to swarm your county. Who knows, maybe it'll be you who's wearing handcuffs come this time tomorrow. Honestly, I wonder what Lockhart's gonna think."

"I don't even know Sam Lockhart, smart guy." He released Tiffany then gave her a little shove. "You're not worth the trouble."

"On that, we agree."

"You two want to hang around the church, go on. I don't care. But this investigation is local now. Sure, the ATF can investigate the gun trail all they want, but Mike Bray lived in my county, and the crime happened here. Heads are gonna roll, and I'm gonna roll them."

Cyrus forced his animosity down. "Understood. Sorry we got off on the wrong foot. I got what I came for."

"Then piss off." The sheriff wheeled, looked both ways, then crossed to his cruiser.

Tiffany watched him go. "If it's all the same to you, I'm going to take his advice."

"Which advice?"

"I'm gonna go back to the church. He just gave me an idea. What time's your return flight?"

Cyrus checked his watch. "Three hours."

"Then we have time for a late lunch." She tucked her arm inside the crook of his elbow then smiled up at him. "What do you think of some Texas barbecue?"

"I could eat."

CHAPTER 14

The renovated hospital's interior polish and shine contrasted the dilapidated exterior to the point it bordered on subterfuge. Misty immediately tied it to how Lockhart hired 1099 contractors instead of full-time employees to hide his investment until the outfit was up and running. They hadn't even removed the aged ER sign she strolled past to enter the building.

Why bother walling the place in?

With marble columns and polished concrete floors, what had been an emergency room was now a welcoming, sprawling lobby with four receptionist's chairs behind a huge wooden counter she might have found at the Four Seasons, but only one of them was occupied. A familiar face waited just inside the sliding doors.

She'd watched YouTube videos to pick up tips about how to contour her face, to change her appearance so the familial resemblance between her and Anna would be less obvious. She'd even donned a pair of fake glasses. Tasker wouldn't notice because he'd known her before. But she didn't want anyone else at LPS picking up the resemblance.

"Tasker." She thrust out a hand.

His enveloped hers as he pulled her forward to give her a quick, one-armed hug and slap her on the back. A light behind him cast her in his shadow, but Tasker White towered over most people.

"Daniels. Welcome to LPS."

She put on her best smile. "Glad to be here." She set a hand of splayed fingers on her chest. "I'm grateful you got me in so fast."

"No prob. We've got a real whiner handling the interim duties until we find someone new, and Ed Xavier wants to shut him up. He's the XO. My boss's boss."

"His title carried over?"

White chuckled. "Sure. He was second in the chain for a highly decorated unit in Fallujah, 2004. They don't let us forget the highly decorated part."

"First Stryker Brigade?" It was no secret the Alaska-based Army unit out of Fort Wainwright had been tasked with killing or driving out insurgents during the early years of Operation Iraqi Freedom.

"That's them. Bunch of them work here. Since they still called him XO, it just kind of carried over to the rest of us."

"Those guys went through it."

"To hell and back, to hear the stories." He gestured toward a bank of elevators. "IT is in the basement."

Since she stood in a refurbished hospital, Misty thought of Marsha. "The basement? You mean the morgue?"

"Ha." He pressed the call button. "Check your six. Does this look like an ER to you?"

"No, it doesn't."

"Right. The morgue is gone. Servers are down there. Everything has been primed, painted, and polished. New infrastructure. Gigabit everything. The server room looks like the inside of an alien spaceship. Nothing half-assed."

"Sounds expensive."

"If you meet the boss, try not to remind him. He's burning the candle at both ends to make it profitable. Although I'm not in the know, I suspect he has investors to please."

Like Ethan Pierce.

If Tasker didn't know about that, it spoke to the level of compartmentalization at LPS.

The elevator doors closed when Tasker punched the B button. They hadn't gotten around to refurbishing the interior of the metal box. Misty's mind blazed in wonderment over who did the construction and how long Lockhart had been planning this project.

"Those Stryker guys have to be getting up there. That was like twenty years ago."

131

"There's no shortage of gray hairs. But age commands respect."

She eyed all the buttons and noted the hospital was 17 floors, including the basement.

"Are there patients in the wings upstairs?"

"Not enough employees yet. We're still spinning things up, and the top floor is for Lockhart and the XO. He wants to expand, with smaller installations across the country to comply with local laws and licensing. It's an interesting concept, right? Vets we employ who need more intensive care, like cancer treatment and the like, can be flown in and cared for. We want to hire veteran docs, nurses with military experience. But until we've expanded, there's little point."

"Does he think he can replace the VA?"

The elevator doors parted and a bell rang. They stepped into a low-lit hallway with tile floors.

"Why would he want to? The VA's a mammoth enterprise. Lots of waste. Government at its finest. That kind of undertaking would suck money right out of the company. Besides, we can't hire everyone who served. But younger veterans, the kind he wants to send into the field, are in better shape. Everybody on staff agrees to weekly PT as part of their contract. Wellness cuts costs."

"They sign a contract?" That didn't mesh with the taxation approach Misty had assumed.

"More of an agreement. You know, in some roles people have to be able to lift fifty pounds. Like UPS or

FedEx, right? We just lay the requirements out so there's no mistaking the core principles. Sound body and sound mind. LPS is going to be one big family, and by providing health care in those rare instances where it's needed, we don't pay insurance overhead. We take care of it ourselves."

He led her up a wide corridor then gestured toward an open doorway on the right.

"What if they want to get care somewhere else?"

"If Lockhart has his way, they won't want to. He plans on only hiring the best. The better the staff, the more recognition in the medical community. Good PR. But the less-evasive answer is, they can always go to the VA."

"Sounds like he's really going wide."

"It's about time someone did. This is the tech center. Heartbeat of the operation." He led her to another door on the right. The name Justin Watson was stenciled in small letters in a frosted sidelight. He knocked twice before entering the room without waiting for an invitation.

The guy inside stood to greet them. He wore a pair of wire-rimmed specs and a green tie over a checkered shirt.

"Tasker, how's it going?" His low tenor didn't match his wiry build.

"Good. This is Misty Daniels. She served with me in Afghanistan, and she's here about the IT Security Manager position."

He scanned her high to low, skipping much of the middle as he scampered around the desk then thrust out a hand. "Justin. Nice to meet you. Maybe you can take the load off."

Tasker gave his narrow shoulder a playful shove. "Don't scare her off before she gets her bearings, dude."

Watson chuckled. "Right. My bad. Have you shown her the office?"

"Nope. Hemingford will be down in a few for the grand tour and interview, but no one knows the job better than you. Thought you could show her the ins and outs."

"Happy to." Tasker squeezed Misty's shoulder. "Glad you're here. I've got a meeting, but you're in good hands. We'll have lunch."

Misty got the impression Tasker White's referral carried some weight, and that might be a shoe-in.

"Thanks, Tasker."

"C'mon." Justin led her across the drab, open area they'd entered from the hallway and across to double, metal doors. Fans hummed on the other side. He swept his card then led her through. The air was cool. Rows of servers neatly slotted into five racks filled the data center.

Misty had to speak up to be heard. "No way this place needs this many servers. You guys thinking about taking up where the NSA leaves off, or what?"

Watson's shoulders rumbled with his chortling but the sound didn't carry over the multitude of fans. His words did. "When the other buildings are occupied and this place gets up to full bore, we'll need all the compute capacity we can get. Not to mention it'll be the home office for satellite installations."

He badged open a door then led her down another hallway. The noise compressed when that door closed, and he spoke in a quieter voice that bounced off the narrow walls.

"There will be a lot of moving parts. I manage the Active Directory infrastructure and the email servers."

"Active Exchange, then?"

"Yup. You familiar?"

Misty smiled. "I've dabbled."

"Good to know. I'll need a vacation at some point." The last door didn't require a badge. He turned the metal handle then shoved it open. The lights overhead flickered to life.

"Wow, that's a lot of room."

He nodded. "Yep. And you'll have it all to yourself. As you can see, Chet preferred a sparser setup. Wasn't big into family pictures and the like, but he didn't spend a lot of time in here."

"Where was he?"

"Usually? Jamming with a pair of Beats on his head shoving servers into the racks and configuring them. He liked the hardware piece and configuration more than the admin role."

"That's understandable, really." She walked around the desk and eyed the Secret Labs gamer chair with a felt, magnetic headrest like the one stationed in her refuge.

"Why's it understandable?"

She looked up from the desk to find his gaze locked on hers, and something about the way he cocked a single eyebrow told Misty the query was more of a test. He wanted to know what she knew.

Why wait for the interview? This is the guy who works down here.

"Because server configuration is so automated these days, any fool could do it. Sure, there's other stuff to manage once they're connected, but I'm a security specialist. It comes pretty naturally at this point."

"Who have you done that for?"

"What? Security work?"

He nodded.

"Confidential clients. Suffice it to say everything from mom and pops to Fortune 500. Usually on a contract basis."

"Heh, you'll fit right in. If you get the gig, you'll be signing ten-ninety-nines."

Which she knew.

"That's fine. More money."

Justin flicked a thumb up. "Exactly. Give me cash any day. If I get the sniffles, I can just go up to the third floor and get a prescription. Can't beat it."

He walked her around the basement's maze of corridors, but there wasn't much to see. Open rooms where she could imagine bodies lying on metal tables with black countertops that probably housed all kind of lab machinery and telescopes. Marsha Pilson's kind of place.

"What's the smile for?"

"A friend of mine is a coroner. Reminds me of where she works."

"Makes sense." He checked his watch. "No point making Hemingford look for you. Let's roll back to the elevators so you can meet him there."

Misty got the impression he had somewhere to be but wasn't about to bring it up.

The tour of the facilities revealed the one-time hospital wings hadn't been overhauled like the lobby and basement. But they were clean, and modern computers and flat screens adorned the counters of the nurses' stations, reinforcing that Lockhart really was planning to fill the place out someday.

Too bad the tech might be outdated by then. Then again, hospitals didn't always boast the latest. She imagined getting the nurses and doctors to use electronic tablets instead of clipboards to register patients' updated metrics and the like was like pulling teeth.

CHAPTER 15

Ethan Pierce eyed the green light perched high on the sidewall with a modicum of disdain. Country club prison or not, there were rules, and Sam Lockhart knew them perfectly well. After all, it was his prison.

If one of Ethan's or Lockhart's lawyers were sitting at the table, that light would've been red. But since Sam had come alone, everything they were saying would be recorded. The question was, why would his business partner—a man in whom he'd invested an outrageous amount of capital—risk that?

The goddamned reporter is why. The Clark woman. He doesn't want me asking. Or maybe it has something to do with the suicide in his ranks.

The vet at the new facility who'd gone home and blown his brains out. The irony was Ethan would've had no reason to suspect anything if Lockhart hadn't come alone to ensure people were listening.

Hell, Sam might have wanted to avoid discussions about the Hope Mills shooter, who spent some time at LPS, according to Ethan's man.

Maybe it was all of it. Things were getting messy, and Sam Lockhart was *handling* Ethan. That would not do.

Sam prattled on. "...but Chicago is all set. We'll have all the major media outlets. The speakers have been interviewed, and they'll all be good on camera. And our friend in the state senate is all riled and ready to go."

Chicago. The first test bed in the second wave.

"Good. Is Country Bank on board?"

"Once they see the press conference in Chicago, they'll be begging to join up. The CEO was brought in to cut costs, and we're the best solution."

"Right."

Lockhart's forehead wrinkled, his eyes narrowed to slits. Had Ethan's animosity come across? He reminded himself to don his poker face... and maintain it.

"Something going on, Ethan? Bubba treating you okay?"

"You know damn well the guards aren't a problem. You saw to it."

"Then what?" Lockhart shrugged, the image of a petulant boy feigning innocence.

"You know what." Ethan glanced at the green light

then back at his business partner. "You're handling me, Sam."

Lockhart lowered his voice, but his growl still came across. "I'm protecting you, Ethan."

"Then why aren't we meeting on the putting green?"

Sam's expression morphed about four times as he tried to conjure an answer, but Pierce waved him off.

"Make sure Chicago comes off without a hitch. Ensure your tracks are covered about"—the green light seemed to flare brighter in his periphery—"anything else that might slow our progress."

As Ethan stood, the metal chair's legs screeched on the smooth concrete floor. "And next time you come here, bring a fucking lawyer."

CHAPTER 16

Two texts to Misty on his way to the airport, unanswered. He tried calling when he landed and let it ring until it went to voicemail. As if anyone checked messages anymore. When he slid into the back seat of the cab, Cyrus deliberated—go to Misty's haven or back to the office?

Since he'd just returned from an unsanctioned trip to Texas, and since Shauna Edenborough had enlightened him about political strings being pulled there, he made a career decision, choosing to fill Blake in on his trip. Although he'd been excited when learning the shooter applied at Lockhart, he'd had too much time to think about it on the plane. At the end of the day, it proved nothing. But it was one hell of a coincidence that Michael Bray ended up on the wrong side of one of LPS's guns after applying there. That couldn't be ignored.

Cyrus had to wait outside Blake's office for ten minutes while his boss wrapped a call with DC. Then he was beckoned inside.

The SAC's mood was obvious from the scowl on his face and the heat in his glare.

As Cyrus sat, the full weight of his predicament came down.

On one hand, he'd learned Michael Bray had applied at Lockhart Security. A hell of a coincidence. On the other, he'd gotten into a dust up with a local sheriff who either had political connections with DC politicians hailing from Texas or to Sam Lockhart. Or both.

"You want to guess who that was?" Blake flitted his eyes toward the phone.

Cyrus's brain jumped into overdrive, but it came up with too many possibilities for a guessing game.

The SAC took up the slack. "My boss. You want to tell me why you got into a territorial pissing contest with a sheriff in Hope Mills?"

"Because he's a puppet."

"For whom?"

"He denied knowing Lockhart, and I believe him. So I'm going with Ethan Pierce."

"Based on what?"

"Do you remember Shauna Edenborough?"

"Sure. ATF."

"The sheriff started his BS with her. Next thing you know, her boss is getting phone calls from

Congress. Before I left Hope Mills, Sheriff Newsome mentioned how he didn't care if ATF looked for the gun source, which tells me some kind of deal was broached. If you got a call, I'm betting Edenborough is about to be hamstrung. Told exactly what she can and can't investigate."

"So you go to Texas, and you come back with a new conspiracy involving the guys you have it out for."

"I can't really argue with that."

"And now you've got the brass looking at me."

"Are they pulling us off?"

"Like I've said before, a missing reporter who happened to be investigating LPS piqued their interest, and the one thing they don't want is to have that come back to bite them when she ends up dead. Now that we've started looking into it, DC knows we can't risk the press getting wind that we abandoned the investigation without finding her. Imagine the scandal, the airtime given to it considering she's one of their own. That would be bad PR at a time when the phrase *deep state* pervades one side's culture. So, did you get anything in Texas that will help us find Anastasia Clark?"

The trip Blake warned against left them with more questions than answers, and despite supposition that Michael Bray applied at LPS weeks before his dirt nap, Cyrus had nothing to tie that to the missing reporter.

"I get it," Cyrus replied.

"Do you?"

"You're worried about Washington."

"I'm worried about Misty Daniels's sister, Cyrus."

The answer caught him by surprise, and he wondered if he'd underestimated Blake.

The SAC scooted his chair forward. "Lockhart Industries quietly buys up real estate, builds a wall around it, starts hiring veterans in droves, then turns them loose to do law enforcement's job. All in our backyard. Without a single red flag. DC is up in fucking arms, Cyrus. The chain of command is getting it from both sides. The liberals want Lockhart shut down, the Republicans want us to stay out of the way so they can pretend they care about deficit spending."

Cyrus's heat rose. "And that's the kind of tribalism that powerful people like Ethan Pierce use to influence voters. His bankrolling of LPS to create the controversy then use it on the back end borders on evil genius."

Blake remained composed. "Funding you learned about via Misty's illicit activities."

"Message received. Direct me."

"Find the reporter so I can get DC off my ass. Go downstairs and check in with Daniels, find out what she's learned about Clark, then drag ass back up here and fill me in."

"Wait, Misty's here?"

"Saw her getting coffee an hour ago. You need to keep track of your people."

As if Cyrus hadn't tried, but it didn't seem like a

great time to be defensive. He'd screwed enough pooches for one day.

"Roger that. I'll do better."

Blake shook his head in derision then maneuvered the mouse on his desk while scanning his monitor. "I have an opening in about thirty minutes. Don't call me. Don't text me. Come back here so I can look into your eyes."

So much for trust, but Cyrus knew he deserved it. All of it.

"See you then."

Misty's chair was drawn forward so its arms were nestled under the desk. When the heavy door latched behind him, she didn't turn. This had been Byron's workstation. The kid had sat the same way, but with his eyes inches from the screen.

A pang of loss hollowed Cyrus's chest, but he set it aside.

"Where have you been?"

She spun her chair to face him. "Is there some-where we can talk?"

Cyrus craned his neck. Two analysts worked in the far corners of the space, but they were out of earshot. Not private enough, he supposed. "Sure."

Misty hustled past him, shoved the bar to open the door, then ambled up the hallway without waiting. She badged into a secure meeting room.

Cyrus pulled up a chair. "What's with the secrecy?"

"I feel like we've established trust since the fiasco in the mountains."

A sense of foreboding swelled, but he nodded. Misty had brought the feds to bear on the warehouse where he'd been bound and beaten. She'd saved his bacon. Now she was cashing in on what he owed her.

"I always told you trust was a two-way street. You earned mine."

"Ditto. But when you told me you hadn't looked into my background, well... it felt good to have an ally. And I don't want to fuck that up."

"Why do I get the sense you're about to do exactly that?"

She sighed, and her shoulders dropped. "Let me get this out, okay?"

"Shoot."

"You wouldn't have found much on me even if you had checked into my background. Before I was sent to Afghanistan to join my unit, I was stationed in Fort Belvoir, Virginia."

"Why does that ring a bell?"

"Because you were in Quantico. I was Military Intelligence Corps."

MIC.

It came flooding back. He saw her in a new light as he filled in blanks. "Intelligence and electronic warfare. That fits."

"After I completed my training at the Army Intelligence Center of Excellence, they dropped me in Kabul to join a Rangers team."

"Is that common practice? To drop electronic warfare specialists in war zones?"

"Of course. I was HUMINT." She caught herself just as Cyrus began to tilt his head. "Human Intelligence. I maintained informants in the field."

"Holy shit."

"I rolled into villages under the cover of night with the Rangers outside the perimeter to back me up should shit go sideways."

Cyrus leaned back in his chair and dropped one palm on the table. "You were a fucking ninja."

"Something like that. I've been called many things. It goes without saying the Army would protect my identity. When I got out, I went to college on the GI Bill. Finished in three years, but more important than the degree, I met a friend who plugged me in with the white hat network."

"Byron."

She nodded. "That's the abbreviated story, but I figure you've earned the right to hear it. It's about trust."

A klaxon whirred between his ears. While Misty's story was mind-blowing and he longed to know more, his gut twisted up, and he knew she was about to drop a bomb. This wasn't just about trust.

Despite his curiosity, he had to meet with Blake

again soon, and the SAC would want answers about the disappearance of Anna Clark.

"Out with it."

Misty sighed again. "Try not to lose your mind all at once."

"Out with it."

"I got the grand tour of Lockhart Public Security while you were in Hope Mills. They interviewed me for the IT Security Manager position, and I start Monday."

Cyrus shot out of his chair. On his feet, he doubled over and slammed both hands on the table. "Bullshit!" He shoved off the surface then paced toward the door and back. Hot blood rushed to his cheeks, and he could *feel* the lightning-bolt-shaped vein in his head pulsing. "You went to Lockhart? Are you fucking crazy?"

Misty leveled her gaze. "How was Texas, Cy?"

He wagged a finger. "No. Don't even try me. You went behind my fucking back. You're so far over the line right now, I doubt you'll ever see the inside of this building again. What the hell were you thinking?"

Misty pushed her chair away with the backs of her legs and she rose. "That my sister could be dead!" Tears welled in her eyes. "And that Sam Lockhart might be why!"

Cyrus shoved open the door and burst into the hallway. He stormed to the other end, back, then repeated the circuit. The silence surrounding him in the corridor swelled as he fumed. After two laps, he threw the door open again. "You fucker."

Misty's face turned from red to pink, her breaths slowing. When she spoke again, it was in a lower tenor approaching a whisper, but without the rasp. "This is what I was trained to do. I infiltrate. Locate sources. Gather intel. Report to my superiors."

"In that case, show me your badge."

She glared.

He met it with equal heat. "I don't have time for this shit. Come with me."

When Cyrus erupted into the hallway, he shoved the door so hard it slammed against the wall then banged shut behind him. It took a moment before he noticed Misty hadn't followed. He didn't slow until he reached the elevator, then he stared down the corridor seeing red.

She appeared a moment later, the wrinkles in her clothes gone like she'd pulled them taut before leaving the room. There was no eye contact when she reached him, and they rode the elevator in silence.

Cyrus led her up the hallway to Blake's open door. His heart beat his ribs, and a hole formed in his throat as he considered what he had to do. But this wasn't one of those times he could go rogue. To hide Misty's subterfuge with more would get them both run out of Denver on high-speed rail.

CHAPTER 17

After Cyrus filled in Blake about Misty's infiltration of LPS, the boss gestured toward the door. Misty closed it then stood at parade rest, her feet shoulder width apart.

Blake's tone was level, but Cyrus knew he forced his composure. "Do I need to lose my temper to relay the gravity of this shit?"

Neither answered.

"Right." Turning, he stood by his window as he ran his hand through his hair while peering at the Denver skyline. Two minutes of thick silence ensued before he spoke with his back turned. "Let's break this down. Misty, how'd you get into LPS?"

"A Ranger I served with got me in. He's high on the LPS food chain behind Lockhart, a guy they call XO, and another guy I haven't met."

"At least you didn't go in half-assed. What's the job?"

"IT Security Manager."

"So you're qualified. Good cover."

"You've got to be kidding me," Cyrus blurted.

Blake ignored him. "What's the facility like?"

Cy rolled his eyes.

"Refurbished. Polished interior from the server stacks to the lobby. They're outfitting nurse's stations on some floors, re-purposing others as offices, best I could tell. But the exterior hasn't been touched. Like they're hiding their progress. The goal is obvious. Shroud everything except what you want to be seen. Gather only the attention you want. Control the narrative."

"And you'd have run of the place?"

Cyrus's chin dropped. The SAC couldn't seriously—

"Not only that, but I could create technical problems to get access to the top floor where the XO and Lockhart have offices, and the dolt working in IT with me is clueless. Highly confident, sir."

Her military bearing pissed off Cyrus that much more.

Blake pivoted to face them then leaned on the windowsill. "And they want you to start Monday?"

Misty dipped her chin in the affirmative.

Blake shifted his attention to Cyrus. "Do you see the position I'm in?"

"Yes. Misty has gone rogue."

"Don't be dense. Temper your... temper and

analyze. Look at that situation. Tell me what happens if she doesn't start Monday."

Cyrus boarded that train of thought. Misty applied for the job. She accepted the offer. All in one day. Another indication Lockhart wanted to speed things along, and considering the huge undertaking of providing vets with health care while stomping out gun violence, there was only one way to ensure the job got done.

Executive-level micromanagement.

LPS expected Misty to report in three days. They were practically a military outfit, and soldiers reported on time. If Lockhart's new tech manager didn't show up, someone might start asking questions. Misty would get unwanted attention, and Cyrus didn't think her lack of social media profiles worked in her favor. If anything, they'd become more suspicious.

Lockhart hadn't made all this progress so fast without access to intelligence. And with Ethan Pierce's money to grease axles, LPS's reach would extend beyond Facebook and Insta. Far beyond.

Even if the government had protected Misty's identity, how many congresspeople on the Intelligence Committee might Ethan Pierce own? After all, the whole Gabby Sutton fiasco had been about putting into positions of power politicians who fit his mold so he could control them. How many did he already fund?

The judge who'd dropped Misty into the FBI's lap had sealed the order, but judges had clerks.

And the SAC had seen all of this in a few moments of silence as he stared out the window.

Jesus. Blake is a beast. Who's the teacher now?

"I get your point. If she doesn't report Monday, she risks exposure. LPS finds out who Misty is working for and starts blabbing in the media about the bureau's overreach, the deep state's efforts to maintain its stranglehold over veteran's affairs, and limiting gun rights."

"It scares me how accurately you spoke the words streaming through my mind." Blake shoved his hands into his pockets. "So, this is what we're going to do. Daniels starts her new job Monday. Because she has exposed the bureau to deep state conspiracy theories and God knows what else, this is the only way to keep DC in the dark until we find Anastasia."

Even though he accepted the SAC's logic, one glance at Misty twisted Cyrus up. "I do not want her at LPS. If they disappeared a reporter, what do you think they'd do to her on the outside chance they caught her snooping?"

"The inherent risks of undercover work. We're investigating a possible kidnapping."

Did Blake know more about Misty's service record than him? Probably.

"But if you need a reason to get on board, consider this. Anything illegal Misty finds while following her sister's trail could expose Lockhart. That must be a pleasant tune to your ears."

Manipulation. That's what it's come to.

The SAC didn't wait for an answer. "Daniels, when this is over, you're going to pay a price for going off on your own. Screw with me, and I'll drag you back to the judge. Are we completely clear?"

Misty nodded. "Crystal, sir."

"Take the weekend to get ready. Get out so I can talk to Cyrus."

Misty closed the door behind her.

The SAC shoved his hands in his pockets. "I knew she'd end up twisting my balls."

"Nice visual."

"Oh, is it funny time, Cy?" The SAC's lips trembled, though, and Cyrus let his shoulders drop. "I know you're not thrilled, but we were asking for it when we got involved in this. If I were you, I'd find a way to support the mission so you know you did all you could for her. Otherwise, if the whole thing goes south, you're going to regret it. Remember Byron."

It was like a husky Russian named Truth had punched Cyrus in the face.

CHAPTER 18

Misty followed Tasker White down a hallway and into an office with a lone cubicle wall, where she was photographed and presented a badge she clipped to her blouse.

White led her to the elevator, and Misty noted its neighbor's door yawned wide as yellow tape cordoned it off.

"Upgrades galore," White informed. "Now the fun stuff."

Misty didn't ask.

Tasker thumbed the button for the fourth floor, and the elevator's soft tone announced the beginning of their ascent.

"Watson's glad you're here. Caught him smiling in the break room earlier. Rare sight."

Watson...

She scrounged through her mental file system.

Right. Justin Watson.

The interim IT Security Manager she'd relieve so he could go back to his Microsoft-oriented duties. She'd have to reacquaint herself with the common militaristic use of last names, because she'd remembered him as Justin.

When the elevator arrived, they crossed the hall to a heavy wooden door with a golden name plate announcing it was the office of Dr. Clayton Burroughs. Before knocking, White faced her. "Usually we put new people through a battery of tests, but the boss trusts I wouldn't refer just anyone. I told him about how you worked for us, but I didn't mention your actual role. I know that kind of thing isn't public knowledge."

"Thanks."

"But everyone talks to the doc. It's mandatory."

Misty's heart ratcheted up a bit, but she forced a smile and nodded. "I understand."

White knocked twice then entered. They walked through a barren reception area then through an open door. A finished oak desk reflected soft light, and a manufactured lilac scent sifted into her nostrils. The doc stood behind his desk, framed on either side by tall splatter paintings. The reckless display of primary colors left her guessing the shrink had a weekend hobby. His form of therapy, maybe.

"Good morning, Miss Daniels." He reached across the desk. "I'm Clayton Burroughs. Call me Clay."

Although his clothes were silk, the brown tie against the white shirt left a muted finish. She watched him for any indication he saw a resemblance to the reporter who'd spent time at LPS. There was none.

She grasped the offered hand. "Misty."

Tasker threw Burroughs a lazy salute. "Thanks, Doc." He patted Misty's shoulder. "Welcome to the outfit. You can take the elevator down to the basement and check in with Watson when you're finished here, assuming Burroughs doesn't find out you're a psycho." He raised a hand to one side of his mouth and whispered, "A real possibility, in your case."

Misty chuckled but didn't feel it.

Once he'd left, Burroughs swept an iPad from his desk then gestured toward a leather chair with one hand and a matching sofa with the tablet. "Sit where you like. I'll keep our first talk short so you don't tire of me too quickly."

"That sounds... promising."

Burroughs's laugh was open, bordering on boisterous. "Not the first time I've heard the sentiment. Don't sweat it. We're just going to get to know each other."

Said the lion to the gazelle.

Misty opted for the chair. Burroughs settled onto the couch then dropped the iPad in his lap. He rubbed his palms on his pants like they were clammy.

She could've predicted how the conversation started. He asked about her military background. She told the requisite, practiced lies. The way he asked if she saw any action in Afghanistan came off as ignorant. Everyone saw action in that backward shit hole. But again, she told her half-truths with the most confidence she could muster.

Things were rolling along nicely until he cleared his throat, swiped on his tablet then, without looking up, asked about her childhood.

Where had she grown up?

West Virginia.

When had she left home?

At seventeen, the earliest possible age to join the service. She bypassed her forgery of the required parental consent.

"Why did you leave so young?"

"Seventeen-year-olds go to college all the time."

"But you weren't going to college. You were joining the US Army. I think you'd agree that's much more of a commitment. One many teens would face with apprehension. Maybe even fear."

Although Misty had told the story before, her brain stuttered and stumbled when she tried to form the words.

Calm down. Don't fuck this up.

She reminded herself that some form of the truth made for the best lie. "My father was a cop. Service was in the family blood."

"I see. Any siblings?"

"Nope. Only child."

"Are your parents still alive?"

"Both dead. My mother in childbirth, my father in the line of duty." She tossed in a second lie. "Near poverty from a single income was another reason I joined up when I did."

"Oh." He frowned. "I'm sorry for your losses."

"Thanks."

"Does it bother you?"

"That my parents are dead? Sure. I don't remember my mother, of course. My father died shortly after I enlisted. That was about twelve years ago, now. Time dulled the pain, but it would've been nice to have him around."

She was happy with how that answer had come off.

"Of course." He glanced at his tablet. "And you went to Georgetown after the service?"

She nodded.

"How'd you like it?"

"I like learning, but I'm not the most sociable person. Transitioning from the discipline of the military to college life with a bunch of young party animals was a culture shock."

Burroughs chuckled then swiped the tablet and sat up straighter. "Well, Misty, I think I've got everything I need, for now. I meet with each employee on staff every two to three weeks, depending on my schedule."

"It's required?"

He nodded. "Does that bother you? Talking to a shrink? Am I so bad?"

She forced a smile and squinted a touch to make

sure it reached her eyes. "Not at all. When you're sending armed men into the field, especially in-country, you probably need every assurance. But why would you need to talk to an IT Manager?"

"Because Sam wanted to match the military's ideals. Everybody is treated the same."

As a woman, Misty knew that was a fucking lie. It seemed the doc was an exception to the rule. He'd never served.

"Understood."

"Do you have any questions for me?"

Her overactive brain conjured the name Chet, the guy who'd killed himself while working in her new role.

"You met with the man I'm replacing, right?"

He nodded. "Yes. But I can't talk about my other patients."

"Of course not. I just wanted to know, in a general sense, if there's anything about this job that's going to..." she trailed off, lending the appearance she was looking for the words while leaving a gap for him to fill in.

He bit the hook. "Drive you crazy?" He chuckled then rose.

She stood to face him on even ground.

"Nope. It's just a job. But it's an important one. You'll be managing a lot more than computers and networks. You're the center of technical security for this installation, and it's a lot of responsibility. The cameras have to stay online. Alarm systems. All of it. But you served. Responsibility isn't new to you. As I understand it, they're creating two new requisitions to hire engineers to work for you."

She couldn't have asked for a better answer. Security management meant more access, and she'd need it.

When she reached for the knob of the outer door in the vacant reception area, it turned on its own. She flinched when the door swung open to reveal a towering man in a crisp white shirt with an open collar and a pair of black, wool slacks.

"Whoa!" He raised both hands. "Sorry about that. Tasker sent me to ride down with you, make sure you got settled in." His eyes flared, then the towering man froze. He scanned her face, his eyes working a bit hard for introductions. His lingering gaze was... off. He cleared his throat. "Sorry, you remind me of someone. I'm Tom Rhymer."

Shit. Worst-case scenario. I look too much like Anastasia. This was a bad idea. Too late now.

She nodded. "Misty Daniels."

His smile lit up the hallway. Rhymer's chin and jawline could've been chiseled out of granite. They rode the elevator down.

"You from around here?"

"Not from, but I live in Denver."

"Roger that. I love the city. Colorado Springs isn't bad, but Denver's the bomb."

"People still say 'the bomb'?"

He chuckled. "Guess I'm old school. How're you finding the place? I mean, I know you're just getting here, but what do you think?"

"Seems like a nice outfit. Lobby is pimped out. Doc seems like the okay kind."

"Yeah, he's all right. But I try not to see him more than I must."

Misty wanted to pry, but gossip wouldn't do on her first day, and she knew better than ever to appear like she elicited whisper campaigns. Drama.

So she turned the idea on its head, took a more empathetic approach.

"Military types like us carry baggage civilians could never understand. I don't envy his job."

"Imagine if you counseled someone who blew his brains out." His expression tightened as the gossip engine ignited. Misty's mind raced for the right words. She decided simple was best.

"Like the guy I'm replacing?"

"Yeah. Chet. A good guy, if you ask me. Always willing to help. My machine disconnected a few weeks ago, a hardware failure, and he was up there replacing my network card in half an hour. He seemed happy here. I don't know what happened."

"I guess you never know with people."

Rhymer cleared his throat. "It's never been said better. You never know."

The elevator doors swung open, and her escort led her through the server room to her office, bypassing Justin Watson's office altogether.

"We're not checking in with Justin?"

Tom smiled. "You understand he works for you now, right? You don't need to check in with him. And if he gets out of line, starts a bitch-fest—as he's prone to do—feel free to set him straight. I wouldn't have guessed that guy served, for the way he complains."

"One of those, huh? I'll take it under advisement."

"Good." They arrived at her office. "Test your badge."

Misty swiped. The lock disengaged with a thunk, then he swung the door open.

"Your workstation's new. Tasker figured you'd want to configure it yourself, but I made sure Watson got you set up in the directory services thing so I could send you an email." He pulled a neatly folded slip of paper from his trouser pockets. "This is your temporary login and pass-word. You'll be prompted to reset it. I'm sure your snooty Georgetown diploma is proof you can handle the rest."

She might have taken offense if he hadn't accentu-ated his words with that winner of a smile.

"It'll probably take you half the day to get through the corporate onboarding. You know, programs to explain the culture, some multiple-choice stuff to make sure you comprehend it all. The SOPs for your job role are in a network directory with your user ID. Chet was still writing them, and you can expect weekly meetings with the team to make sure you understand what we're going for so you can finish the job. If you need Watson to fill in any blanks, remember he works for you now. You don't need an appointment."

She nodded her understanding. "Thanks, Mister Rhymer."

"And thank *you* for that flash of my father's face. It's Tom." Again with that fucking smile. Misty wondered if he practiced in the mirror.

CHAPTER 19

The charismatic senator serving in the Illinois state house had tweeted up a storm over the weekend about the attempt on his life, and a crowd of spectators and gun control advocates filled Hyde Park to hear his ideas. Lockhart's interviews with right-wing talking heads, pundits, and whatever the narcissistic Alex Riddle considered himself had reached for the low-hanging fruit. But, while Republicans represented a more nostalgic, bootstrap tugging, gun-loving demographic, liberals were suckers for sadness. All he had to do was tug at the ol' heartstrings, let their tribe speak to them in their own language.

The faculty at the University of Chicago had tripped over each other to accommodate the Democrat, and what Sam feared would turn out to be predominantly a press event looked more like a Trump rally in an alternate universe. The vast expanse of Hyde Park was a sea of humanity, its collective energy pulsing through the air. Anyone could feel the palpable sense of unity and purpose binding them together, their faces alight with anticipation and determination.

The tricky part would be swaying them just enough to meet Sam's objectives.

Banner had been true to his word, rounding up the parents of victims of gun violence for the show. Each wielded a poster of their deceased child's face.

The politician donned his wide smile as he stepped up to the microphone. The spiel he dropped about the scourge plaguing America played well. Everyone could agree gun violence was a problem. Banner's all-pro speech writers engineered his pauses so the crowd could applaud at the right times, and Lockhart was pleased to hear a few whoops and whistles as well.

The senator introduced a man named Harry Baker. Sam recalled his dossier with clarity. A plumber by trade, Baker had lost his seven-year-old boy in a drive-by in Englewood. Lockhart thought of his own fourteen-year-old, Thomas, a reminder of why he'd gotten involved in this enterprise to begin with. His boy's life had been violently cut short, and since the government wasn't going to do anything about it, he'd been left to navigate the politics, ignore the tribal naysayers, and solve what the idiots wouldn't.

The Second Amendment crowd—who apparently didn't bother reading the document with a discerning eye—were a bunch of sheep who took their talking points from politicians whose funding came from organizations like the NRA and gun manufacturers. 'More guns' was their stupid answer. The Libtards wanted all the assault weapons melted down, as if people would turn over their weapons in some kind of kumbaya moment. Neither side had practical solutions. Meanwhile, the funeral business was booming, and one of Sam's sons rotted in an airtight box.

If every liberal in Hyde Park that afternoon drove down the street to a pawn shop and filled out the paperwork to buy a pistol, that would've been just fine. But if he had his way, an army of well-trained veterans would take up the slack where law enforcement failed. Defend people at private schools and corporations across the country. Not just to make them feel safe, but to ensure they were. If this showing went well, he'd sign a major bank, Lockhart Public Security would soon be in the black, and customers would be lining up. If the reduction in gun violence in the states where LPS had already saved lives swayed twenty percent of the population from both sides, it'd be downhill from there.

Ethan Pierce had suggested signing enough clients and showing what LPS was capable of might even bring political campaigns to the company's customer list. Maybe local government contracts were too much to wish for, but who knew the limits? Where Ethan Pierce was single-minded, concerned only about adding to his reserves in the eternal battle among the rich to die with the most toys, Sam wanted the violence to stop.

But he wouldn't refuse a boat-load of cash.

Baker stepped up to the podium, raised a fist to his mouth, cleared his throat, then leaned toward the mic.

"My name—" the mic burst with feedback, and plumber Harry stepped back like it'd taken a swing. "Sorry about that." His self-conscious chuckle couldn't have come off better if he'd planned it. "My name is Harry Baker." He raised a glossy poster of a blond-haired boy with piercing blue eyes and a gap where his front teeth had been. "My son's name was Ronny. He died when a gang member drove past my car in Engle-wood one day, firing a semi-automatic weapon at the adjacent sidewalk as we rode by, no care for who he hit."

Sam could've heard a pin drop.

"His killer's name is Rip Johnson, a known felon who'd received early release from prison for good behavior. A felon who went home, beat his wife, got arrested, then had the charges dropped instead of being dumped back in prison where he belonged.

"I'm here today because I love my son, and I want him to be remembered. Fitz Banner is going to make sure that happens. And he seems to be the only politi-cian around here willing to do whatever it takes. He got shot at himself recently, if you recall. Guess that woke you up in a hurry, huh Fitz?"

He gestured toward Sam. "But the guys from Lockhart Public Security saved his skin."

A few boos rose from the crowd. Sam maintained his stony expression.

Harry took it in stride. "Sure. You've heard about his guys thwarting shootings in three states. And you've heard other democrats tell us that's the government's job." A couple cheers rose from the crowd. "But how long are we going to wait for the government to get its act together? How many years has it been since Columbine? How many since Sandy Hook?"

The crowd quieted.

"I understand how you all feel. But I've met with Sam and here's something you might not know. Lockhart Public Security has created a vast network of people and technologies to track these scumbag crazies who shoot up the streets, schools, and synagogues. They monitor social media and other sources without violating peoples' privacy to do it. Now, who would you rather have on your side? Someone who hires veterans, provides them free medical care, and requires psychological counseling to ensure they're sound before they go into the public with guns? Or a government who invades your privacy and sends out inexperienced and sometimes racist cops who open fire under the slightest perception of a threat, just like the gang members and White supremacists?"

This guy wasn't pulling any punches. Hell, he was doing Banner's job for him.

"Well, I'm with Fitz Banner because he's gonna work *with* Lockhart instead of against him. I hope you'll join me in honoring all the boys and girls across this country who've needlessly lost their lives by calling your representatives and insisting they vote for the Banner Bill."

Lockhart flinched in surprise when the crowd burst out in applause.

Fitz Banner shook the plumber's hand vigorously then stepped up to the podium.

"Well, I think he just stole my thunder."

Laughter filled the park.

"Like the man said, it's time we do something instead of just spouting off about injustice. I can sit back and complain on cable news, or I can introduce legislation to allow companies like Lockhart Public Security to bring our challenged city back into balance. To help us put violent criminals where they belong. Most of all, to protect our children."

Then Banner dropped the A-bomb.

"Remember the guy who stopped the mall shooter in North Carolina? What if I told you he was LPS? And all of you remember the nightclub in Tallahassee, where the gunman got one round off before a citizen took him down? Yes, that was LPS, too. If that isn't surprising enough, gun violence in all these areas is down to almost zero. Now, imagine a world where some psycho with an AR-15 has to think twice because he never knows when he's going to run into an Army-trained, stable actor whose only interest is in public safety."

Sam allowed himself a subtle smile as Banner rolled.

"We need the government to get with the act. They should be protecting our schools and other government-run institutions. But if companies like nightclubs, strip malls, and private academies want to hire LPS to provide security, that could only benefit all of us. LPS could set a standard the government could learn from.

"I plan to submit the Child Protection and Security bill on the floor next Monday, and I hope each of you will contact your representatives to insist they support it."

The crowd burst into applause. Lockhart scanned them. Some clapped their hands over their heads. Others pumped their fists. Sure, many stood idle, and there were a few slow-clappers with hands dropped low, but it was a fine start.

His phone buzzed in his pocket. He checked the screen. Country Bank was calling. Sam smiled.

CHAPTER 20

It was for the better that the two analysts Cyrus often shared with other agents in the Denver field office had their cases under control, because his third charge was over at Lockhart Public Security's Colorado Springs campus with her ass hanging out, and he couldn't focus. He'd spent half the morning summoning visions of the worst scenarios.

Misty caught snooping. Lockhart having figured out who she was working for before she'd strolled in the door to report for work. Her body ending up next to Anastasia Clark's in an unmarked grave.

Cyrus knew he was being ridiculous. He had no evidence Sam Lockhart had done anything with the reporter. To the contrary, footage from outside the compound had shown her car leaving LPS that Tuesday night, and she'd never returned. Her editor had even said she had a way of going dark. If he'd fired her over voicemail after a couple days of absence, maybe she'd packed up and taken a vacation.

Or maybe she found something at LPS, they got onto her, and her twisted-up body ended up in a barren field.

After spending most of his day bullshitting around, the SAC had called him in. Blake asked if Misty had reported to LPS. Cyrus said he'd assumed so, but they hadn't spoken over the weekend.

They actually hadn't uttered a word since Misty left the boss's office that Friday afternoon, three days ago. Two stubborn bastards, like a couple high schoolers unwilling to be the one to break the silence.

Blake had suggested he act like the agent instead of the analyst. For all intents, she was his charge. But the SAC had ordered her to report directly to *him*, not Cyrus.

He decided not to point out the irony.

Late that afternoon Tiffany Brooks had called to announce she was back in town for a day. It'd taken her less than two minutes to home in on his attitude, and she'd suggested they have dinner.

Cyrus stood when she entered the restaurant, and they were seated. He'd worn his suit, she wore a matching green plaid jacket and shirt with just a touch of gold around her neck to fill it out.

She'd suggested the oyster bar. He'd never been. The mixed aromas made for a thick olfactory experience, and he couldn't place a dominant scent.

Tiffany ordered a scotch. Cyrus, water.

She unfolded a linen napkin and dropped it in her lap. "You see this Fitz Banner thing?"

"The shooting? Old news." Cyrus recalled the assassination attempt, how LPS had saved the state politician's bacon.

"No, the other thing. Bastard is dropping pro-Lockhart legislation next Monday so they can operate in Chicago. Probably the whole state. I haven't been able to get my hands on a draft yet, but his speech spoke for itself. Surrounded himself with victims of gun violence, shameless prick."

"Isn't he a democrat?"

She nodded. "Would I be so... perturbed, otherwise? A damned turncoat is what he is."

"He *was* shot at."

Tiffany narrowed one eye. "Yeah, and the shooter in Texas was trying to get a job at LPS just weeks before one of Lockhart's guys punctured his lungs with bullets. Whole Banner thing might've been set up."

"That's a stretch."

Her lips parted as if she'd come back full force, but she pressed them back together then blew a long breath through her nostrils. "I sound like a conspiracy theorist. I know it."

"I want Lockhart in prison as much as the next guy. Seeing as you were Gabby Sutton's best friend, we're like peas in a pod on that account."

"Yes." She turned the napkin over in her lap. "That, we are." When she looked up again, her piercing eyes scanned him for a few seconds. "So, what's up your ass? You look... sullen."

"Is it that obvious?"

"Think Greek tragedy."

"Thanks."

She didn't smile. "Anything I can help with?"

"Not unless you have contacts at Lockhart Public Security who hate their jobs enough to keep a watchful eye for me." Cyrus perused his surroundings and decided the noise of the collective patronage would drown out their chat.

"That's something I don't have. I'm still getting plugged back in. Tell me anyway."

"Who are you getting plugged in with?"

"Maybe I'll tell you someday. Don't try to distract. You look pissed. Let's deal with that."

Cyrus huffed, and he made no effort to hide it. But it was her genuine expression of concern as she stared across the table at him, the friendship, that swayed him

"I have this analyst who used to be a covert operator in the Army. She and my boss have decided to insert her at LPS."

Tiffany's pencil-thin eyebrows shot up. She scanned the crowd in the same way he had then leaned across the table.

"At the new facility? Colorado Springs?" When he nodded, she leaned back in her chair, spine straight, then folded her arms across her chest. Although her gaze was locked onto him, he could see the cogs turning. "And you aren't on board?"

"Not in the least."

"Can I ask what the mission is?"

"You can ask."

The country came out in her accent. "Don't fuck with me Cyrus. You're either gonna share or you aren't."

"A reporter is missing."

"Who?"

"Let's reserve that piece."

She waved a hand. "Fair enough."

"She was last seen leaving LPS."

"Jesus. Does the bureau suspect a kidnapping? Is that why you're involved?"

His shirt collar seemed to tighten the more he spoke. But who would she tell? He slipped a finger behind his tie and loosened it a bit.

"Possible kidnapping, but we have exactly jack shit."

She unfolded her arms. The waitress brought their drinks and asked if they were ready to order, but Tiffany sent her away with the smiling southern charm of a pro operator. The kind a politician would turn on when the red light blinked to life above a TV camera.

"What's the problem?"

"I'd think it would be obvious."

"Then tell me like I'm stupid. You said she was

covert ops, right? So, she's obviously qualified. I assume she's a good snooper."

"She's technically sound."

"So, I repeat. What's the problem? Just afraid one of your girls could get hurt?"

Cyrus mused. Tried to come up with the words. "She went behind my back to get the job."

"Ah, you feel betrayed."

"That's a bit simplistic."

"Bullshit."

"What?"

"You heard me, Cy. It's bullshit. She went behind your back. Betrayed you. Then your boss went along, which must feel like a second bit of treachery. That about sum it up?"

When he didn't answer, she nodded with self-satisfaction. "Right. So, you feel like she's being rewarded for bad behavior."

"Well, yes."

"And since you've never gone off on your own like that..."

Heat flooded Cyrus's neck.

"That's what I thought. Tell me, Cyrus, why is this analyst of yours so interested in LPS?"

Cyrus contemplated holding out, protecting the familial angle, but since he didn't have to reveal any identities, he came out with it.

"She's related to the missing reporter."

Tiffany's jaw dropped. "Jesus Christ on a golf cart."

She picked up the napkin then tossed it onto the table. Reaching into the pocket of her plaid jacket, she withdrew some cash from a small purse then dropped it beside her half-empty glass. She was marching toward the door before he had a chance to react. Heads turned to watch her go.

Cyrus weaved through the tables, hustled past the greeter's station, then through the glass doors and onto the street. Tiffany stood with her arms folded across her chest, leaning against a blue Prius.

Cyrus turned his hands over. "Guess we're not eating."

"I thought you'd be more comfortable out here, where no one could hear us when I start laying into you."

"How did I turn into the enemy?"

"You're not my enemy, you're my friend. You just told me you want Lockhart in prison. That we're"—she made quotations with her fingers—"peas in a pod in that way. So, why are you bellyaching about betrayal when you've got this woman on the inside?" She shoved a finger into his chest. "You should be using her, Cyrus."

"Using?"

"Are we really going to parse words? It's time to grow up, mister."

"The southern mama effect is wearing thin."

She dropped her hand. "Oh! Well, excuse me!" She feigned clearing her throat and, when she spoke again, her accent vanished. "Maybe this will suit you better. It's time to grow up, Agent Jennings. Lockhart is dangerous. What he's trying to do is outrageous. Who the hell does he think he is, assuming he can outperform government law enforcement? What's worse, he works for Ethan Pierce, and that bastard is sitting in a Lockhart country club. He's probably carrying a cell phone around. Internet privileges? Forget about it."

"You're ranting."

"Well, fucking excuse me. Maybe you've forgotten I worked with Pierce at one time. The way he betrayed me? He killed Gabby, staged the suicide of the DNC's national chair, and funded the Republicans behind my back!" She folded her arms again. "Now he's the wizard behind this new curtain, and you're worried about your analyst's *etiquette*?"

"She went without asking me!"

Tiffany flinched.

Cyrus sighed. "Sorry."

"Don't apologize to me. Apologize to your asset, because that's what she is. A fucking asset, Cy." She pointed again, but her finger came up short of his chest. "You're behaving like a child. But she didn't steal your football, she got into LPS. Who else could've pulled that off? What kind of ingenuity must that have taken, especially without FBI support?"

The air escaping her nose plumed in the cool night as she took a step forward and grasped his arms.

"You saved my backside, Cyrus. And you did it without anyone's permission. You marched up that snowy mountain, took out Pierce's guards, pulled me out of there, then sent Ethan to prison for what he did to me, consequences be damned. I'm grateful, and I will prove it to you for the rest of my life. But if you'll turn off your ego and realize what a hypocrite you're being, it'll serve you better."

He nodded. "Anything you'd like to add?"

She considered him for a minute, and Cyrus wondered if she wouldn't bring another verbal assault, but her mouth formed a sideways smile.

"Yeah, it's her fucking family. What would you do for your family?"

"Fine."

"Go get something on Lockhart before that legislation drops, or the dominoes will fall in his favor across the country. In short order."

That was a scary thought.

Her smile widened. "You know, you wouldn't be half as pissed if you didn't love her like you do."

"Love her?"

Tiffany cocked an eyebrow again. "I didn't say you wanted to fuck her, Cyrus. But I don't think you'd be so pissed about her going behind your back, especially considering your history, if you weren't fretting about the danger she's in. After all, I know about your girlfriend, the coroner. I know about your parents gali-vanting across the US in their RV. But you've never mentioned this woman." She shook her head. "You're protective of her. I'm certain of it. Whoever she is, you care about her."

Cyrus smiled. "Your fucking intuition is off the charts."

"You don't think I've come this far by being dense, do you?" She kissed his cheek. "I'll grab a burger on the way home."

"I thought you were a vegan."

"Jesus, Cy. I'm not *that* liberal." She chuckled, circled the Prius, then tapped the key fob to unlock it. "Tell the coroner I said hello, and I hope to meet her someday." She pulled the door open. "And call your girl, Cyrus."

CHAPTER 21

Misty spent her first day at LPS getting oriented, figuring out directory layouts, then analyzing the Microsoft Exchange setup to measure the competence of the man in the office up the hall. After that, she got to work on network security, looking for vulnerabilities, closing holes so gaping they might have been left as tests of her abilities. But she doubted Justin Watson would've been capable of that.

That he handled the Microsoft Infrastructure was a blessing because, between him and the now-deceased Chet Parsons, security at LPS was trash. If it hadn't been Misty's plan to infiltrate the system, the half-assed setup would've miffed her. She could've hacked the place from the outside, after all. But Cyrus had been clear about law-breaking, and Watson might have been just competent enough to detect the intrusion.

Maybe.

Then she happened upon the folder containing what she was there for. The parking lot cameras were not only operational, but also well-distributed. No blind spots. When she scrolled the video directory to the date and time of Anna's disappearance, she frowned. The video file names were sequential, but one was missing.

Uh oh.

Misty clicked inside the directory address bar and typed in

.snapshot

She sighed with relief when she found camera footage was backed up, and they kept a month's worth of video before purging. *Manually* purging. Misty put an end to that practice with a simple script. Anything of interest would be backed up to a password protected directory and a USB stick.

She ordered video of every external camera so little windows filled the screen, placing the one someone had tried to delete in the center. The guard's gate at the main entrance—the only way in or out of the compound. Wide views of the front, left, and right sides of the hospital. Front door views of the pair of new, unoccupied structures she hadn't visited yet. As an afterthought, she nestled the lobby cam among the others before starting the show.

Winding the footage back to the date and time revealed by the traffic cam footage the SAC had provided, she slapped the space bar. Still images burst into motion.

Her sister first appeared walking toward the sliding glass doors in the lobby. Her hair was pulled back into a ponytail, and she wore slacks and a light jacket. There was no escort, and she wondered if someone had left her at the elevator or if they'd actually given a reporter full run of the place. She'd wind it back to find out later, but she let the video roll for the moment.

When Anastasia disappeared from the lobby cam, the window in the top right reacquired her as she strolled along the exterior wall to the side lot, where her car was parked four rows back. The lights blinked when she pressed her fob, but then Anna turned, her keys dangling from one hand. Someone moved into view.

The area might have been covered by the camera, but the lighting over there was shit. If she'd been a real LPS employee, Misty would have put in a requisition. She maximized the window then leaned toward the monitor. The man held his hands out and made patting motions, as if to indicate he wasn't a threat. Anna shrugged then pointed toward the building, like she wanted the taller figure to fuck off. Misty tried zooming, but the guy was cast in shadows. No way she'd identify him from this.

Anna drew her phone from her pocket then tapped the screen. The guy snagged it, threw it on the ground, then stomped down. Misty's sister gaped and shoved him with little effect. The man drew his own cell from his jacket, tapped, then held it out so the white light shone on Anna's face.

She drew back, raising one hand to her chest.

The man withdrew the device, pocketed it, then waved toward her car.

Anna turned her gaze toward the building, twisted her head to look over one shoulder toward the guard's booth at the entrance, then nodded. The man circled the ride then slid into the passenger's seat. Less than a minute later, the headlights flared. She backed out of the space then drove slowly toward the gate.

Misty slammed the space bar, flopped back in her chair, then resumed viewing at the image of Anastasia's car passing through the gate. The video Blake had requisitioned would've picked her up a moment later. So, Anna had been driving, but she hadn't been alone in the car.

Although she'd checked her father's router logs to verify he'd been at home watching Hulu that night, the woman she'd spotted walking from his house to the mailbox daily could have accounted for the internet traffic while her father had driven halfway across the country to Colorado.

But now that Misty had seen Anastasia drive off with someone else, she saw her theory for what it had been. Paranoid. Ludicrous. Any relief she felt now that she'd ruled out their abusive prick of a dad barely registered.

Misty reached for her phone. Not the one LPS provided, but her personal cell. She scrolled down her contacts until she saw the icon of Cyrus's face. The only person she'd bothered to snap a picture of for his contact card.

When she'd left the SAC's office, he'd been fired up. Shoulders tensed. Jaw working.

And why not? You went behind his back. It's one thing to evade the SAC, but isn't Cyrus more than a pair of eyes looking over your shoulder?

But he'd also traipsed off to Texas with no leads while her sister was God-knew-where, and she'd had no breadcrumbs to follow.

She scrolled to Blake's contact card, gazed through the phone, blurring her vision and sharpening the replay of her sister arguing with someone in the parking lot, then slammed the phone back onto her desk.

"Quite a gig, ain't it?"

Misty jerked. Justin Watson stood in her doorway, peering at her over the glasses perched near the tip of his nose.

"Anything I can help with?"

"Personal stuff."

"Oh." He scratched the back of his head. "Yeah, I get it." He eyed her personal cell phone lying on her desk. "Hey, I'm guessing no one told you, but we're in kind of a lock down state until we're fully operational."

"What's that mean, exactly?"

"The boss wants us to put our personal cell phones into a locker upstairs when we arrive. I guess Tasker forgot to mention it. We should probably add it to the onboarding documentation until Mister Lockhart removes the restriction. Anyway, the lockers are down the right-hand hallway when you reach the lobby elevators. You just pull a key, open the locker, shove personal effects in there, then close it."

"Like a train station."

"Exactly like that. Even the same little orange keys." He smiled, but it didn't reach his eyes. "So, hey, I noticed you logged into the Outlook server earlier. Need anything?"

Misty's face scrunched. If she wanted to keep him out of her way, she'd need to establish her dominance in the pecking order. "You getting territorial on my second day?"

"Not at all." He raised a hand to wave away the sentiment. "Just checking in. I'll let you get back to it. Let me know if you need anything."

He ambled back up the hallway toward the server room and his office on the other side.

Little shivers of intuition cascaded up her neck.

Watch that fucking guy.

She rewound the video to when the figure first appeared in the parking lot. Judging by the man's height, she ruled out Justin Watson. Tasker White wasn't tall enough. A gentle tap of the space bar brought the video to life again. The stomping of the cell phone. The man walked around the car, pulled the door open, then slid into the passenger seat. Misty paused and noted how low he'd had to bend.

She went back a few frames at a time. When she froze the playback halfway through his descent, his broad shoulders stood out. Her heart ratcheted up as she realized the man in the video was the same one who'd towered over her during the elevator ride from the fourth floor to the basement the day before then escorted her to her office to make sure her badge got her in.

The video played again, and Misty watched as Tom Rhymer rode away with her younger sister until the Subaru disappeared through the gate.

Snatching up her cell, she scrolled to Cyrus's contact card again. Her thumb hovered over the call button. For the second time, she scrolled to Blake's card. This time, she pressed call.

"Blake."

"You asked me to report to you. I'm reporting."

"What do you have?"

When she'd initiated the call, Misty planned to spit it out. But what did she really have? Who was Tom Rhymer, and what had he wanted with Anastasia?

"Not much. I've been sweeping their network security, closing some holes. Doing the job. I found video of her leaving the compound with some guy that Tuesday night."

"Any idea who?"

She deliberated, but knew hesitating would draw the SAC's suspicions. Say what you would, Blake hadn't earned his job with dull instincts.

"Unclear."

"You on site?"

"Yes, sir."

"Think that's safe? To be calling from there?"

"I swept the office for bugs."

"Good. But from now on, let's play it cool. Call after hours. Did you tell Cyrus?"

"No."

His sigh came across the phone in a burst of static. "You two need to bury the bodies. No, the hatchet. Duh. Look, I'll fill him in, but I think it'd be best for everyone involved if you just return to standard practice."

"In other words, call Cyrus if I find anything else."

"Oh, did you need more clarity, Miss Daniels?"

"Message received."

"Good. Because even though I let you walk in there, you're still on a short leash. Work fast, be as efficient as Cy claims you are, and get the hell out. I was serious about prices that would be paid for this little fiasco. I know Cyrus might have gone rogue before I came onboard, but you'd do well to ignore those lessons and fly the straight-and-narrow like he has over the last year."

"Understood." She ground her molars.

"Thanks for the report. Get an ID, talk to Cyrus."

He hung up.

Misty threw her phone into her backpack, logged out of her computer, stood, shrugged the pack onto one shoulder, then broke for the elevator. The remote login she'd set up earlier would allow her to check the employee files of Tom Rhymer when she got back to her place, but she doubted she'd find much there. Probably a dead end. But what else did she have?

Maybe Cyrus would think of something.

Dammit.

The sun was down by the time she reached the lobby. Part of being a basement dweller was how a windowless environment shrouded time.

Unlike Anna, she'd parked under one of the two-story streetlights in the front lot. Her car horn chirped when she thumbed the fob. Remembering the figure who'd approached Anna, she threw a look over one shoulder as she tossed her backpack into the rear seat.

A tall, broad-shouldered man stood one row back, the high streetlight painting a shadow across his features. Shivers cascaded down her spine.

"Hi, Joanna. Is your tank full?"

"Rhymer?"

"Glad you remembered. Is your tank full?"

Wait, he just called me Joanna.

She nodded. "Damn near full. Why?"

"I'm driving a blue Toyota truck. If you'd like to see your sister, pull out after me and follow."

He turned and made a beeline for the back row, closest to the gate.

"Wait!"

He didn't turn around.

Heart pounding her ribs like it really wanted out, Misty thought of Cyrus and the cell phone she'd shoved into her backpack. But he'd never let her follow the guy, and a she didn't want to risk adding another car to the procession lest he notice. She left the cell in the pack, fired up her engine, then followed Tom Rhymer's truck through the gate and out, into the dark night.

CHAPTER 22

Cyrus set his hand on Marsha's leg and squeezed while he worked the remote in the other. When she set hers atop his, he found himself smiling, realizing Misty's jokes about his domestication hadn't been far from the mark.

He'd take it.

But when he pressed the play button to get the movie rolling, Misty's face was still plastered to his mind's eye. Somehow, watching *Sixteen Candles* with Marsha made him feel unfaithful. Eighties movies had been Misty's and his thing.

On screen, the Baker family's morning chaos erupted to life, the group milling at the bottom of the stairs, Samantha Baker's younger brother calling up to her.

Hey, birth defect!

Marsha chuckled.

"How have you never seen this movie?" Cyrus asked. But his mind was split.

He reached for his cell, checked the screen for missed calls, then dropped it back onto the sofa cushion.

"Still nothing from your protégé, huh?"

"No."

"Why haven't you called her?"

One side of Cyrus's mouth twisted up.

Marsha reached across him for the remote and paused the film just as Molly Ringwald descended the stairs.

"It's bureau stuff. Misty's... not in the open right now. I don't want to compromise her."

Marsha twisted on her cushion. "Are you saying Misty is undercover?" Her mouth gaped. "I didn't think she did that kind of thing." She slapped his leg. "Cyrus! No wonder you've been pouting around here like a..."

His cell buzzed. Cyrus snatched it up and read the screen. With a sigh, he answered.

"Boss man."

"Cyrus. Just wanted to touch base. Misty found something. You should reach out. She's probably left LPS by now. I told her to report to you going forward. I'm heading out for a late dinner with my wife. Stop acting like children."

He hung up then peered at Marsha's slanted smile.

"Guess he told you. I'll give you some space. Call her."

She was out of the room in seconds, and Cyrus heard the gentle catch of the bedroom door's latch a moment later.

Drawing the phone up before he could think about it, he dialed Misty.

It rang six times then went to voice mail. His lip twitched. He tried again. Then again. Nothing. He brought up the texting applet.

Time to get the gang back together. Call me when you're in the clear.

He paused, checked the time. They'd fallen out before, had little tiffs here and there. But the first time she hadn't picked up had been when he went to Texas. Misty always answered or sent a text. He read the unfinished message then added:

Or just shoot me a text to let me know you're okay.

CHAPTER 23

Various scenarios played out in Misty's head as she followed the Tacoma out of Colorado Springs heading west. Anna tied up in a basement somewhere. Anna in a ditch, decomposing. The slide show expanded as the roads grew darker. An hour and a half later, they ascended up a narrow, winding road, and she checked her cell. Still no bars.

Then a ping of familiarity. A giant tree washed in her headlights at the apex of a hairpin turn. The sky-reaching sentry's thick branches creeping wide, like it'd bullied any opposing growth out of the area to create a singular opening in an otherwise dense forest. Then, a glance through a break in the trees revealing a huge lodge nested near a cliff on one side.

I've seen all of this before.

It hit her—her grandfather, Owen Reed. Her mom's dad, who'd only been allowed to see his granddaughters a few times after his daughter died in child-birth. Misty conjured an image of his face, younger than she'd expect, but age was relative to the youth of the viewer. He couldn't have been, what? Forty-five back then? Fifty?

Last time Anna had called, it'd been to announce he'd passed. She'd wanted her big sister to come to the reading of the will, but Misty had declined, choosing to leave the past behind and suggesting Anna do the same.

No links to your past, she'd reminded her sister. *That's how he'll find you.*

Now that their father had shown up at the newspaper, the warning struck her as ridiculous. Anastasia was a reporter, and a good one. It was inevitable.

When Tom Rhymer pulled his truck onto a narrow, winding dirt road moments later, it all came rushing back.

Misty, about seven years old, riding in the back of a car with her sister beside her. Thick, dark hair covering the back of Pop-pop's head as he drove. Her mother long dead. This had been the last time she'd seen him.

She recalled the dirt road winding uphill until...

The antiquated cabin perched on a craggy ridge. Snow would cover it soon. Its exterior was time-stamped with weathering, a testament to the harsh elements it had endured over the years.

When Tom Rhymer pulled onto a freshly graveled lot on one side, his headlights painted a Subaru. Even through the relief of seeing a place Anna had to have chosen herself, her heart raced as she parked and the story came together. Flickers of orange light danced on the window glass from inside. Misty snatched her flashlight from the glove box then jumped out and clicked it on, passing its white beam over the facade.

The roof was patched in one spot, but fresh tiles indicated someone had begun renovations. The surrounding trees creaked in a high wind.

A rusty axe was wedged into a tree stump, and cords of wood were stacked neatly against one wall. Smoke rose from a brick chimney. The front door, a recent addition of polished wood with a window cut into its surface, swung open.

Anna stood in a fuzzy robe, her face washed in the light of two high-wattage bulbs set into the facade on either side of the door.

"What in the hell are you doing here?"

"Why do you sound surprised? Didn't you tell Rhymer to bring me?"

"Yeah, only after I found out you were working at LPS. Let me rephrase. What the hell are you doing *there?*"

"I was looking for *you.*" She mounted the stairs then crossed the threshold.

Anastasia pulled her into an embrace. The interior was humid, bordering on suffocating. When Anna closed the door, Misty surveyed the surroundings.

The interior of the cabin contrasted its weathered

exterior. A stone fireplace dominated one wall, its split logs burning high with reserves neatly stacked in a rack nearby. Bark dust littered the surface. The polished sheen of the hardwoods shone in the firelight. The scents of wood smoke and fresh paint struggled for dominance.

A small kitchen was tucked into the back right corner. Its counter tops were ancient Formica, but the appliances were state-of-the-art.

The contrast between modern and antiquated was jarring, but it also lent the cabin a unique charm, like it was caught in a time warp, suspended between past and present.

A dusty canvas drop cloth covered the kitchen table, a hammer and strewn-about nails suggesting renovations were still underway. A patchwork staircase led up to the loft.

"I'm guessing our grandfather left you the place."

"He left *us* the cabin. You didn't seem interested, and I didn't want to hear any shit about connecting to my past, so I spent weekends up here over the last year."

Misty gazed toward Tom, who'd slipped past when the women embraced to stand on the opposite side of the fireplace.

"So, what's your role in all this?"

"It's long-winded."

Misty plopped down on a leather sofa. "Well, I'm not going anywhere until I know what's going on." She focused on Anna. "You had me in a fucking state. What the hell? Why are you hiding up here?"

Anna nodded, and Misty found her empathetic expression annoying. Patience proved challenging, but she waited while her younger sister gathered words.

"Someone broke into my apartment."

Misty straightened, sliding her backside to the edge of the sofa cushion. "Broke in?"

Tom interjected. "Back up. Start at the beginning."

Anastasia sighed. "I was sent to do a piece on Lockhart Public Security."

"This, I know."

"Oh. Well, it was an unusual opportunity. The way my editor described the enterprise, what LPS was trying to do, I knew I had to jump at it. He promised Lockhart would give me full access to the facilities." She waved one hand toward the towering figure across the room. "Tom was my escort. First, Sam Lockhart brought me to his office and dropped his spiel about what he was trying to do with his new company. I interviewed employees, talked to the staff shrink, checked out the basement, etc.

"Then I met Chet Parsons. The IT security manager. He showed me the server room, told me about his time in Fallujah. Great guy. Smiled a lot."

"Until he shot himself in the head," Misty added.

Anna didn't respond. Tom frowned.

"Go on."

"My editor wanted something comprehensive.

Heavy on the word count. Imagine it. A company that wants to put the screws to gun violence, one that predominantly hires vets, provides medical care—it was so far-reaching it bordered on being a fairy tale.

"I had all kinds of questions. Did they weed out vets with PTSD? Not according to Lockhart. What if they had criminal records? Depends on the seriousness of the crime. So I wanted to see how on-boarding worked from beginning to end. How veterans were brought into the fold. They let me interview a guy applying at Lockhart. I followed him around with Tom in tow.

"Then the applicant I'd interviewed ended up dead outside a church in Hope Mills, carrying an AR-15 and a pistol."

"Michael Bray," Misty said. "Dead at the hands of LPS."

"You see why I'd get a little..."

"Apprehensive."

"You're still finishing my thoughts. Some things never change. Yes, apprehensive is the right word. Since I'd talked to Bray, and I knew most applicants met with the shrink—"

"Clayton Burroughs."

"Yes. Shut up so I can finish. So, since I knew he'd been assessed by Burroughs, I went to talk to the doc about Bray. Of course, doctor-patient privilege is a thing, but I wasn't sure Bray qualified as a patient. No money had changed hands, and LPS never hired him.

But the doc was mum. Resistant to everything I asked. I don't know if he has a beef with reporters, but he seemed... annoyed I'd even come to his office."

Anastasia slid onto the opposite side of the sofa. Leaning forward, she rested her elbows on her knees while the fire painted her features in an orange glow.

"Two days later, Chet killed himself."

Misty slid puzzle pieces around. Michael Bray applied at Lockhart. Got rejected. Went to shoot up a church. Then the IT manager ended up dead. She lacked the intel to connect the two, but a thought emerged.

"I'm guessing that's when Lockhart regretted letting a reporter inside."

Anna nodded, leaned back on the sofa, then crossed one leg over the other. "How right you are. And we come full circle. I drove home two nights after I'd learned Chet was gone. At first, nothing seemed amiss. But when I was changing into my pajamas, I noticed something strange. You know how regimented I am. I have a bedtime routine. A bottle of melatonin sits on my nightstand next to my phone dock. Always on the left so it's within easy reach, close to my hand lotion. But that night, the pill bottle was on the right."

"Maybe you moved it." But Misty's words carried little conviction in her own ears. Her sister bordered on obsessive-compulsive. Everything in its place.

Anna gave a long sigh though nostrils. "I entertained the possibility, despite knowing better. I took a tablet, rolled over, and went to sleep. The next morning, while I was getting ready in the bathroom, I noticed the edges of a hand towel I keep on a ring over the sink were uneven. I might have set that aside, too, but I'd just washed that towel, and I specifically remembered folding it neatly, slipping it into the ring, then hanging it so the edges were even. It wasn't remotely close to how I'd left it."

"So, you think someone was in your apartment. Looking for what? Face cream?"

"Your snide bullshit is unnecessary, Joanna."

"Misty." She cast a glare at Tom. "And could you stop towering there? Sit down or something."

Tom slid into a recliner. "No problem."

Anastasia ran a hand through her long, black locks. "Look, just hang with me. Okay?"

Misty frowned before finally nodding.

"After seeing the towel, I pulled open drawers. Looked in cabinets. Nothing was out of place. Still, I kind of freaked out. I checked in with my editor. Filled him in about Michael Bray's link to LPS, Chet Parson's suicide. Told him I thought someone had been in my apartment."

"How did he respond?"

"He called me paranoid. Really pissed me off."

"Understandable. That it made you mad, I mean."

"In retrospect, that call to Will was my first mistake."

"I think that's where I come in," Tom said, and

Misty might have detected a tone of impatience, but she wasn't sure. Instead of expanding, he reached into his jacket pocket, withdrew a cell phone, then tapped in the code. After a few swipes he offered it to Misty.

A landscape snapshot. She flipped the phone sideways so it filled the screen. A soldier troop lounged in the shadows of overhead netting, all wearing desert camo, but not hats. No smiles. The lone standing figure towered over the rest. Tom Rhymer.

Misty zoomed in on the faces while Tom narrated.

"Fallujah. My unit was sent in to root out terrorists back in 2004, clear the city."

Something Tasker White had said the day she reported to LPS for her tour rang out in her mind.

"You were First Stryker Brigade."

He shook his head. "No, but that's what we say for cover. My team was special ops, sent in to support First Stryker, but we reported to a different commander. Edward Xavier."

"The XO at Lockhart, right?"

"One and the same."

"Why a separate unit?"

"Dark Ops."

Images of a small village in Afghanistan flashed in her mind. A woman in a hijab, looking over both shoulders while feeding Misty information. Chills ran up her spine.

"We'd gotten flash intel on a target one night, a real son of a bitch from Pakistan who wasn't in the deck of playing cards soldiers used to identify enemy targets in Saddam's power structure. The US had wanted him for years, but they couldn't go to his home country to get him."

A strategy that had changed when it came to a new president and Osama bin Laden, but Misty didn't mention it.

"Now that he was in Iraq, the target was fair game. This was early in the campaign, and we came upon a group of civilians. But in Fallujah, the enemy dressed like civilians. One of them spotted us, and the crowd swarmed in our direction. A young guy, probably about sixteen, moved faster than the rest. He was dressed in robes, covered from head to toe. We had protocols."

"I think I know where this is going."

"You're probably right. We raised our rifles and ordered them to stay back. Most of them complied, but the kid kept coming. Our LT got antsy, trigger happy, and he mowed the kid down. The rest of the crowd erupted. Raising their fists in the air. Shouting. Chanting. Chaos ensued. A pair of guys appeared from around a corner, waving AKs. Lieutenant-be-damned, I tried to order a retreat but was drowned out by more gunfire. The whole episode was crisp and blurry at the same time. When it was over, all my guys were upright, and not one of the Iraqis had survived."

"Jesus. Did you hit the target or withdraw?"

"We took the fucker out."

"What did command say?"

"It was Fallujah. Hell on earth. But I still tried to take responsibility for my unit mowing down a bunch of non-combatants. The XO cursed me out. Said no one knew we were there. Not even First Stryker. Instead of reprimands, he put us all in for Silver Stars and told us from then on, we should tell people we were First Stryker."

Misty's nose twitched. When a commander of a black ops unit put his men in for awards then told them to lie about who they'd operated with, he was concerned about word getting out. If the media learned a bunch of civilians were mowed down, the XO's bosses would have to give some kind of answer. Saying it was a CIA-backed, black ops unit wasn't the kind of answer the military gave.

Anna nodded. "If that isn't enough, they're called the Silver Stars at Lockhart."

Misty eyed the photo, but it was grainy, rendered from paper to digital, and she couldn't make out any familiar faces from LPS at first glance.

"Right," Tom said. "The XO of our unit is second-in-command at LPS. Shameless bastard knows the Fallujah event wasn't on the level, but he still paints the heroic image. The Silver Stars were the first hires, right after him. He'd talked us up, so Lockhart made me his fixer."

"Fixer? That sounds ominous."

"It's... interesting. After Bray lost his shit in Texas, I was in the XO's office. He told me Lockhart wanted damage control, and the XO was passing it on to me. That's when Chet showed up, asking how a guy from our unit ends up dead by Lockhart Security."

"Chet was a Silver Star?" Misty asked.

"Yes. The XO asked me to stifle Anna's coverage. He specifically wanted me to keep her off track. Told me to talk about how crazy Bray was. But she'd interviewed him when he applied at Lockhart, and your sister isn't stupid.

"Like I was saying, I was in Xavier's office when Chet barged in and lit into the XO about a guy from our unit ending up dead in Hope Mills, Texas, killed by some green LPS agent."

"Green?"

"That's what he said. His name's Chance Baker, and he's young. But he was put on paid leave after the shooting."

"Did he break protocol?"

Tom shrugged. "No idea. The XO is keeping that information close to his vest."

Misty deposited that for later.

"Anyway, Parsons threatened to quit. Said he was going to talk to Anastasia himself. I think the XO would've talked him down, but Chet said something that, in my opinion, sealed his fate."

Rhymer's rapid monologue had Misty struggling to order the information so she could stow it away in her mind.

"He told the XO that Anna would find the whole Fallujah thing really interesting."

The big picture came into view, and Misty rubbed her temples. "How long before Chet was found dead?"

"That night."

"Jesus."

"I found out the next morning. No one called me when he was discovered. Lockhart had left word at reception that I was to come up to his office as soon as I arrived. The ride up seemed to last forever because I had every intention of resigning. Something was fucked, and I wanted no part of it.

"No doubt, the XO had told Lockhart about the argument in his office. My suspicion was he'd want to lend me assurances it was actually a suicide. But after the church dust up and Chet killing himself, Lockhart's lone interest was to scratch Anna's story. He offered no consolation over the deaths of two brothers from my unit. No mourning of the loss of a Lockhart family member. He wanted the story dead. Family, my ass. And the way they talked about Anna's story, especially in light of Chet's sudden death, made me worry how far they might go to squash it."

"So you didn't resign."

"Right. I wanted to dig up some intel. Find out what happened to Chet so I could go to the cops. But in the meeting that morning, I noticed Lockhart never quite says enough to implicate himself, even when we're alone or talking on the phone. He counts on the

XO to run day-to-day operations... and do the dirty work."

"I'm not surprised."

Tom's eyebrows shot up at Misty's words.

"Lockhart is a criminal. One of his guys killed a politician. It doesn't surprise me he wouldn't want the press."

"Right. But that's where it gets interesting. The one guy Lockhart didn't hire from the Silver Stars was the LT. The XO probably made it clear we wouldn't work with him. Hell, we'd all left the service because of that prick. He was the one who shot the kid in Fallujah, setting off the whole thing. When Anna and I compared notes..." He pointed toward the phone in Misty's hand. "He's the guy on the right."

Misty zoomed. A ping of familiarity. Another shiver. Then she recalled the framed medal on the shelves behind Will Bresnan's desk at the *Post*.

"Anna's editor was a Silver Star."

Tom jerked. "You've met him?"

"Yeah. Saw the medal on the bookcase in his office."

Tom refocused on Anna but spoke to Misty. "How'd you get him to talk to you?"

Misty started thinking up excuses. She didn't know Tom from Adam, and revealing who she was actually working for was *no bueno*.

When she turned her gaze away from the fireplace,

Anna was leering. "How exactly did you end up at LPS?"

Thankful she'd redirected them from Tom's question, Misty shrugged. "Your friend used the bat phone."

The moniker for the secure messaging system.

"Shit! Dane?"

"We didn't exchange names."

"He's the only one with the info. Are you telling me you found out I was missing then applied at LPS?"

"You're my sister."

The firelight reflected tears welling in Anna's eyes. "Always protecting me, aren't you?" She sniffed. "Shit. I should've called him. The last thing I wanted was to drag you into this." She looked away then whipped her head back around. "Wait, I thought you served with a guy from LPS. Isn't that what you said, Tom?"

Tom nodded. "Tasker White recruited her."

Misty melted into the couch. "Not exactly. We served in Afghanistan together. But I found him, not the other way around. When I heard you were missing"—she paused to form the words without giving away her position with the feds—"I started looking into Lockhart. Saw Tasker in one of his media photos. I was between gigs, so I thought I'd kill two birds with one stone."

The long silence that ensued was broken only when the burning logs popped and sent fiery motes up the chimney. All three of the cabin's occupants flinched.

Tom scooted forward. "But if you got in through Tasker, and you haven't talked to Anna in a year, how did you get into the paper to talk to Bresnan? Did you tell him you were sisters? I thought you two kept that quiet."

The only conclusion Misty could draw from his words was that Rhymer and Anastasia had established trust. She wouldn't tell anyone else about their past.

Anyone who could read body language would've intuited that Tom was going into protective mode. The strong interest in Anna's safety lent Misty some comfort. But hesitating before she answered might set him off.

Not wanting to reveal the circumstances surrounding her visit to the paper, Misty answered selectively. "The paper was a dead end. Bresnan said he'd fired her last Friday over voice mail."

"I shouldn't be surprised, but I didn't know he'd axed me. Someone crushed my cell phone." She threw Rhymer a mock squint.

"I saw that on the parking lot video."

Tom perked up. "Wait, what? I deleted that video."

"There's a backup that's purged every thirty days."

"Shit. If you found it—"

Misty waved him off. "Those half-wits wouldn't notice if their lives depended on it. I was surprised they'd set up a schedule to manually purge the files every month. Don't worry."

Anna balled up a fist. "Will Bresnan told me he'd served with someone at Lockhart when he gave me the assignment, but he's a newspaper guy. When I filled him in about Chet and Michael Bray, he should've wanted me to finish this story. Total click bait, not to mention how, with LPS's controversial nature, the article would go viral. But the morning after Chet died, he pulled me off the story. And his excuse? He was suddenly worried about the apartment break-in. He thought I was fucking stupid. Boy, did I lose my shit!

"I threatened to quit, to take it to another outlet. If he'd been on the level, he would've fired me on the spot. Instead, he told me I'd done the work for the *Post*, and he'd file an injunction if I tried. He put me on two days' leave to cool off before reassigning me. I haven't talked to him since. That he eventually did terminate me doesn't change anything."

"So, that's why you're holed up. You've got it coming from all sides."

"Someone was in my apartment. Damn right."

Tom rang in. "The morning after Anna's editor put her on leave, the XO called me to his office. He said she could come to campus to get anything she'd left in the locker we'd loaned her. They're single-key deals, so he didn't have a key to snoop through her shit. But I'll bet he would have. He asked me to escort her wherever she went, watch what she pulled out of the locker, then take her temp badge, thank her for her interest in the story, and show her to the gate. I had her card, so I called her to ask if she had left anything on campus. She'd left her iPad in the locker. If she hadn't, we probably wouldn't be here."

"Why is that?"

"When she arrived late that afternoon, she told me the company I was working for was trash. Shady. I agreed something was way off, but I didn't say so. Then she told me someone had been in her apartment, and my brain kicked into overdrive. I wondered, had the XO wanted me to watch her at her locker because they hadn't found what they wanted in her apartment? After Fallujah, I knew what an ass-covering prick the XO could be, but breaking into her place?

"Then she cursed Bresnan, and hearing his name, my alarm bells went off. That's when I realized her editor had been the murdering field commander in my unit. The guy who started the whole fiasco in Fallujah with his itchy trigger finger. We all left the service with only our worthless Silver Stars to show for it. None of *us* display them, and Will Bresnan is the last guy who should."

"Why go back to work for your XO if he covered up a war crime?"

"It's going to sound bad, but the pay was incredible. It'd been almost twenty years since Fallujah, and I had assurances they would never hire Bresnan." He waved a hand before she could reply. "Anyway, when

Anastasia told me about the break in, I didn't want to say anything inside the facility. You never know who is listening. I waved goodbye from the elevator, stashed my company cell phone in my locker, then took the side exit to catch up with her in the parking lot."

Misty handed him the phone. "Then you showed her that picture. I saw it on the video."

"I see why Tasker White referred you for that job."

"Thanks?"

"Right. When I showed her the picture, as you saw, she whipped out her cell to call Bresnan. I asked if it was a company cell. She said it was. So, I stomped on it to get her attention and snap her out of her delusions. We needed a place to talk. I didn't want to go to my place, so she told me about this cabin. Said it belonged to your grandfather, and she's been restoring it since it left probate. No cell reception, but an otherwise perfect place to hide.

"She dropped me in town, and I took an Uber back to my truck. I knew they monitored the parking lot, so I slipped in after hours to delete the video. Good thing you're on our side. Can you delete the video files?"

There was a conundrum. She could do no such thing. Blake and Cyrus would lose their shit if she destroyed evidence, and she was already in the frying pan with those two.

"The video doesn't show you doing anything illegal."

"Yeah, but what if they figure out I rode off with her?"

"Little late in the game for that, isn't it? I mean, you're here for some reason and, if you're still working at Lockhart, you must have a plan."

"We're still working it out. The morning after she came to the cabin, the boss called me in. Lockhart himself. Told me the reporter had disappeared after leaving the previous night. It confirmed my suspicions that Lockhart, the XO, and Will Bresnan were in cahoots. That, along with news someone had broken into her apartment, erased my doubts about his intentions. Since I fall right under the XO in the food chain, Lockhart asked me for a favor. Asked me to be a good soldier, if you can believe it. Then the bastard mentioned Fallujah. Said he'd heard the stories from the XO. That it was good to know he had someone in-house who'd proven he was a team player.

"The message was clear. He had four guys from Lockhart Tactical who'd flown in that morning. They were scoping out the newspaper and her apartment."

Lockhart Tactical. Misty's scrunched up her nose.

"He put me in charge. Told me to use them how I saw fit. I could handle the op. He called it a fucking op, if you can believe that."

"So what did you do?"

"I left them where they were. Told them to work in shifts to ensure there was constant coverage, in case she returned."

Misty smiled. "Since you had her tucked away in a cabin no one would find."

He returned the grin. "Exactly."

"Shrewd. I kind of like it. So, coming back to your plan."

"I've been waiting for Sam to say something incriminating so I can go to the cops. I called him after his interview with Alex Riddle, trying to fish it out of him. But he told me to keep watch, refused to give me the order to break into her apartment. He even authorized me to pay her off in exchange for her walking away from the story. He called it 'comfort for silence.' Nothing illegal about that."

"Right. Say what you will about Lockhart, he's careful."

"Very."

"How much was he offering?"

"A quarter mill."

"That alone tells me he's desperate." She turned toward Anna. "How come you didn't call me?"

Anna shrugged. "What were you gonna do? You're an IT person."

If her sister had known how much had changed for Misty in the last year, would she have called?

She was going to have to sit down with Anastasia for an extended conversation about her military service. It was overdue.

Anna went on. "Besides, I think you've bailed me out plenty for one lifetime." She grasped Misty's hand. "I probably wouldn't be here if it weren't for you."

A memory surfaced in full HD. Their father, face down on the floor beside a bed. Blood trickling from the back of his head. They'd stayed separated for a reason, but if their father had shown up at the newspaper, as Anna's editor had said, it was time for a new strategy, anyway.

Tom perched an elbow on the arm of his chair. "When I told Anna I'd seen a woman who could pass for her twin at the LPS, and we realized who you were..." Tom stood up and threw a log on the fire. He spoke while he stoked it, and little embers flowed up the chimney. "I just wanted to warn you off. So, are you going back?"

That was a damned fine question. If Blake had made anything clear from the beginning, it was that she was investigating a missing person. That case was solved. But all the new info about Lockhart, the Silver Stars—specifically the XO, the dead IT manager, and the shooter in Texas—brought a crisp image of Cyrus's face to mind.

He hadn't wanted her anywhere near this op. Would the SAC want any part of it, considering the new information?

Tom racked the fire poker then turned his back to the high flames. "The break-in is the puzzle piece that's bothering me. With Lockhart being so careful, I just can't figure out who was in her apartment."

Misty mulled that over.

The pill bottle on her nightstand. Like someone had read what she was taking. If the culprit was thinking an overdose might play, melatonin probably wouldn't do the job. Which brought her to the towel. Not very interesting to someone trying to dig up dirt on a reporter. Why would an intruder care about a towel? And assuming it was a trained operative, why would they touch it at all?

Then, a message from the past. The echo of a cold day. A mental image worn and distorted by the passage of time. Rain. Misty squeezed her eyes closed, remembering. A door. A brass deadbolt with Schlage engraved beneath the cylinder's face.

A sledgehammer of realization slammed into Misty, and her breath hitched in her chest. The room tilted on its axis. She shot up from the sofa, paced into the kitchen, and peered out the window into the dark.

"What?" Anna asked.

"Tom is right. It wasn't Lockhart who broke into your apartment. The timeline doesn't track, and if he called on Tactical to keep watch, he wouldn't have wanted to risk having someone from LPS caught inside when they're already under scrutiny."

Anna slouched on the sofa. "Yeah. So, who was it?"

Misty turned, leaned her hip against the Formica, then folded her arms across her chest. "Who could get access to your apartment address?"

"Will Bresnan had it on file. He could tell Lockhart."

"You're running in circles. We've ruled out Sam Lockhart. But Bresnan tipped me off."

"How'd my editor tip you off?"

"He told me you had a visitor at the paper."

Anna's chin dropped, her eyes flared, then she splayed her fingers against her chest.

"Shit. Father knows where I live."

CHAPTER 24

It was after eleven when Cyrus's phone rang. Marsha grumbled something under her breath, but it lacked conviction. It went against her nature to complain. Cy reached for his nightstand, snagged his phone, then blinked against the assault of the light as he checked the screen.

Misty.

His shaky finger tapped three times before it made contact with the right button.

"You're alive."

"Hey, Cy."

"Where are you?"

"Driving back to Denver. Can you meet me at my place?"

"Kind of late, isn't it?"

"I found her Cyrus. She's alive. Stashed somewhere safe. I don't want to talk on the phone. Can you meet me? It can't wait until morning."

Marsha was measuring him from beneath the blanket, a hint of moonlight streaming through the Venetian blinds casting her light complexion in a cool glow.

He sighed. "I'll meet you there in forty-five."

"Thanks, Cy."

"Let me guess," Marsha said.

"Misty."

She smiled then reached out with one hand. He squeezed it. "Guess I'll see you in the morning, love." She rolled over then pulled the blanket up to her shoulder. "Feel free to sleep in her spare."

"I'll be cuddling you by sunrise."

"That's the right answer."

CHAPTER 25

They sat in the dim light of the cage after midnight, Cyrus running back through Misty's story, trying to piece it into a coherent timeline.

"So, the editor was one of these so-called Silver Stars. Practically a war criminal."

"It was Fallujah. Try to imagine."

"Yeah, I shouldn't judge. Fine. But he sent your sis to write a puff piece for his former XO. This Xavier..."

"Edward. That's right."

"And Michael Bray, another Silver Star, applied at Lockhart. For whatever reason, they turned him away, despite having hired all the others, except for Bresnan."

"Right. Since Bray went after a black church in Texas, Anna asked the shrink about him."

Cyrus tapped text into his cellphone's notepad. "The shrink, Clayton Burroughs. He a star, too?"

"Nope."

"Okay. I think I have it all. But something doesn't fit."

"That someone broke into my sister's apartment before the Hope Mills shooting, and before Chet Parsons got himself unalived."

"You not buying that Parsons committed suicide?"

"Fuck no. I think someone offed him, and I don't care how it sounds."

"Right. But I'll come back to it. Who broke into the apartment?"

"My father. Almost certain. The items Anna found out of place were insignificant to anyone else. The pill bottle I could dismiss. But the hand towel."

"Why the towel?"

"Because I think he was *smelling* it."

A wave of disgust coursed through Cyrus's veins as the implication struck. The sisters' name changes were starting to add up. The urge to press, to learn more about Misty's early life, neared overwhelming. What had this depraved, towel-smelling bastard done? Cyrus could only imagine the worst.

The screens mounted to the cage were all dark, and Misty was gazing at him from her chair. The way her gaze flitted from one of his eyes to the other and back, like she feared he saw inside her, convinced him to tamp down his emotions.

He sat to face her. "Your father is none of my business. He has nothing to do with this case. So, if you're sure it was him who was in her apartment, we can set him aside. If you've told me everything about LPS, we're sitting on a stack of circumstantial evidence. Nothing we could charge."

"Nothing tying the events together but a conspiracy theory."

"Yeah." He pocketed his cell then dropped his arm into his lap. "The bad news is, your sister is safe."

"That's a funny way of putting it." She chuckled. "But I get it. I was thinking the same thing at the cabin. Blake is under pressure from DC to wrap this up, and they don't want him fucking around with Lockhart right now. Politics."

"I don't like it."

She smiled, and he realized it'd been a while since he'd seen that. "I don't either. I thought I'd be happy just to know Anastasia was okay, but after hearing what she and Rhymer had to say, I'm wanting to burn LPS to the ground."

"Right. But I can't let my animosity toward Sam Lockhart affect my decisions. The SAC will likely suspend you for the unsanctioned infiltration, and pushing our luck might get you marched back to the judge. I can't let that happen."

Misty crossed one leg over the other then interlocked her fingers at her waist. The way she chewed her lip while her eyes rolled around the room told Cyrus she was musing. Maybe suppressing her emotions.

A week ago, he might have left her to it, stood up,

gathered his shit, and headed back to the woman waiting for him in a warm bed. But something stayed his hand.

He did some musing of his own. "If Lockhart Tactical's guys are watching her apartment, I assume Anna is staying put, right?"

Misty dipped her chin. "Right. And I think I trust Tom Rhymer to cover her needs, keep her isolated."

"Yeah, but until when? She can't hide forever, can she?"

"Well, I could help her install some solar and—"

"Skip the sass and consider the question."

"Right. Sorry. No, she can't hide forever. But I think I have a solution. Of course, it creates a new problem."

Cyrus chortled. "Seems they often do. Shoot."

"Anna could write her article. I'm sure another rag would take it. It's like she told me at the cabin, it'd go viral. Bresnan's threat of an injunction was posturing. The damage would be done before he could get in front of a judge. But she's in the same predicament we are. Everything's circumstantial, and if she wants to keep her reputation intact, Tom would have to find more."

Cyrus tapped a foot. "Is he up to it?"

"No one's going to admit anything. The XO and Lockhart expect him to be a good soldier without being filled in. Compartmentalization."

"Maybe he could look at internal logs? Communications? I mean, someone had to have written a text, an email about Hope Mills or Anastasia."

"He didn't even know they backed up the parking lot videos, and I didn't get the vibe that he's good with technology."

A little ping rang between Cyrus's ears. "Hmm."

"What?"

He raised a finger, staving her off.

The case was solved. They'd have to report to Blake, and he might even say they'd done a good job. He'd certainly be relieved to have something to report to his superiors, let alone be rid of the case.

But—

"If you reported back to LPS tomorrow, how quickly could you dig through their communications? They gave you a cell, right? Do they back up the phones on site so you can access them? Can you get to their emails?"

"I can get to all of it. I haven't seen any cell back-ups, just images they use for new installs. But the email is on an exchange server. It's not complicated. Sad, really."

Her superiority aside, that was good news.

Cyrus pulled out his phone, checked the time, then shoved it back in his pocket.

"Here's how I see it. Blake said if you didn't report to work, red flags might go off at LPS, right? Well, we can turn that around. You might arouse suspicions if you suddenly up and quit. So, you should go back to

LPS in the morning." He stood then wiped his balmy hands on his hips. "I'll look into the events surrounding Chet Parsons before work hours. I'll bet I can get some photos of the scene."

Misty snapped her fingers. "Because Marsha performed the autopsy!"

He nodded. "You poke around the Lockhart servers and see what you come up with. I'll have to report to Blake when he comes to the office, though, so go early and work fast, just in case he decides to pull you."

"Which he likely will."

"True. But it buys us a few hours. Will LPS be suspicious if you arrive before sunrise?"

She chuckled. "Everyone but Sam and the shrink is a vet. Before sunrise is standard."

"Roger that. Try to get a few hours shuteye. Go in early and work fucking fast. Leave the facility for lunch tomorrow, take your personal phone with you, and update me. If Blake wants to pull you, I'll tell you then."

"But he's not going to like it. If he knows I found Anna tonight then returned to LPS..."

"Leave Blake to me. If it comes to it, I'll tell him I sent you back in, and I'll tell him what I told you. We needed to avoid suspicion until I'd checked in with him."

"What if he says you should've called him as soon as you knew Anastasia was safe?"

"The last time I talked to him, he was out to dinner with his wife. He kept it short, told me what was what and hung up before I could reply. So I can say I figured he was entitled to a quiet night at home."

"He's going to call bullshit."

"Yeah, but for all he knows, we spoke at three in the morning. He'll let it slide."

Misty rubbed her hands together. "This is getting fun."

"You worry me."

She stood and wrapped her arms around his shoulders. "I'm sorry I went behind your back."

He returned the hug. "Then don't fucking do it again."

When she pulled away, tears streamed down Misty's face. Blood had rushed into her cheeks.

Cyrus gripped her shoulder.

"This isn't about our tiff. What is it?"

She set her hand on his, squeezed, then gave it a gentle push.

Misty circled him, slipped between the server racks, then disappeared. Maybe she was going to clean herself up, needed a moment to herself. He slid back into his chair. The low hum of the servers swelled in his ears as his heartbeat thumped a hard, slow rhythm.

Misty returned, flicked something out between two fingers. When he took it, she sat again. A wallet photo.

Two boys with close-cut hair, standing on a covered porch. Weather stains on the support beams, but not on the siding behind them. Although he couldn't make out many facial details, he saw the browning welt beneath one of the taller boy's eyes.

Without looking up, he asked, "Who are they?"

"My sister and me."

Lockhart was forgotten as his brain slammed on the brakes.

CHAPTER 26

Misty stood again, threw her hair over one shoulder, then beckoned for him to follow. She opened a cabinet in a wide corridor of unpainted drywall with metal framing, pulled out two glasses and a bottle of Crown.

Lightweight or not, Cyrus had no intention of declining. He considered texting Marsha but decided to let her sleep. She was not only the coroner for the consolidated city-county of Denver, but its chief medical examiner. Her phone was never in Do Not Disturb mode.

They ended up on the sofa where they'd watched 80s movies, where Cyrus got his ass kicked in Call of Duty more on the regular than he liked to admit.

He only sat once she'd settled in. After sucking back the first pour, she tipped the bottle again, casting a suspicious glance at his full snifter.

"I think you need it more than I do." That and he

wanted to be sober for whatever was coming, but he kept that piece to himself.

After a one-shoulder shrug, she slid the bottle onto the unfinished table, next to the game controller he'd never put away. Misty reached out for the photo he still held. She raised it to eye level with one hand while sipping her drink with the other.

"We grew up in Marlinton, West Virginia. Ever heard of it?"

He shook his head. "The name rings a bell, but it's vague."

"Tourists know it for the Beartown and Watoga state parks. If it wasn't for the house blocking it in this picture, you'd see the Greenbriar river. We lived about fifty yards up from its banks.

"My father was in the Navy. Our mother died in childbirth when my sister was born, and he'd had to leave the service. I was only two at the time. He joined the Pocahontas County Sheriff's Office. He's still a deputy, but I thought he'd have retired by now."

"Right. Getting along in years?"

Misty sipped her drink then interlocked her fingers around the snifter as she settled it into her lap.

"He's fifty-six, and I'm surprised the booze didn't get him a long time ago."

"Alcoholic?"

"Understatement."

Cyrus nodded.

"But he's not one of those fall-over drunks who has

to have it every day. Or he wasn't until we left. He'd pick one night of the week when he knew he didn't have to work the next day. After ordering us to our rooms with a warning we'd better shut the hell up, he'd hit the bottle.

"We shut the hell up, but he'd still come upstairs. Stumbling, leaning on the door jamb of our room. He'd ramble about how it's a good thing my mother hadn't been around to see the weak little girls she'd produced. How she'd been too sorry to give him boys."

"Fucker."

She nodded, jabbed the air between them with an index finger. "Bingo, Agent Jennings. A real fucker, that old man of ours." Once she'd gotten both hands around the drink again, she sucked it down like a toddler with a bottle then poured.

"PTSD?" Cyrus asked.

"Fuck no. He never saw combat. I don't know, maybe his father laid into him. I never met that one, and dear old dad cut us off from our maternal grandfather before I reached double digits." She spoke with the glass, waving it side to side. "No PTSD, just asshole blood."

"Right. A bully by nature."

She admired him for a few seconds then nodded and returned her gaze to the far wall. "An apt description. He shoved us both around. Called us names. Said he'd make men out of us if it killed him. I figured out early that, in his case, booze brought out his true feelings, removed what little filter he had the rest of the time. But don't think for second he was any nicer when sober.

"He made men of us, alright. By ten years old, I could shatter a bottle on a rail at sixty yards. Twelve? One-hundred, easy. How wise it was of my old man to lock those guns up when he wasn't around." She twisted her head toward him. "And the locks weren't pickable, either."

"You tried?"

She nodded, took a hefty swallow from her glass. "That's what tipped me off about Jolene's—Anna's—apartment. One day, when I was around twelve, we locked ourselves out of the house. We walked a half-mile to the neighbors in a cold winter rain and called him. He came to pick us up. I'll never forget the mask he wore, the way he smiled and thanked the neighbor for seeing to his girls, giving us hot cocoa while we waited.

"If only she'd been my parent. Anyway, he packed us into the back of his cruiser, drove us home in silence, led us onto the porch, then turned. He reached out with one hand, offering a leather pouch. He said we were worthless, that we might as well learn a skill so he didn't have to come and bail us out." She side-eyed Cyrus. "Lock picks, you see."

"Are you serious?"

"Dead. He snatched my chin, drew me close, then told me to focus or freeze to death. Explained tumblers.

The tension rod. All that jazz. Handed me the set, told me what did what, then took the rake out and shoved it in his pocket. That's the kind of asshole he was, he took the one tool that hit multiple pins and could be shimmied to pop the lock. Before he left, he turned, unlocked the deadbolt, then shook the knob to ensure it was locked. He wished us luck, got back into his cruiser, and drove away.

"When he came home from his shift two hours later, we were still at it. Jolene was shivering uncontrollably in the corner of the porch, and I was fumbling around with the damned doorknob. He walked onto the porch, shoved me to one side so I landed on my ass, unlocked the door, walked inside, slammed it, then locked the knob again."

"Your teachers didn't know? Neighbors?"

"What would they have done? Called social services on a deputy in Podunkville, West Virginia?"

Cyrus's neck burned.

Although a word slurred here and there, Misty was getting a rhythm. "I was the mother in that house. I raised Jolene. I did our laundry, cooked her meals. He sent us off to school only in pants—never anything that showed our legs. No skirts, dresses, or shorts. Said we'd come home pregnant, and that was just what he needed. Especially since we'd probably have girls because we were weak. He gave us close haircuts to androgenize our appearances."

"You want me to kill him?"

"The question is, do you think I haven't considered it?"

Her lips were thin lines, painted white as she pinched them together. The color returned when she raised the glass to finish it off. Slamming it down on the table, she leaned back, and her body slouched into the leather.

"It was common that a couple days after a night of drinking—or two, if he decided to binge, and hang-overs-be-damned—he'd come to my room while I was sleeping."

"God, please don't tell me he..."

"Not that. But he'd set a hand on my chest. Gentle-like, mind you. Peer down into my eyes. Say he was sorry about how he responded to *my* behavior. You know, the sideways apology of a serial abuser, the *I'm sorry you're such a piece of shit that I can't control myself* kind of thing. But you know what? I think his gentleness in those moments, the softness of his touch, scared me more than the moments right before he'd haul off and slap me. It makes me shiver in revulsion. I try not to think about those moments."

Misty belched, and a sour expression twisted up her face. She refilled the glass.

"When I was six or seven, a shiny new Walmart Supercenter opened in Louisburg, about an hour from where we lived. Father liked it there. That's what he insisted we call him. *Father*. Never *Daddy*. Never *Dad*. It was yes, *Father*. No, *Father*."

Her head drifted to one side then straightened.

"I digress, don't I?"

"You're fine."

She smiled. "Thanks. Where was I?"

"Walmart. Louisburg."

"Oh, good. You're paying attention, and I'm getting a little drunk."

He thought she was past *a little*.

"He'd take us to Walmart on these little apology outings. Insist I buy an action figure." She set her free hand on his knee then leaned toward him. "Never dolls, mind you. Dolls were for weak little girls who didn't want to live in reality. Not that my Star Wars action figures had any basis in reality, but at least they came with weapons. And Father liked his weapons." She pushed off his leg then leaned on the arm of the couch.

"I had every version of Luke Skywalker one could find. But I didn't open the packages. It would've been like recreation with my pain, accepting an apology that hadn't even been one. Besides, I was a woman of the ripe old age of nine, and I had a sister to feed, clothes to wash, a household to keep.

"One day, he walked into our room and noticed the action figures hanging on one wall, asked why I wasn't playing with them. It'd taken him almost a year to figure that out. Of course, any hyper-vigilant kid who didn't want to catch a beating would have foreseen this inevitable scenario coming from a mile away. I told him I was collecting them, to keep their value.

"He must not have hated that answer, because he just left, and I never heard about it again. When I was fifteen, I came home, and they were all gone. I knew better than to ask."

Cyrus ground his teeth. "This...mother...fucker..."

"That sums him up." She checked her phone. "Shit, it's two in the morning." Slamming the glass down a little too hard on the table, she stood, teetered, then dropped back down, bouncing on the sofa once before her back settled in. "Enough booze." Misty raised one finger. "Let us fast-forward this film!" She belched again. "I ever tell you I played softball as a teen?"

"You never told me you'd *been* a teen."

A full-throated laugh erupted from Misty's chest as she threw her head back like she was howling at the moon.

"You're fucking funny, Cy. I never tell you how funny you are." She hummed a long, final note to taper off the laughter then eased back.

"Although he said it was a dyke's sport, he allowed softball. But I quit when I turned seventeen because I wanted to focus on my last year in high school. It wasn't like I could go out with the girls after practice. Or have any kind of social life, for that matter.

"But I'd figured out the only way to escape my father was to do well in school. I loaded up on every elective in computer science, found I had a knack. Spent time at the library to go further, and that's where I started filling out college applications, raiding his wallet in small increments after he'd passed out to pay the application fees. I was the one who brought in the mail, so I figured he'd never be the wiser when the responses came. I'd been accepted to Georgetown, NYU, Notre Dame, UNC, and UCLA right under his fucking nose. UNC and UCLA were offering scholarships.

"This doesn't surprise me," Cyrus said. "You're one of the smartest people I've ever met."

"Aw." She punched the side of his leg. "Thanks, big guy."

Somehow, it didn't come off as sincere.

"So, yeah, I was seventeen, going on eighteen when he found one of the letters."

"Shit."

"Yeah. He kept me out of school for the whole week, until the black eye was gone."

Cyrus growled. "This motherfucker!"

"Yeah, but you have to understand. I went behind his back, right?"

Cyrus flinched, but Misty continued. "I was an unfaithful little girl who'd conspired against him. If I left, who would see my sister through her last two years of high school while he was out there patrolling, keeping the county safe?"

She cleared her throat.

"Irony was, I'd asked myself the same question. I had no intention of leaving Jolene behind with that bastard. I'd spent my life stepping in front of him when he side-eyed her. Taken the brunt when I could. We were born just short of two years apart, but Jolene was softer. More delicate. And he'd been happy enough to focus all his anger on me. I knew which words would redirect his attention. But two nights after my high school graduation—where my father put on the mask of a doting patriarch that should've won him an Oscar—I snapped awake to find him standing at the foot of Jolene's bed. Yes, we shared a room. We felt safer together.

"He was so drunk, he had to steady himself with one hand against the wall. I peered over at her, and she was sleeping on her side, a pair of shorts riding up high on one leg. When I returned my gaze to him, something was different there, maybe in his half-mast eyelids. That was when I realized the hand that wasn't steadying him against the wall was..." her words trailed away.

A sudden biting pain made Cyrus realize he'd been clenching his fists so hard that his fingernails had pierced his flesh.

"We slept caddy-cornered from each other, my bed against the front wall of the room, hers aligned in the opposite corner near the window on the back wall. When my father straightened, eased around the foot of her bed, I lost it. Bats swarming my belfry. Without thinking, completely devoid of any rationale, I threw off my sheets, snatched up the softball bat leaning against the wall, then swung.

"I'll never forget that hollow thunk as I clocked one side of his head. It's only out of pure luck it was a semi-glancing blow. Hard enough to put him on his face, not hard enough to crack his skull. He went down, the front of his head smashing into her little nightstand, and the lamp tumbled to the floor with a crash. Jolene tripped over him when she shot up out of bed, but he was out cold. I kicked him in the ribs to make sure.

"Autopilot took over. Survival instinct. I emptied Jolene's book bag, told her to pack four changes of clothes, and nothing else. No cell phones. No identification. I emptied his wallet, took the debit card since I'd memorized the PIN number he'd received in the mail. Drunken bastard had been so off the rails when I gave it to him, he'd just tossed it to one side without noticing I'd opened it, so he'd naturally assume it'd been him who'd torn it at the perforations while he'd tied one on.

"The biggest mistake he'd made was letting me get a driver's license so I could shuttle myself to the grocery store and back. We stole his beat-up Chevy. Drove to an ATM, withdrew the max, drove to another, withdrew the max. We had thousands by the time the bank security ate the card. Today, we would've been fucked. But in 2011? We got lucky."

"I'd say so. How did you keep him off your trail?"

"Paid cash and stayed in hotels, at first. But our funds were limited, so I made a plan. Wake County, North Carolina, had all kinds of access, good civil infrastructure. I used the public library to get online. Found the names of a couple in California who died childless. Forged a death certificate, then made a copy of it to present to a boarding school in Raleigh. Before we visited it, I studied about the ASVAB. Visited a recruiter, took the test, then joined the Army so I'd have proof of income for the boarding school. Told them I was Anna's guardian. I guess they never followed up. I'd forged some documentation, but they never asked for it."

The stream of information revealed how his every suspicion about Misty's level of genius over the previous year had been short of the mark. Any shrink worth a dime could work it out. Misty's trauma fed her intellect, a common irony. When her father crossed the final line, her body took over, and it hadn't been until he was unconscious and bleeding that her faculties took up the mantle. He wondered if she remembered the swing of the bat at all, or if the sound of its impact was all that stood out.

"Believe it or not, some woman has taken up with him, and I suspect he's controlling her in the same ways. She only leaves the house to get the mail or return with groceries."

Cyrus unclenched his fists, trying to relax. But the idea of someone living with the abusive prick inflamed his sense of propriety, like his protective instinct where Misty was concerned spread out a few hundred miles.

"What do you know about this woman? How long has she been there?"

"No, Cyrus. I'm keeping clear of him. She's a big girl, and she can take care of herself."

"Just curious, is all."

"Bullshit." Misty forced a smile, but it didn't reach her eyes. "Let it go. There's nothing we can do. Even if we could prove a crime, it would be local. No jurisdiction, and I know all-too-well how a small-town sheriff's office turns blind eyes. I'll move Anna when this is all over. Put a place in my name. It's doable. But Father's girlfriend will have to fend for herself."

"How do you know about the woman living with your father?"

"Dammit, Cy," she slurred. "I knew I shouldn't have mentioned it. Do you have any idea how you are about women? It's like you have this drive to save us all, one at a time."

Cyrus frowned, seeing how similar the words were to Tiffany's ruminations. Cyrus and his girls.

Misty's sighed, and her shoulders dropped. "Fine. I used a facial recognition scan from the camera I hid in the woods near his house. Pulled a deck. Nora Aiken. Registered Democrat, if you can believe it. She picked the wrong house. Hell, the wrong town. I wonder if dear-old-dad knows. She only leaves the house to go to the grocery store, best I can tell. Brings in the mail.

247

Seems she has taken my place. I couldn't find any living family."

It shouldn't have come as any surprise Misty had done a full workup, but considering all the new information, Cyrus still found himself wondering what he'd gotten himself into by bringing her to the bureau.

She checked her smart watch. "That's enough story time. I'm fading, and I need to be at LPS in a few hours."

"With a hangover?"

"Nah. I bounce back. Couple bottles of water and espressos, I'll be right as rain."

Something she'd said earlier resurfaced. "And just to make sure I'm clear. Because of the hand towel and the melatonin bottle, you think your father picked the lock to your sister's apartment."

"I know he did. So when this is all over, I'm going to have to move her somewhere."

After Misty retired, Cy poured his liquor down the sink in her kitchen. An image of a demon with horns standing over a teenaged girl's bed ruled his mind as he strolled down the narrow, dim corridor leading to the security door that would let him out into the pre-dawn chill. He slid into his truck then drove off to keep the promise he'd made to Marsha.

CHAPTER 27

Blake's chair rolled then slammed into the wall when he shot upright. "Pull her out of there!"

"Bear with me."

"Cyrus, there's nothing you can say that—"

"Chet Parsons didn't commit suicide."

"Who?"

"The guy from Lockhart who Misty replaced. I went to the morgue with Marsha this morning. Although he's long-buried, she had crime scene photos and the grizzly shots she took."

"Marsha. You mean the county coroner. So, what? You pulled her out of bed to gather evidence before coming in? Are you here to manipulate me into letting you chase down Lockhart, despite my warnings about DC?"

"You know," Cyrus replied, "sometimes I wonder if I'm more of a problem than an asset. All the other FBI offices around the country act like their own little fief-doms but, from the day I arrived in Denver, the"—he made quotations with his fingers—"*home office* has been up our asses."

"That's what happens when you go after an acting director."

"But I was right!" he replied a little too loudly.

Blake's forehead scrunched.

Cyrus brought his volume down to an acceptable level. "The bastard was crooked. It burns my britches that he was covering for Sam Lockhart. And the recording I got of him threatening me if I didn't play ball went straight to the Oval Office. The bureau should be thanking me for cleaning house."

Blake smiled, and Cyrus wanted to strangle him.

"How naive is that? The new director knows all about it, Cyrus. And on some level, I'm sure he's glad you took out his predecessor. But your *methods* weren't on the level. You didn't call for backup when you drove to Ethan Pierce's house, did you?" He didn't wait for an answer. "Before you assaulted two of his guards? Shot a third?"

"He raised his gun."

"Hence, you aren't in prison. And the pictures you took of Tiffany Brooks—who I hear was in Texas—convinced Pierce's lawyers to take a deal. Good move."

"Thank you."

"But the bureau is still going to keep an eye on you."

"I thought that was your job."

"It is. And considering your work before I arrived, I think I've excelled." Blake sat, rolled his chair toward the desk, then planted his elbows. His expression softened. "You've earned latitude. We work well together. The Lassiter fiasco, your willingness to take up a sniper rifle and protect your fellow agents, the way you lured her into a recorded confession... it all really worked in your favor. My boss thinks you're an asset. But that doesn't mean she's going to turn a blind eye to potential conflicts. It's because of Lockhart's connection to Pierce she wants you kept the hell out of it. Tell me how she's wrong."

Goddammit.

Cyrus fumed. He couldn't argue with the logic. Any defense attorney worth a spoonful of salt would paint him as a deep state cop with a vendetta, argue Lockhart's arrest was just the unfinished business of a *rogue* fed. Hell, they might even actually say the words.

Deep state.

"There are many ways to skin a cat, Cyrus. What did Dr. Pilson say?"

Cyrus reached for the leather attaché she'd bought him for his birthday then dropped three eight-by-ten glossies on the SAC's desk.

"They aren't easy to look at."

Blake fanned out the shots. "I give exactly zero shits."

"She made it clear she was no splatter expert."

Cyrus reached across and planted an index finger on one shot. "But you see that stream of blood there, off to the side, away from where the brains painted the wall?"

Blake raised the photo, leaned back, then appraised it. "Hmm. Where did that come from?"

"Right. It's too far away. If we believe the suicide story, he planted the pistol under his chin before firing. Marsha noted the explosion of blood and brains splattered all the way to the ceiling, fanning out behind his head. But that blood..."

Blake set the photo on his desk. "Right. It's thick. Dark droplets on the carpet removed from the rest of the Pollock painting."

"Exactly."

"But who would reach under his chin to pull the trigger?"

"An inexperienced hitman who wanted us to think it was a suicide."

"Any suspects?"

Cyrus nodded. "Edward Xavier. He's the executive officer at LPS, and he hired members of his special ops unit in Fallujah. Chet, the dead guy, was in the unit. Misty told me the story of how this group, nicknamed the Silver Stars because of the awards they got, were part of a civilian massacre there. The guy in Texas, Michael Bray, was also a Silver Star."

Blake rubbed his temples. "Jesus. And he was shot by LPS as he approached the church."

"Right. I can't prove it was a setup, but it sure is messy. Tom Rhymer said the shooter was young, new at LPS. I sure would like to talk to him. But Lockhart is undoubtedly cleaning house the best he can."

"No shit. And how does Chet's suicide tie to Xavier what's his face?"

"Edward Xavier. LPS president. When Chet found out Michael Bray had been gunned down by a company guy on duty at Live Oak, he stormed into the XO's office. Freaked out, if Tom Rhymer is to be believed. And I think he's on the level."

"Tom's the one hiding Anna?"

"Something like that. Apparently, Chet threatened to go to Anastasia with the whole story. Tell her about Fallujah and how the XO covered it up with the awards."

"Wow. That might put his ass in a sling with the military."

"I get the impression most of the unit isn't proud of their Silver Stars. Misty thinks Rhymer is ready to blow the lid on LPS, Fallujah, the whole shebang, because he's seen how Lockhart operates. Hell, he was practically his fixer."

"Really? Would he testify?"

"Doesn't have enough. No kill orders or anything so obvious. He has Lockhart Tactical folks watching her apartment and the newspaper, pretending to do the job. Keeping them busy and out of the way. Which brings me to the next part, and you might want to brace yourself for this one."

The SAC smirked.

"The Silver Star with an itchy trigger finger who caused the Fallujah massacre wasn't hired by LPS because the rest of the unit despised him for what he'd done. They wouldn't have taken their jobs if he was there. Want to guess who he is?"

"I don't have time for guessing games."

"Anastasia Clark's editor at the post."

Blake straightened in his chair. It creaked. "What?" His face twisted up in confusion. "Who? How does he play into... what?"

Cyrus held his response to let the SAC work through it. Blake stood, ambled to the window, then shoved his hands into his pockets.

"The editor's name?"

"William Bresnan."

"Right. A crazy thought just went through my mind, Cyrus. Want to hear it?"

Cyrus nodded. "Of course."

The SAC leaned his backside against the windowsill. His hands moved in the way he reserved for his amped-up moments. A rarity.

"Do you think someone in this XO's position would get his hands that dirty? If he showed up at Chet Parson's house, would he even get in the door?" He didn't wait for an answer. "Ask yourself a question."

"What's that?"

"Who stood to lose the most if Parsons followed through on that threat? To expose Xavier's cover up in Iraq? I mean, sure, the Army might trace it all back to the XO, but that'd get messy. The unit, the XO, they would have different stories. He said, she said. Xavier would claim fog of war. Say his guys did the best they could in the hell that was Fallujah. But I'm sure the Army would be interested in the one thing the rest of the unit agrees on."

Cyrus snapped his fingers. "That Bresnan got trigger happy. That he caused the whole episode."

"You got it. And if Bresnan sent Anastasia to do a piece on LPS, he was probably promised something. Like, a pile of cash in return for a patriotic puff piece. Imagine it. Bresnan might have seen the offer as a chance to serve the unit. To build a bridge, mend fences, make them like him for promoting the company they work for." The SAC went quiet for a few breaths. When he spoke again, his contemplations came in low, almost in a whisper. "No doubt, this Xavier is retired if he's president of the Lockhart outfit. But what about the editor? Is Bresnan in the reserves?"

"I could find out." He stood so he and Blake were at eye level. "What am I missing?"

"I might be adopting your conspiratorial tendencies, Cyrus, but I can't help but wonder what the Army would do to someone who was still active, even if only in the reserves. Someone who could cause them headaches when the media posted 'Military covered up war crime in Fallujah' in all caps on a front page."

"It's an interesting question."

"And if Bresnan, who knows his unit doesn't like him, thinks he could be brought up on charges for something that happened twenty years ago, how far would he be willing to go to keep it quiet? I'll bet he'd be susceptible to suggestions from the one person who stayed loyal to him. The person who offered him access to LPS for a story."

"Xavier." Cyrus organized all of it, double-time. "So, you're thinking the XO makes a call, sends Bresnan over to have a talk with Chet. He talks his way inside. William gets the drop when Chet turns his back —hence, the distant blood spatter that doesn't fit the scene—and snuffs out a witness to his Army crime who's threatening to go public."

"Maybe. I mean, it could have been Edward Xavier, himself, who pulled the trigger. But if Sam is trying to protect the new business, he could use Lockhart Tactical to keep LPS personnel uninvolved with staking out the reporter. Compartmentalization. It follows someone outside LPS would need to do the wet work."

"And unlike the rest, Bresnan displays his Silver Star. I saw it on the desk behind him when Misty and I went there. He values it."

"Right." Blake nodded. "So, Daniels is still at LPS,

but her sister is alive and well enough in a cabin somewhere. Our stated mission is complete."

"I hope there's a 'but' coming."

Blake cursed. "Of course there is. Look, I know it's going to piss you off, but she's not an agent. Military qualifications or not, I should have never let her go in. Thankfully, it paid off. Rhymer led her to Anastasia Clark. But if the XO would have one of his guys whacked, which might still be a stretch, I don't want her in there. Tell her she has until the end of the day. Then I want you to do something else for me."

"What's that?"

"Find out if this editor fuck is in the reserves. If he left the service, he probably wouldn't care about Chet Parsons. But if he's still in the Army…"

"Command would be less likely to ignore it. They'd burn him alive for what happened in Fallujah when they read what Anastasia Clark published about it. That also supports why he'd fire her—to cut her off before she learned too much and keep any articles from being published."

"Good, you've been listening."

"And if he is in the reserves?"

Blake smiled. "Head straight for the paper and do what you do best. Look the fucker in the eye so you can read him when you ask where he was at the time of the murder. Then report back."

CHAPTER 28

Caution would be cast aside in the interest of expedience. Efficiency. Misty'd spent the morning listing the vitals for her exploratory surgery. The timeline of events. A theory of the conspiracy and its participants. Their possible roles. She skimmed the list.

The Silver Stars unit. The massacre in Fallujah.

Will Bresnan, the former trigger-happy instigator of the whole ordeal and now editor who'd sent Anastasia to write a supportive piece about Lockhart Public Security's mission.

Edward Xavier, the XO of the unit, now president at Lockhart's new outfit, who'd hired the former members of the Silver Stars at LPS. Except for Bresnan, who was omitted because his unit despised him. Tom Rhymer, anyway.

Chet Parsons had raised hell in Xavier's office when he found out Michael Bray, a Silver Star who'd applied at the company, had been mowed down by Lockhart forces in Texas on his way to shoot up a church. Her research had revealed Chet, who'd wound up dead by Desert Eagle, died in a new house he'd bought when he landed the gig.

Misty had also looked into Donnie Worth, the foiled shooter at the Fitz Banner rally, but he'd never served in the military. That he'd been stopped in his tracks was a point in Lockhart's favor. The school shooter had also never served. As much as it pained her to admit, Lockhart's service seemed to be working. Too bad he was such an asshole.

After reviewing the involved parties, Misty put together a list of tasks, reordered them, then interlocked her fingers and cracked her knuckles.

If she worked fast, no one would notice her intrusions until she was long gone. But she recalled Justin Watson coming to her office, asking if she needed any assistance because he'd noticed she'd logged into Outlook—although he had meant Exchange. Exchange was the server handling emails on an organizational level, while Outlook was just a desktop client. While she might have concluded the misnomer suggested some shortcoming in his understanding of his work, the fact he'd noticed her login called for some modicum of caution.

But Misty's need for speed conflicted with that notion. She needed to find communications reaching the highest level of the company. Anything implicating Sam Lockhart.

Work fast. Collect data. Pack your shit. Get out.

Because she didn't want to tip Justin Watson off too early by searching through emails, she ran queries on the mapped drives across the organization. Before she knew it, she'd burned the morning. She glanced at the system clock. Almost noon. She'd have to call Cyrus from her personal cell in the parking lot and hope Blake wasn't going to pull her before she could get anything done.

CHAPTER 29

Cyrus had taken Misty's call right on the hour as he sped across town to the *Denver Post*. He'd relayed Blake's orders. She'd been defensive. But by the end of the call, she capitulated, and he took his first steadying breath of the drive.

What's four hours? She'll be out in a beat.

A quick search of the Defense Manpower Data Center's Military Verification service revealed William Bresnan was the lone Silver Star who remained in the reserves.

The SAC's theory was still intact.

When he strolled into the lobby, Cyrus made a beeline for the reception area.

"I need to see William Bresnan."

The bespectacled woman behind the counter tapped a few keys then spoke into her headset while Cyrus scanned the lobby.

"Mr. Bresnan is out of the office. Would you like to leave a message?"

Cyrus flipped open his cred pack. "FBI. Where is he?"

The woman's eyes flared. She tapped the keys again, informed the person on the other end of the line that the FBI was on-site, and asked where Bresnan was. Then she nodded and tapped her earpieces.

"Mister Bresnan is following up on a piece at Lockhart Public Security. Do you need—

Cyrus's back straightened and the blood pumping through his heart might have reversed direction. He sped back across the lobby, burst through the doors, then made for his bureau ride. The memory of Misty's impatient demeanor when she'd sat beside him in Bresnan's office took center stage.

He reached for his phone before remembering she informed him she'd have to stow hers in a locker on campus. Did he risk calling the Lockhart cell? He stopped in the middle of the sidewalk, eyeing the screen, his thumb hovering above the call button.

Scanning the street as he deliberated, his gaze lingered upon a pair of guys sitting in a GM truck. The one on the driver's side was watching the newspaper's front door. The other seemed to be snoozing. Though he longed to make trouble for the Lockhart Tactical assholes, Cyrus brought up another contact on his phone, then dialed as he passed them by.

"Blake."

"Bresnan is still in the reserves. I went to the *Post*. They say he's on the way to LPS."

Blake made the connection in an instant. "Shit. Misty was with you in his office."

"Exactly what I was thinking. She was snappish, too."

"So he'll likely remember her."

Silence ensued, and Cyrus figured Blake was mulling it over, probably going through the same mental rigmarole.

"Text her then drive over to LPS, wait outside the gate, and make sure she drives through it. If she doesn't, well, don't break the law, but get her out."

CHAPTER 30

A stab of annoyance at the sight of her empty coffee thermos told Misty the imbibing of the night before was catching up to her. She yawned, cursed, then returned her focus to the screen. But the text seemed to take on a new form. English words, but blurred and meaningless in her disheveled state, and she was working on an emaciated timeline. So much for bouncing back.

She grumbled, brought up the login for the Exchange Server, then paused with her fingers resting lightly on the keys. This needed to go fast. Her gaze meandered to the steps she'd plotted out on a rumpled sticky note.

Another yawn. Another curse. Snatching up the thermos, she made for the door. On the other side of the server room, Justin Watson's office door was wide open, but he was utterly focused on whatever took up residency on his screen. All the better. Misty wasn't sure she could form coherent sentences.

Note to self—lay off the fucking booze.

She watched the numbered lights over the elevator as it meandered up its shaft. The other was still under maintenance, and Misty started forming a conspiracy theory about the working one being programmed to service the higher floors. Basement dwellers came last. But she was just irritable. No sign of the resilience she'd promised Cyrus in the wee dark hours of the morning.

The elevator finally arrived. She stomped on and smashed the button. Even the soft tone as it reached the lobby annoyed her. With two employees in the basement, they'd never have their own break room.

Why are you thinking like an employee? Focus!

The doors split open. A man with a shining dome wearing a shirt and tie stood there, and he stepped to one side then waved an arm to let her through. Recognition dawned a moment later, and she almost gaped.

Oh no.

Will Bresnan. Anastasia's editor. She forced a smile, lowered her gaze, dipped her chin, then hurried past him.

"Thanks," she said, her voice a register lower than usual.

He didn't answer, and she didn't dare look back. Makeup contouring or not, she'd sat right across his desk at the *Post,* and she wasn't about to give him a second gander. The elevator tone sounded again when she reached the corner of the corridor, and Misty waited until she turned the corner to glance back in its direction.

No one. He'd boarded.

Was she being paranoid? Had she caught a hint of familiarity in his eyes?

Misty stopped outside the breakroom door, peered up the hallway toward the exit through which Tom Rhymer had gone the night he met Anna in the parking lot, then at the sign about halfway down the corridor indicating the stairwell.

Her heart was pumping at full bore, the lump in her throat in full bloom. The exit. The stairs. The exit. The stairs.

Cyrus would tell her to take the exit.

Anna would tell her to exit.

The voice of self-preservation screamed, *Take the fucking exit!*

She'd gotten herself into this by going behind the bureau's back. Betraying Cyrus. Sure, she'd found her sister, but if she came up empty on Lockhart, could she forgive herself? More importantly, could Cy forgive her?

The least she owed him was a phone call.

Misty slapped the hip pocket where she kept her company cell. Her heart ticked it up a notch. She'd left it on her fucking desk. The elevator would soon reach its destination.

"Fuck," she muttered.

The exit. The stairs. The exit.

She jogged up the hallway, shoved the bar on the door, then descended the stairs.

At least she didn't need the coffee anymore.

CHAPTER 31

Cyrus gave the engine some juice, whipped around a lollygagger in the slow lane, then gunned it. The GPS timer showed a tick over ten minutes left in his drive. He'd just see about that.

Sure, the odds were low Misty and Bresnan would cross paths. She worked in the basement with one other guy. No reason for the newspaper editor to go down there, especially since the one other person in the bowels of the building wasn't a member of the Silver Stars. No reunion to be had.

His cell phone chimed. Cyrus eyed the hands-free display.

Tiffany Brooks.

Nine minutes to LPS.

He thumbed the answer button set into the steering wheel.

"Yo."

"Yo, yourself, mister. You might want to leave your girlfriend when you hear what I have to say."

"Tempting as that would be to any straight man with a pair of eyes, no shot."

"That's why I love you, Cy."

He had nothing to say to that, and the sudden awareness of his amped heart rate made small talk seem frivolous.

"What you got?"

"You know Rodney Hinson?"

"Doesn't ring a bell."

"Well, I do. He's the preacher at the Live Oak Church, where Michael Bray got aerated."

"You have a way with words."

"I've been told I'm blunt. Anyway, you remember when I said I wanted to go back to the church after we had our altercation with the sheriff?"

"Clearly."

"The good reverend hadn't been around. I called later, tried to make an appointment. Never heard back. After our barbecue dinner in Denver, I reviewed the street interview he did with a reporter the day after the shooting because I had one of those little itches I get. Couldn't quite put my finger on it. Probably happens to you all the time. Your work tunes you for it. Since I was coming back to Texas to talk to a reporter on behalf of my employer, anyway—"

"Ready to tell me who this employer is?"

"Focus, Cyrus. On a whim, I called my boss to ask

for a favor then drove back to Live Oak, surveilled the parking lot in back for about an hour, and caught the rev walking out. I'd done some homework, you see. Found out they help fund a non-profit that manages low-cost housing. I told him I was interested in donating. Showed him a check for twenty-grand, asked if he'd mind having a cup of coffee."

"Twenty-thousand dollars? Just like that?" He paused. She didn't answer. "Just tell me that associating with you... promise me your financial sourcing isn't going to throw shade on my investigation."

"Well. I call to give you a gift and..."

"Okay." He waved a hand despite her inability to see it. "Go ahead."

"We had a nice chat. Learned about his family. His background. Seems like a good man. I mean, an upstanding one."

"I'm sure it was a lovely chat."

"Shut it. I'm trying to tell you a story."

And in true southern style, taking the long way around.

"When I mentioned the shooting, he clammed up. Let me tell you, Cy, when you peddle drugs to doctors, you learn to read people. Rodney Hinson's attention went to the window. The cars passing. The waitress behind the counter. Everywhere but me. That was when the thing he'd said during the interview hit me. Not what he said, but how he said it. I shoved the check across the table to refocus him."

"You didn't think he'd see through that?"

"No, I knew he would. But, like I said, the rev is an upstanding guy. Real nice, bordering on sweet, like you. I suspected a fella who'd misrepresented himself on national TV, a man who preaches to his flock three times per week about biblical principles, might *want* to come clean, given the right motivation. Maybe it would be eating at him. That, or I could be way off the mark, and the twenty grand would go to a good cause."

The idea that her funder wouldn't care about the twenty thousand netting jack for her trouble brought flashing red dollar signs to mind.

Tiffany paused for effect. "Let me quote his words from the interview. He said, 'We'd be dead without their service.'"

Cyrus rolled the words over in his gray matter, but nothing rang out. "So?"

"Yeah, it's not obvious. If it were, I'd like to think I would've caught it the first time. But how do we thank soldiers for fighting for our country? We thank them for their *service*. But something he said a minute later brought me back around. I have it right here. One sec."

A moment later, Tiffany cleared her throat.

"Until the United States of America figures out how to protect the people of this nation from the scourge that is assault weapons, we need citizens who will stand up for what's right and protect the meek."

"Almost like Lockhart wrote it, right?"

"Exactly. But this guy's a southern preacher, not

some PR rep. That's why I watched the interview a few times. That's when I wound back to the beginning, where he said, 'We'd be dead without their service.' Like it was a service to our country, not *services* Live Oak paid for."

Cyrus felt his forehead wrinkle. "Wait. You mean, like... you've gotta be fucking kidding me, Tiff."

"Nope." He could hear her smiling.

"Let me make sure I have this right. You heard the word service instead of services, and you suspected if he'd been a customer, he would've used the plural? That's a fucking stretch. I mean, you just handed over twenty grand based on a single letter of the alphabet."

"And I was right, Cyrus. Rodney Hinson never paid for Lockhart Public Security. He admitted it over a cold cup of coffee. He didn't even know they existed until they showed up and planted Michael Bray. Oh. There's the bluntness again. Pardon me."

"Holy shit. You should be a cop."

"I'm afraid I've become accustomed to my lifestyle, and I've got a Tesla on order."

"It's not the car I'm jealous of. I would've never caught that."

"Right. So, does it help?" The hopeful tone of voice endeared him further.

He eyed the GPS. Three minutes to the LPS gate.

"Yeah, you just gave me a new direction."

"Which is?"

"Before, I was looking into a missing person. The

plan has changed, and I'm on a tight timeline, but now I have a new plan."

"What plan?"

"Well, I'm from the South, too. So, I'll save my story for next time we have coffee."

"Make it drinks, and you're on."

"Fair enough."

"One more thing, Cy."

"Yeah?"

"Lockhart offered the church an LPS agent every week, free of charge."

"No wonder the rev played ball. A guy rolls in to shoot up his church, these guys thwart him, then they offer the gift. Memorize a few lines for an interview, and you can keep your parishioners safe at no cost."

"Yeah, and like I said, Rodney is a stand-up guy. Under the stress of the moment, I don't think he set out to mislead anyone. He just cares about the worshipers. They're his family."

Cyrus pulled off the exit leading to LPS.

"If you believe it, I believe it. Thanks, Tiff. I can use this."

"You got it, babe. Keep me in the loop."

"I'll do my best."

The second the call disconnected, he brought up Blake's number.

"Blake."

"I just got a call from Tiffany Brooks. Wondering if you could get me an interview."

"Let me guess. The young guy who shot Michael Bray."

"It's like you're psychic."

"You mentioned him before."

"Yeah, but before we weren't investigating Hope Mills. Name is Chance Baker. If he works for LPS, he's probably local. If you could get someone to pick him up for a chat, I'd appreciate it."

"What's the angle?"

"He wasn't hired by the church. So, I'm wondering what the fuck he was doing there."

A moment of silence ensued. "Is that solid? They didn't hire LPS?"

"Roger that."

"Oh, that's making me feel warm and fuzzy all over. He'll be here when you get back. Just make sure you drag Misty back with you. No side stops. We still need to have that chat I promised her."

Cyrus swallowed. "I'm pulling up now."

CHAPTER 32

The automatic lock on Misty's office door clicked into place. Her chair rolled when she dropped down, and she planted her feet to stop it. Scooting forward and shoving her legs beneath the desk, she glanced at the crumpled sticky note. Then she shoved it into her mouth and chewed while she worked.

The taste of glue really added something to the experience as she brought up the Exchange Management Console, drilled down into Edward Xavier's email archive, then typed 'Texas.' A general term, for sure, but she didn't have time to rack her brain. She'd narrow it down as she went.

She swallowed the gummy note then mumbled something foul under her breath.

As president, Xavier was also the operations guy. Second-in-command at Lockhart, but he ran the day-to-day. She figured she better cut right to it.

She wrestled a USB stick out of her pocket then shoved it into her machine. The drive window popped up to confirm it was connected, and she closed it.

A list of emails appeared on the screen. Misty scanned the subject lines and stopped when her eyes landed on 'Bray."

Michael Bray. The shooter.

She popped it open. The headers showed it was an email from Dr. Clayton Burroughs to Xavier. She read.

When is he coming for his assessment?

This was taking too long. If Bresnan had recognized her, she was cooked, and they'd be coming. So Misty sent a system request to export the entire PST file, which would offload the entire mailbox, and set the target for the USB drive.

Her mouse shot to the X button, and she returned to the list of emails. Heart still pounding, she ran a new query for 'Bray.'

Narrowed results. Good. She scanned until she saw the doc's name again.

XO,

Attached is my assessment of Michael Bray, but let me add a little emphasis. I'd say a place like LPS offering the return to discipline and proximity to other ex-soldiers would be good for a guy like him. He was disheveled. His eyes were bloodshot. I got the impression he isn't sleeping well. This guy needs a schedule! But no

way in hell do you bring him on board as a field opera-
tive. PTSD is the least of it. He was hesitant to talk
about the service. Didn't want to talk about combat at
all. Went into a tirade about how he was the best
marksman in his unit, and that should be enough for
"Xavier."

You put him in the field in a pressure situation and
things could go sour fast.

Like I said, the assessment is attached. If I can meet
with him weekly, we can dig in, and he could probably
do something administrative. He's not stupid. But guns?
In this guy's hands?

Hell no.

Clayton

Misty ordered the Bray emails by date then scanned
for anything that came after the doctor's warning.

A faint beep sounded, and her head shot up.
Someone had just accessed the door down the hall, on
her side of the server room. Popping open the USB
drive's window, she dragged all the emails over.

She checked the PST status.

87%...

Voices on the other side of the door, hushed. Low.

93%...

Misty pinched the USB stick and eyed the door,
listening as her heartbeat thumped in her temples.

97%...

Maybe they'll knock.

The badge reader outside her door beeped and the lock clicked. Misty yanked the USB stick and shoved it in her bra as the door swung open.

She snatched up her cell then stood, trying to look casual while she shot off a text.

"Daniels."

Tasker White stood in the doorway. Just behind him, a security officer in a crisp white shirt and black trousers stood with one hand perched on a holstered 9 mm.

"What the hell, Tasker?"

"No idea." She found the almost-bored tone of his delivery unconvincing. Nothing to see here, except for the guy behind him with a gun. "Mr. Lockhart would like a word, if you'll please come with me." His formal tone said it all.

Her mind raced. If she got on the elevator, she could press the lobby button at the last moment then bust out. Would they really try to restrain her?

Will Bresnan told them you came to his office with an FBI agent. They're going to try.

Misty had tactics. She could belt Tasker one, kick the guard in the nuts, then haul ass. But her former comrade hadn't done anything to Misty. Hell, he'd referred her for a pretty sweet gig, all things considered.

She thought about Lockhart. Then about Cyrus.

Misty shoved her cell in her pocket then, as she rounded her desk, she cast a glance at her monitor.

Download Complete.

She patted Tasker's shoulder, adopting the most relaxed tone she could muster. "Let's go see the boss."

CHAPTER 33

Heavy, wooden double doors mounted to thick frames secured the suite on the top floor, and Misty wondered why they hadn't gone the last leg and installed metal to complete the bomb shelter motif. Funny how an entryway could reflect a guy's insecurities. She divined Sam Lockhart was one of those rich guys who thought his money made him a target. It was, after all, the top floor.

Her rampant heartbeat had steadied halfway up the elevator shaft, her military training bringing focus in tense moments. She was able to shut the shit down so, by the time the door swung open and she spied the two executives standing inside, they might as well have been meeting for dinner.

But Xavier's expression didn't reinforce that idea, the stony mask he wore completed by the flexed nodes in his jaw. Her throat dried out when she thought about how Chet Parsons had come to the man's office to raise hell about Michael Bray's death in Texas only to wind up slouched beneath a bloody splatter painting in his brand new house.

"Miss Daniels," Sam Lockhart said in greeting. He swept an arm toward a chair then cocked his chin at Tasker White and the guard. "You two can wait outside. The XO and I have it from here."

"Roger that," Tasker said. Misty thought she caught a hint of regret in the milliseconds their gazes matched, but she might have been imagining it.

With her adrenaline amped and the XO glaring at her like he might start swinging at any second, Misty had to remind herself this was *not* the military. It was a corporate outfit despite its employee base. Lockhart made a life out of hiding his complicity in sour situations, and she doubted the XO would act out in that office.

Will he?

Misty declined the offered chair.

"I'll stand, if it's all the same."

A muscle under the XO's nose twitched. "Sit down."

"I'll stand, if it's all the same, *Mister Lockhart.*" Some part of her hoped Xavier would get on with it. Come at her full tilt so she could reduce the number of adversaries in the room.

Instead, Xavier parted his lips like he'd repeat his

command, assert his dominance, but Lockhart preempted him. "Imagine my surprise, Misty."

He paused like he was waiting for her to complete the thought. But she wasn't going to respond until she knew what he knew.

"Will Bresnan popped by, but you know that, right? You know Will?"

"Know him? Name doesn't ring a bell."

"Well, he seems to know you. He says you showed up at his office asking about one of his reporters, one who was doing a piece on LPS before she vanished from the face of the earth."

"Oh, someone is missing?"

"We're not buying it, Daniels," Xavier said.

Misty didn't spare him a glance.

Lockhart continued. "I couldn't help but wonder why someone who shows up to question a newspaper editor about his rogue reporter would end up working here, where said reporter was researching her story. What a coincidence. But imagine my further surprise when I learned the agent accompanying you at the *Post* was Cyrus Jennings. We have a history, you know. Agent Jennings and I."

"Romantic past? Racquetball buddies?"

Misty found the repeated cock of his chin toward the XO annoying, but she didn't let on.

"You see it?" Lockhart asked.

Edward Xavier wore a dumb expression. "See what?"

Lockhart smiled like he'd found the crucial piece of a jigsaw he'd been working. "The familial resemblance. That's why she never showed Will a badge."

"Shit," the XO said. "How did Will miss that?"

The sense Misty should remain silent was trounced by a sudden desire to even the playing field. "Because he's incompetent. I'd think you would've learned that in Fallujah." The gig was up, they knew who she was, and she wasn't going to listen to Lockhart's egotistical banter for any longer than she had to. Although it'd only been minutes since she sent the text prior to leaving the office, the bureau would be spinning up its wheels by now.

Xavier inched forward. "'The hell do you know about Fallujah?"

Misty clenched her fists. "Take one more step toward me, asshole."

Lockhart raised his hands. "Let's take it down a notch. Bring me into the loop. What's all this about Fallujah?"

Misty's shoulders slouched. "Jesus Christ. I'm not buying your bullshit, Sam. Bresnan was a trigger-happy dolt who should've been charged with a war crime, and your president of operations—or whatever he is—covered it up with Silver Stars for all."

Xavier punched the air between him and Misty with one finger. "Fuck you. You don't know shit."

In contrast to his second-in-command's posture, Lockhart slid into the high-backed leather chair behind his desk, crossed one leg over the other, then inter-locked his fingers. "The question is, how would you know that? Who do you think she's been talking to, Ed?"

The XO's expression morphed like his brain had finally switched on, but he didn't answer. Misty could almost hear the rusty cogs grinding in his cranium.

Lockhart pressed. "Certainly not Bresnan. Parsons isn't around anymore. Who's left?"

The XO filled in gaps. "Tom Rhymer."

Considering he'd been using Rhymer to look for Anastasia, Misty longed for the moment when Sam's incompetence smacked him in his smug fucking face.

But his expression remained stony. "Interesting theory."

"Not a theory, Mr. Lockhart. Tom's the only one left who could've told her."

"Well, Misty?"

"Feel free to call me Miss Daniels."

That got his face twisted up, but only for a moment. Lockhart drew a deep breath through his nostrils then blew it through a small gap in his lips.

"Do you understand what we're trying to do here, Miss Daniels?"

"I think I have the gist. Profit from gun violence."

"That's a lie, and you know it. We're providing vets with gainful employment after they've served our country with distinction."

"With distinction," Misty echoed. "Guess that

explains why you didn't hire William Bresnan. Oh, wait. That's right. No one from his unit in Iraq would've worked with him."

The XO's face darkened, but he dropped into one of the guest chairs. She wondered how much effort it took to suppress his urges and let Lockhart take the lead. Couldn't have been easy for a former military commander to stomach her blatant disrespect. She hoped it hurt.

"Humor me," Lockhart said. "Tell the truth. What do you really think of the mission?"

The ego on this fucking guy.

"What do I think of the mission? I actually love it. It's stupid to think you're going to stop gun violence in a country where there are more guns than people and more mental illness than sanity, but jobs and on-site premium health care services for vets? In anyone else's hands, it would be great."

"Why not my hands?" Lockhart asked.

"Because you conspired to murder a state senator?"

The XO's head whipped around, his eyes flaring toward his boss.

That did the trick. Lockhart shot out of his chair. "I was cleared in that investigation. Jake Ramon went rogue."

Misty continued like he hadn't said anything. "While working for your old buddy, Ethan Pierce, who happens to be funding this little shindig. Do you really think we're that stupid?"

"So, you *are* FBI?"

Images swept through her mind. Cyrus's face. Blake's office. The exterior of the Denver Field Office building. The basement office where she'd taken Byron Jenkins's place after he died.

Holy shit, I'm FBI.

It was like Lockhart's question had raised the curtain to reveal the wall she'd put up between herself and the bureau. How she'd used the judge's court order as a shield, a writ of indentured servitude that excused her for working with the people she'd railed against for so long. Badge or no badge, she'd become Bureau.

She was surprised by her own smile. "You know, I guess I am."

Lockhart planted his hands on his desk then leaned in. "You deep state motherfuckers are going to ruin this country. We've got people opening fire in elementary schools! Shooting up movie theaters! Dance Clubs!" He raised one hand then swung it out to the side. "Veterans who serve their countries living in fucking tent cities! And what are the politicians going to do about it? Congress is too busy infighting to pass bills into law. Vacating the speakership while the world is on fire!

"The days of party platforms and pretty ideas are over. They rail against spending out of one side of their mouths while saying they support the troops out the other. And what does the federal government do when someone steps in to take up the VA's slack? Instead of aiding law enforcement by putting trained soldiers where they're needed, Big Brother sends you. For what?" He flung the arm again. "To dig up dirt on the only guy trying to solve problems?" He tapped his own chest.

Despite telling herself she'd keep her cool, Misty fumed. Her fingernails dug into her clammy palms. "And where did you serve, asshole? You've never served anything in your life but yourself. Two of the veterans you claim to adore are fucking dead! You think I believe Chet Parsons killed himself? That Michael Bray was some White supremacist who just happened to apply at Lockhart before going to shoot up a Black church in small-town Texas? Shit, can you hear your own bluster? Do you really believe you're so much smarter than the rest of us?"

She spun then marched toward the door but, when she turned the handle, it didn't budge.

"Time to open up. I'm out of here."

"You stupid bitch," Lockhart growled. "You think you know so much. But tell me, where's your proof?"

As much as she hated to admit it, Misty didn't have enough. All she'd seen in the XO's emails was a message from Clayton Burroughs rejecting Michael Bray for armed duty. But her investigation had been cut short, and she had his whole inbox on a PST file on the USB stick in her bra. They'd take it over her dead body. But she had to accept that possibility. She doubted there were any lengths to which Lockhart wouldn't go to keep her quiet.

Lockhart chuckled. "That's what I thought. All conjecture. You don't have any proof." He twirled a finger. "XO, I'd like you to drive Miss Daniels to the local PD and have her booked for trespass until Justin Watson can download proof of her espionage from our logs. Take our in-house attorneys along."

"I'll be out by morning, assuming they arrest me at all."

Lockhart nodded. "And my favorite newspaper editor will publish a story about how the deep state infiltrated my company by the time your cell door opens. Your little mission failed, Miss Daniels." He thrust a finger toward her. "Get this bitch's locker key, take her cell phone and anything else in there with you, and make sure no company property leaves this building."

Misty let her full smile beam. "Your hands come anywhere near me, and you'll be choking on your fingers."

"I look forward to finding out," Ed Xavier said.

"Yeah, how's that going to look to Tasker White? You know, the guy I served with in Afghanistan."

Lockhart returned to his chair. "We're making a citizen's arrest. That'll do for now. Get her out of here."

CHAPTER 34

In lieu of driving right up to the gate, Cyrus nosed his car off the left shoulder then backed across the road so he was parallel to the LPS compound's wall. Ten minutes passed, and he stared at his cell's screen, debating.

When leaving the *Post*, it'd been his intent to drive right up to the gate, flash his badge, and tell them to open the fucker. But he didn't have a warrant, and he lacked any proof Misty was in distress. Besides, it was likely she hadn't crossed paths with Will Bresnan at all and, if she was down in that basement collecting evidence, the last thing he wanted to do was tip her hand.

His nerves grated on him. Blake would be trying to get the LPS guy who'd shot Michael Bray in Texas into an interrogation room, a legitimate new angle he could chase even if Misty's snooping came up nil. What was more, if he found Lockhart was complicit in the shooting, the killer's testimony would get the Bureau a warrant to dig into the whole enterprise. The idea of snuffing out Lockhart's attorneys' Fourth Amendment arguments before they started was attractive.

If nothing else, it would keep DC at bay, give Blake some cover. The man had earned some loyalty by letting Misty and Cyrus get involved in the case in the first place.

But with Misty inside that building, everything else was secondary.

He was trying to distract himself by calling Tiffany for more details about the reverend in Texas when the gate lurched and its gear started winding as it crept open.

A headlight. A black Suburban. Tinted windows. Hands gripping the wheel, he waited. If Sam Lockhart had been willing to kill a politician, why would Misty be any different.

As the gate yawned wide, it revealed a second SUV, the perfect twin of its predecessor.

His cell rang.

"Jennings."

"Tom Rhymer just called the switchboard. Misty's blown. Sent him a text. I guess she didn't want your number showing up from her company cell, so she wrote him. Get her out."

Cyrus cranked his engine, yanked the gear shift to *drive*, then stomped down on the accelerator. The lead

Suburban driver slammed on the breaks to avoid a collision. The trailing vehicles lurched to a halt.

When he jumped out of the driver's seat, he raised his badge over the roof of the car. At first, the metal beasts sat idle, their running lights glaring at the side of his car while God-only-knew what was going on inside.

Cyrus reached into his jacket then unsnapped the strap over his holster. The rear doors of the front vehicle flew open. A tall man with a high-and-tight slid out first. A guy in the kind of high-priced, tailored suit only a lawyer would wear appeared on the other side.

High-and-tight spoke first.

"Who are you with?"

"FBI."

The pair shared a look and, when the military type's head came back around, he was smiling. "You're Cyrus Jennings."

He raced for an answer. "Nice to know my reputation precedes me."

"Your reputation is a discussion for another time, and I'm sure it will come up," the suit said in the nasal tone of an Ivy League mouth. "Move your vehicle. You're blocking the road, and we've made a citizen's arrest. You could be charged with obstruction."

So, Misty was in one of the vehicles.

"Do you really think I'm that stupid, dipshit?"

"Who're you calling dipshit?"

"A dipshit with a bad poker face. See this?" He tilted his badge back and forth. "This is the trump card, so you can fold your hand. Produce Misty Daniels. Now."

The other guy had moved close enough that Cyrus could make out deep crow's feet at the corners of his eyes, the gray bags beneath reflecting the sleep deprivation of a military lifer.

"What are you, fucking deaf? We've made an arrest. Your services aren't needed."

The balls on these guys.

Cyrus considered producing his more convincing credentials from the holster inside his jacket, but they were unarmed, and it wouldn't play well back at the office.

"What's your name?"

"I'm Edward Xavier. President of Lockhart Public Security." Although he only presented half a smile this time, it was still a smug one. "And you're on private property."

"I'm on a public road. Produce Daniels or I'm going to search both vehicles."

The lawyer leaned on the front SUV like his suit was of little value. "With what cause? You don't even know if Daniels is here."

"Is she?" It was Cyrus's turn to smile. "Please lie to me."

The counsel's nose scrunched up. "Fine. She's here. But unless you have a warrant for her arrest, we're taking her in."

"In to where? On what charge?"

"We'll start with trespassing, since she's here under false pretenses."

"Right. She's listed as an employee. Try another."

The prick let that one twirl around in his spongy brain for a few ticks before answering. "We're going to turn her over for violations of the Computer Fraud and Abuse Act."

Cyrus circled the car then shoved his cred pack back into his pocket. "Perfect. Unauthorized access to computer systems and data, right?"

The lawyer's expression melted as realization dawned.

"Yeah, that's right, *counsellor*. That's a federal crime. I'll be taking the suspect into custody. Now pull her out." Cyrus produced a pair of cuffs, raised them, and let them dangle.

Edward Xavier shook his head. "That might work if it hadn't been for how we caught her. You see, we have a witness that says she was in his office with you."

"So?"

"Sounds like a conflict of interest to me."

Cyrus laughed then cocked his chin toward the lawyer. "You actually let this guy talk out loud?"

The attorney waved off the corporate president. He strode to the back vehicle, opened the door, then gestured to the people inside.

Misty slid out then stomped toward Cyrus, kicking up dust plumes from dirt on the road. But when she passed Edward Xavier, he snatched her arm.

"She's not going anywhere."

The rear door of the back vehicle opposite where Misty had appeared slid open and another crew cut wielding an AR-15 stepped out.

Cyrus dropped the cuffs then yanked his weapon from his holster and leveled it. "Drop the fucking weapon."

The guy raised his gun. "I'm licensed to carry this!"

"Are you licensed to wield it at a federal officer?"

Misty whipped her head around. "Put it down, Tasker."

The LPS soldier didn't take long to consider it. He lowered his weapon.

Xavier clutched Misty's arm and yanked her closer. "Don't drop that weapon."

Misty balled up her fists.

Cyrus showed her his free palm like he was directing traffic. "No, Daniels. I got this." He reached down, his sight line still trained on the guy wielding the psycho special, and snatched up his cuffs. The Tasker guy raised both hands without being asked, but Cyrus moved toward the one grasping Misty. "Let her go, Edward, and do it now."

Xavier shoved her toward the SUV. Cyrus cocked his head in that direction.

"Hands on the hood."

"For what?"

"Obstruction, to start."

The lawyer threw his hands up. "Based on what?"

"You wanted to prosecute this lady under the Computer Fraud and Abuse Act. I said I was taking custody. He obstructed."

"That's thin, and you fucking know it."

"Then you shouldn't have any problem springing him." He waved his weapon toward the car. "Don't make me say it again, asshole. Hands on the vehicle."

The lawyer nodded at the Lockhart president. Xavier's face turned an interesting shade of red that contrasted with his dark complexion.

Cyrus frisked him, eyes still trained on the Tasker guy.

"We're going to burn you for this, Jennings," Xavier said. "You have no idea who you're messing with."

"Keep talking, and maybe we'll see what the Army thinks of your legacy."

Xavier clammed up as Cyrus shoved him toward his ride.

The lawyer circled the front of the vehicle but kept his distance when Cyrus shot him a warning glare.

"Where are you taking him?"

"Denver Field Office."

"I'll have you out in a couple hours, Xavier. Don't say anything until I get there."

Cyrus shoved his prisoner in the back of the car then slammed the door.

Misty jumped in the passenger's seat, but Cyrus eyed the guy who'd been wielding the weapon for a long moment. As if reading his mind, the guy raised his hands even higher.

"Hey, I didn't know. My bad."

Cyrus rolled his eyes, circled his car, jumped in, then peeled out.

CHAPTER 35

From Cyrus's side of the two-way window, Chance Baker more resembled a high school wideout than a soldier who'd shot Michael Bray in Texas. Sure, he was husky, but his youthful complexion and clean shave contradicted the image Cyrus had conjured in his mind.

If he'd been investigating Lockhart earlier in the game, this pending interrogation would've happened a lot sooner. But that was federal politics, and now he had some cover.

The suit sitting beside him checked his watch.

"I love it when they get impatient," Blake said.

Cyrus flinched. He'd forgotten the SAC was standing there while he'd taken the kid's measurements.

"Yeah. Was he any trouble?"

"Came voluntarily. Didn't even hesitate. Agents

told me he called the lawyer from a card in his wallet on the ride over."

"And what do we know about *him*? Someone the kid called after the event in Hope Mills, or is he one of Lockhart's?"

"The latter. Introduced himself as in-house counsel. Doubt he's ever seen a murder case. Then again, look who he works for. I'm sure he'll call someone else if you get anything on Chance Baker."

"It isn't going to be like that."

"What do you mean?"

"Too young. Misty told me *green* was the word Rhymer used. No way he's a Silver Star, which means we're dealing with a foot soldier. They'd only tell him the minimum. I'm willing to bet he was sent to"—Cyrus made quotations with his fingers—"protect the church, saw this guy with the AR, and pulled the trigger before he could think about it. I wonder if they're even trained to call out a warning. Anyway, I doubt he served more than one tour. I'll find out."

"You got all that from his youthful glow?" He clapped Cyrus's back. "Go get 'em, tiger."

Cyrus nodded then headed for the door.

"Oh, where's Daniels?"

"Downstairs. Scouring something she called a PST file that has all of Edward Xavier's emails."

"You know they'll probably shred it in court, right?"

Cyrus shrugged. "Then why'd you send her in?"

Blake returned the gesture. "I think we covered that. The damage was done. I was screwed either way. If she didn't show up and Lockhart got curious, his connections in DC could prove fatal to my career."

"Still could."

"Yeah, but this way we have some leverage. It's all about how we play it. I hope to hell she finds something. But if she doesn't"—he pointed through the glass —"you sure as shit better."

Cyrus pulled open the door.

"Oh, and Cyrus?"

He turned. "Yeah?"

"There will still be recompense for Daniels. You get that, right?"

"You know boss, I was pissed off when she went behind our backs. You don't have to sell me. I'm still learning life lessons every day, and she's obviously due one."

"Glad we're on the same page. If you see her, tell her where I am."

"Will do. Any idea what her life lesson is going to entail?"

Blake smiled. "Fuck off, Cyrus."

After taking a moment outside the door to refine his angle of approach, Cyrus pushed into the tight conference room with a flat expression.

"Evening, gents. I'm Cyrus Jennings. Sorry for the late hour."

The suit checked his watch. "We've been waiting for a while. What's this all about?"

Cyrus pulled out the chair across from Chance Baker. "This your attorney?"

The suit answered in his client's stead. "No, I'm here to sell Girl Scout cookies."

Cyrus maintained his light demeanor. "I'll take a box of Caramel Delights and some Thin Mints."

He allowed a few seconds of silence for the lawyer to continue his snark, but he didn't.

"Don't worry, I'll try to keep it short. Maybe you could start by telling me your name."

"I'm Edmund Fox."

"What firm?" Cyrus asked.

"I'm in-house counsel for Lockhart Industries."

Cyrus winced for show, aiming it at the younger man. "You brought a company lawyer for this?"

"For what, exactly?" Fox asked.

"Questions about the shooting at Live Oak."

Chance finally spoke up. "I've only had the gig for a couple months, and I'm not rich... yet."

"Ha. I get it."

"Something wrong with company lawyers?" Fox asked.

Cyrus showed the subtlest one-shoulder shrug. "Depends on Chance's—can I call you Chance?" His target nodded. "It depends on what he has to say about the shooting. His answers about the events surrounding Michael Bray's death."

"Answers about the nut job my client took down before he could shoot up a church." It wasn't a question.

"Yes. We'll let Chance decide if a company lawyer is in his best interests."

"I hope you're not trying to drive a wedge between me and my client."

"I think it's up to Chance to decide if he's your client."

Chance's eyes flicked toward his attorney then back at Cyrus.

And there's the wedge. Baker doesn't know this guy from Adam.

Cyrus jumped in. "What were you doing at Live Oak that day?"

"Protection detail. My first one."

The lawyer rang in. "We answered that question in Texas."

"With Sheriff Newsome asking, right?"

"Yes."

"Well, you understand I'm with the Bureau. Federal outfit. We have our own I's to dot and T's to cross."

"Then dot and cross them," the lawyer said. "But I wonder why you didn't question him sooner. What's changed?"

"I wasn't investigating the shooting earlier. We

were interested in another matter that led us here, and that's all you're getting for now." Cyrus gave Chance a single nod. "Who sent you to Texas?"

The lawyer interrupted again. "Lockhart Public Security sent him."

"Is your client planning on answering any questions, or should we just send him on his way so I can talk to you?"

"Don't tempt me."

"Like I said, we'll let Chance decide." He gave Fox a couple seconds to spout off, but the suit held his tongue. "Who at LPS sent you to Texas?"

The lawyer raised a finger. "He was sent by the company. Your question is irrelevant. Are you questioning my client about a crime, Agent Jennings? As far as I know, the shooting was ruled legit. He's licensed to carry in that state, despite lax requirements."

"Nice to know you're in the loop, counselor."

"Can't do my job if—"

Cyrus interrupted, addressing the shooter. "I've already forgotten what your voice sounds like, Chance."

The younger man side-eyed his lawyer. "Yeah, I'm getting what you mean. Yo, how about letting me answer so we can get out of here. If he asks something out of bounds, let me know, yeah?"

Good news. The kid had a spine.

"Fine. But we need to know why we're here."

"You're here because I'm conducting an investigation into a public shooting in Hope Mills, Texas, and the local sheriff isn't amenable to sharing his interview video." He hadn't even spoken to Newsome, but Cyrus figured it was a good story to cut through the shit, especially since Fox wasn't going to call to verify the lie while he sat in that room. "So, we're tying up our own loose ends. Now, Chance, who from LPS sent you to—"

"How is that relevant to anything? Are you investigating LPS or Chance?"

"And there's the real question. Right, counselor? Because you seem hell-bent on protecting LPS, but I wonder if you'll be so fierce if Chance's interests part from theirs."

Blood rushed to Fox's cheeks. "That's out of line."

"Really? I think I'm being a pretty stand-up guy, here. I'm not after Chance. I just wanted to ask him some questions. But you're starting to make me wonder if he has something to hide."

Chance displayed both palms. "I absolutely don't."

Cyrus continued on his roll. "I'm starting to wonder if your lawyer does. Oops, I mean LPS's lawyer."

"I know who you are, Agent Jennings. And I know you have it out for Sam Lockhart. Believe me when I say I'll make use of that information. I'll slap you with an injunction so fast—"

Cyrus interrupted, engaging Chance. "You understand, right? If anything you say shines a negative light on your employer, I want you to be aware of your rights. It's nothing against Mr. Fox. We just like things to be tidy in court."

The suit leaned toward his client. "He's just trying to split us up because he has an axe to grind, and separation between you and the company suits him better. It's not going to work."

Chance's forehead winkled into fleshy waves as he glared at Fox, and his attorney backed away.

"Who sent you to Texas?"

Before Fox could chime in, Chance Baker spat, "Edward Xavier."

The answer Cyrus had been waiting for. "Great, we have him in the room next door."

The lawyer bit his lip.

Baker frowned. "Next door?"

Cyrus nodded. "So, Chance, what was the mission?"

"At the church? To provide security. What else?"

"I don't work at LPS, so any insight is welcome."

"Yeah, sure. I don't get peoples' hang-ups. They hire vets. We're field-ready. I had to pass range qualifications, undergo psychological batteries, and the like. They aren't sending out just anyone."

"I'm sure you're all upstanding citizens. No question."

"Damn right."

"And have you gotten to know the other guys at LPS well?"

"Like I said, I'm new to the outfit. I was benched after Texas, with pay."

"Why?"

"I shot a guy. I'm told it's procedure, same kind of thing law enforcement does."

"Law enforcement benches officers pending investigations. Is there an ongoing investigation at the company? Did they say that?"

Chance nodded. "They assured me I had nothing to worry about and sent me home. I still draw a paycheck."

"How generous of them. But why send you home? They didn't assign you to desk duty? Something to do around campus? I wonder why they'd want to isolate you."

Chance shrugged in response.

"I'm not sure I like your insinuations," Fox said.

"Were the LPS guys who thwarted Fitz Banner's assassination put on leave, counselor?"

One pregnant pause later, the lawyer's chin ticked up. "I'm not here to provide information about my client's operation."

"Oh, I forgot, it's LPS you represent."

Chance side-eyed his attorney again.

Fox didn't like it. "One more time, Agent Jennings, and we're ending this interview."

"So, you're not willing to tell me if the LPS contractor who stopped the school shooting in Missouri was put on paid leave, either, right? Not in front of

Chance, anyway. Because then he might wonder why he was. Hence, my use of the word, *isolated*."

Fox opened his mouth to protest.

Someone rapped on the door. "Well, damn," Cyrus said. "Sorry, Chance. I need to step outside for a sec. You mind waiting, or would you like to come back tomorrow?"

The lawyer checked his watch again. "He's not coming back. That concludes the interview, unless you plan on making an arrest."

Chance raised a finger. "I'm going to wait."

"Mr. Baker. I represent—"

"Maybe I should get my own counsel then."

Fox's face contorted. He checked his watch again then sat. "Let's hurry this along."

Chance shot the attorney another side-eye, pressing his lips into a white line. "We'll wait."

Cyrus twisted the knob then stepped into the hallway wearing a grin. Misty waited with a folder in one hand, the full span of her pearly whites on display.

CHAPTER 36

"You look like the cat who ate the canary."

Misty opened the folder then flicked through a stack of crisp paper with single-spaced text inside before handing it over.

"What's this?" Cyrus asked.

"Emails. What else would it be?"

Some documents had colored stickers to divide them, probably by topic. Her data collection speed should've stopped surprising him months ago, but Cyrus wasn't in the mood.

"Stifle your snark."

"Guess I earned that. Take a second to read those before you go back in. They're self-evident."

"Take a second? With all this shit?" He raised the folder then wagged it. "Walk me through it. Give me the CliffsNotes."

Misty snatched the folder, flipped it open, then

tapped the first page. "Since you said the SAC was pulling in the LPS guy from Texas, I queried his name in the XO's inbox. I found two interesting things. First, this is the only time Xavier wrote to Chance Baker, to give him marching orders. Second, he says 'welcome to LPS.' Looks like it was his first time in the field. Think about that for a second."

Although he hadn't had a moment when Chance said it was his first operation, he took one now. "A young guy with a new job. He's been through the evaluations at LPS, and they've sold him on the big picture. The grandiosity."

"Right. They're all ex-military, so they know how to prod his gung-ho instincts."

"Yeah. He's there to thwart bad guys, to be the solution to gun violence. That would amp a guy up. Then they sent him alone. Made him feel special."

"Now imagine how he'd react when a middle-aged guy rolls onto the scene with an assault rifle and a pistol." She paused the flipped over a page. "I also found this while I was still on campus. It's from Clayton Burroughs, the shrink at LPS. He's warning Edward Xavier against putting a weapon in Michael Bray's hands. No uncertain terms. But the doc isn't rejecting him outright. To the contrary, he says a regimented routine would be good for him, to return to a more military bearing."

"And the XO decided not to hire him at all."

"Depends on how you look at it." She flipped over

another page. "I think this one's pretty revealing, but you should skim it, yourself. I want to know if you see what I see."

Cyrus took the offered page.

Xavier,

Thanks for wasting my time. I was loyal, and this is how you repay me? Well, so much for all that shit about brotherhood. About honor. It makes me wonder if you and Lockhart give a shit about veterans at all. Even less gun violence. But, hey, that's fine. You're a bullshit artist who covered up for a guy who should've never been in our unit, and now you're casting off one of the soldiers who stayed loyal to your team. I served my country. But what happened to all that grand talk about LPS providing counseling to people like me? Was it all just bullshit? I'm willing to bet the Lamestream Media would pay for a story like mine.

Fuck you very much,
Bray

"He doesn't sound happy."

"Right. And I'm willing to wager the former XO doesn't like being threatened. But remember the pamphlets found at his place? Xavier is Black, and Bray doesn't sound the least bit racist, even less like a White supremacist. I mean, how many opportunities are there in that email to slur the XO? He calls him a bullshit artist. That's it." She paused, probably to order her words. "What do you want to bet the paper found in his apartment was crisp? Shiny and new."

"You think they planted it to discredit him."

She fanned through the pages then held up a sheet with a swastika icon.

"You have got to be shitting me. No one caught that?"

"Which leads to this one." She handed over another sheet. Cyrus started to scan it, but she slapped a hand over it. "I'll save you the trouble. Xavier wrote to apologize to Bray. Told him Lockhart agreed they should hold to their values, and he thinks he'd make a perfect addition to the team. Then offered him an assignment."

Cyrus sucked breath. "The church!" He snapped his fingers. "Same place he sent Chase Baker, and that's why the XO reached out to assign the job to the rookie, himself."

"Yup. After I saw that downstairs, I skimmed local press coverage and found a photo of Chance Baker wearing a tactical vest with LPS insignia."

"Damn. You're about to tell me Michael Bray was in plain clothes, right?"

Misty nodded with enthusiasm. "End result? You have Ed Xavier by the balls."

Cyrus called after her. "Is this the lot? You still searching?"

She pivoted to face him. "There are a couple more emails in there, but I didn't recognize the names, and I was discovered before I could parse. They're marked with the red dividers. If I'd had more time before you started the interrogations..."

He flipped through the pages.

"How about that GPS on William Bresnan's car? Was he at Chet Parson's house the night of the suicide?"

"He was not. But in light of the emails I found at LPS, I requested another ping. I won't ruin it for you, but it's in there. Blue stickers." She pointed at the folder.

"You're pure gold, Daniels."

"Good to hear."

Cyrus pointed toward the observation room door. "Blake wants to talk to you."

Her expression went slack, like she knew what was coming.

"Best to get it over with. I hope he keeps you out of prison." Cyrus gave a rueful chuckle. "I've kind of gotten used to having you around."

"Think he'll take me to the judge?"

"Why would he do that?"

"Because I went off on my own, and he doesn't like rogues?"

"Think about who you're talking to. My work in Denver won't be used to train new recruits on procedure."

She still didn't smile.

"Watch the interview with him, and let's see how the information you got serves us before you fret." He tapped beneath his bottom lip. "Chin up."

Misty swiped her badge then stepped inside.

Back pressed against the wall, Cyrus scanned the pages, checking the timestamps and ordering events in his head. He spotted the name of the reverend at Live Oak Church, Rodney Hinson. Then, as if the divine had intervened, another name he hadn't expected jumped off the page. He read the paragraph twice. His brain cycled scenarios as he queried his mind for the best angle, then the answer came.

He yanked out his cell, looked up a number, then dialed. The line rang, and he was transferred. A woman with a nasal pinch to her voice answered.

"United States Attorney's Office, Denver."

Once the call was over, he tucked the sheet in the very back, then pushed through the door with a fresh smile plastered on his mug.

CHAPTER 37

After grumbling about the extended delay and a pending dinner date, Fox quieted so Cyrus could do his work. If he knew about the emails, he'd try to get them tossed out of court. But the nature of undercover work allowed for some latitude. If the Bureau had cause—and a disappeared reporter was just that, even if it turned out she'd fled on her own under duress—a judge might let it in. The crime wasn't related to the Bureau's original suspicions, but law enforcement discovered crimes while investigating others all the time, and if the legal question was a tossup, judges often erred on the side of justice.

Much had changed during the interlude in the hall, and he'd decided to alter his plan of attack.

Chance Baker would be central to it.

"Let's rewind so we can speed this up for your

attorney, Chance. Run me through it. This was your first assignment, right?"

Chance nodded. "Yep."

"And we established Edward Xavier sent you to Texas."

"Correct."

"Any special orders? Did he say anything about the job beyond where and when?"

"He assigned it via an email, but he called me the morning I took up the post." Chance's head swiveled a little to the left, like he'd consult with Fox, but he returned it to center. Maybe he was tired of the lawyer's voice, too. "He said I should keep my eyes peeled, reminded me of the profile."

"What profile?"

"He'd wanted to confide in me on the phone. That was the word he used. Confide. They had an anonymous threat against Live Oak, and the XO didn't have anyone else in the area. He said he'd be sending someone down the next day, but he needed me to hold down the fort. Asked me if I could handle it."

"Why were you in Texas in the first place, if not to protect Live Oak Church?"

To Cyrus's surprise, Fox held his tongue.

"I was completing the LTC course."

"License to carry? Texas is permitless."

Chance nodded. "Yeah, but there are still some restrictions that a license gets past. I'd done the training and passed the written exam, but they needed my fingerprints. So, I went to get it done."

"I thought Mister Fox said you were already licensed... despite lax requirements."

"He'd completed all the requirements," Fox said.

"Fair enough. Let's get back to the profile Xavier told you about. The anonymous threat."

"It wasn't anything I hadn't learned at LPS during my onboarding week. Average shooter is a middle-aged White guy. You know, statistics and shit. Xavier reminded me about recent mass shootings, like the mall in Allen, Texas, the school in Uvalde... he specifically reminded me of a church shooting in Sutherland Springs. They all involved AR-15s. He said shooters come in with a plan and go to work, so hesitation on my part could put me and everyone in the church inside boxes."

"Almost like he was predicting trouble."

Fox snapped his fingers. "Out of line. The XO wanted to make sure Chance was prepared."

Cyrus found it interesting he'd adopted the XO moniker for the president of LPS.

"Fair enough. Tell me, Chance, what were you wearing the day of the shooting?"

"The Lockhart loadout. Cargo pants, long-sleeved shirt with a Kevlar vest, and a black ballcap."

Cyrus grinned. "A real *Guns and Ammo* fashion show, right?"

Chance chuckled. His lawyer frowned.

"What was Michael Bray wearing?"

Chance sighed, and his shoulders dropped. Fox, however, straightened in his chair, and his lips parted like he'd interrupt. But his shifty eyes turned toward the wall behind Cyrus, and he stared like he was mulling something over.

"It's hard to forget. Long-sleeved flannel shirt. Also wearing cargo pants. No armor like the Columbine guys, though."

"Did he come from a car? Walk up the sidewalk?"

"A truck. Pulled up to the curb right in front, like he owned the place. Yanked his rifle out of the passenger's side then slammed the door. He had sidearms holstered on both sides."

"Dual-wielding, huh? What did you do?"

The suit chimed in. "Don't answer that."

Cyrus leaned back in his chair. "Why not? Does he have something to hide?"

Fox didn't answer.

Chance dragged a trembling hand from the table to drop it in his lap.

Cyrus pictured the scenario in front of Live Oak from Baker's perspective. Despite his service time, he was basically a kid. Early twenties. Entrusted to protect a church because of a specific threat... as far as he knew, anyway. A rugged-looking guy who fits the profile he was given jumps out of his truck with a purpose. He's armed with an assault rifle and a pair of handguns.

"Chance, did you see combat in the military?"

"Don't answer that."

Cyrus ground his teeth. He wasn't about to let up. "Are you aware the guy you shot applied for a position at LPS?"

"What?" His head swiveled toward Fox then back.

"Did you know he was one of the Silver Stars?"

"What?"

The suit shot up. "This interview is over."

Cyrus ignored him. "Sure was. Served in the XO's unit in Iraq."

The younger man pushed back in his chair so hard its legs screeched, and the sound echoed off the walls. "He was at LPS?"

The lawyer reached for his briefcase. "We can discuss that on our own. It seems Agent Jennings has no cause to arrest you. Let's go, Chance."

The kid folded his arms across his chest then slouched in his chair.

"Chance? We're out of here."

Cyrus kept quiet so Baker could work through it on his own. Blake had said the kid came to the interview willingly, and that lent a little insight.

When he spoke again, his voice came in a low drone. "The XO set me up, didn't he?"

"Chance! Let's go."

Cyrus stood then eyed the attorney. "Actually, Chance can leave if he likes. But you're not going anywhere, counselor. Hands on the table."

Fox's expression melted then morphed into disbelief. "What? Are you out of your mind?"

Chance jumped from his chair then backed into the opposite corner.

Cyrus rattled the cuffs. "Hands on the table, counselor, or I'll put them there."

"This is outrageous."

"Finally, we agree."

The attorney planted his hands. "On what charge?"

"Conspiracy to commit murder." He swiped open the folder, reached for the last sheet, then drew it toward his face.

"This is a chain of emails between the man you call XO and Tom Rhymer. The thread starts the night before the shooting at Live Oak. It reads, *Make sure Edmund Fox is in Texas. I doubt Bray will show up, but I want to play it safe.*"

Cyrus spun Fox around so they faced each other.

"I remembered something when I saw that order. Lockhart's quite the Boy Scout. Be prepared or some such shit? Seems he always has someone like you nearby when he's planning something."

"Hey man, fuck you. That means nothing."

"The language of the email to Tom was careful. You know"—he made quotations with his fingers—"'I doubt Bray will show up.' But a deleted email shows the XO sent Michael Bray to Texas. He thought *he* was acting as LPS's security detail that day. Their solo detail."

"None of that implicates me in anything."

"Were you told about the threat?"

"Do you have an email showing I was?"

"Do I need one? You flew to Texas, and I have an email from the XO telling Rhymer to send you. Funny, Chance can tell me why he was in Texas, but why were you there?"

"Circumstantial. You have no proof I knew about the threat. I'll never be charged."

"You could clear all this up by telling me why you were there."

Fox didn't answer.

"Tell me counselor, who writes up the contracts for LPS clients?"

The crow's feet around Fox's eyes deepened in concert with his forehead wrinkles. "What's your point?"

"Was Live Oak a client of LPS?"

The lawyer's lips pinched into a white line.

Chance Baker, who'd been standing as far from the pair as he could get, stepped forward. "Yo. Answer him." Fox didn't spare him so much as a glance. "Dude. Are you telling me the church didn't even hire us? That you fuckers sent me in there with my ass in the wind? You set us both up?"

Fox unclenched his jaw, but his words came out

strained. "Shut the fuck up, Chance. You have just as much to lose. More, even."

Cyrus slipped between them. "I called the US Attorney before I came in. I can offer you immunity in exchange for your testimony against Xavier."

Chance took a step back, pulled his shirt taut.

The lawyer laughed. "He doesn't need immunity. He didn't break the law."

"Let's focus on you, Fox. The emails my associate printed out and stuffed in this folder had been deleted. She pulled them from a backup."

"So what?"

"The XO has thousands of emails marked as 'read' sitting in his inbox. He's a real hoarder. But *these?*" He raised the folder. "The ones about Texas? About Bray? He deleted them. Xavier broke his pattern. And my associate checked Doctor Burroughs's sent items. His recommendation regarding Michael Bray was deleted. Imagine how a jury would see all this."

Fox clammed up.

"I'm willing to bet the email ordering you to Texas has been deleted, too."

The suit didn't answer.

"And in light of the way Xavier broke his pattern, I wonder. Do you keep a clean inbox, or will that deletion stand out?"

"Even if that were true, you'd never get that warrant based on conjecture, Jennings."

"I wonder how the Bar is going to look upon an

officer of the court who flew into Texas the night before the shooting knowing there was a potential threat, knowing who the man was and where he'd show up, but not reporting it to the authorities? Aren't lawyers supposed to report potential crimes? Did you call the local sheriff?"

"You should save your fairy tales for children."

It was time to improvise. Cyrus turned his head to throw a nice long stare at the two-way glass, knowing Misty was on the other side.

"I have Tom Rhymer in a safe place, ready to testify about the email he sent you. He was told Michael Bray had gone off the rails and was threatening Live Oak Church in Hope Mills. The US Attorney is very interested in what both he and Chance have to say."

Fox's expression flattened, but he couldn't hide the rush of blood to his cheeks.

Cyrus smiled. "But here's the fun bit. I spoke with one of Michael Bray's neighbors. He said there was no way Bray was associated with the Truth Tellers. At first, I doubted him. Why would their literature be at Michael Bray's house after he was shot? But, as my luck would have it, I have the best analyst at the FBI working with me." He looked at the two-way glass then held up the paper with the swastika. "Turns out, with just a little digging, anyone can download the Truth Tellers' manifesto from the Internet. I'm starting to think it was planted there to cast shade on Michael

Bray for the media. But while I was out in the hallway, I kept asking myself, who was in Texas to plant it?" He tapped the sheets inside the folder. "Then it clicked. Rhymer sent you to Texas the day before the shooting." He tugged one of Fox's arms behind his back, cuffed it, then reached for the other. "I'm sure you wore gloves, counselor, but I wonder... did you delete your internet search history when you were looking for a local supremacist cult to tie to Michael Bray?"

Cyrus spun him around. Any fool could've seen reality dawn on Fox's face.

"Edmund Fox, you have the right to remain silent."

CHAPTER 38

Blake stood in his favorite spot by the window in his office, and Misty sat in one of the chairs by the desk, picking at her fingernails while Cyrus recounted the nothing-burger interview with the XO after he'd arrested Fox.

Despite the emails and threats of testimony from Chance Baker and Tom Rhymer, Edward Xavier refused to roll on Sam Lockhart. His lies came freely, despite the absence of an attorney. He never discussed Texas with Lockhart. He simply forgot to tell one LPS soldier about the other, was all. If the cops would've asked him, he'd have said all that. He blamed Tom Rhymer who, by his account, was responsible for logistics. Chance Baker was too amped up. His itchy trigger finger cost Michael Bray his life. Too bad, so sad.

It wasn't lost on Cyrus how the Fallujah story resembled the events in Texas and, while it might have presented some short-term pleasure to choke the life out of the guy sitting across the table, imagining the prick behind bars sufficed.

When Cyrus revealed he knew there was no contract with Live Oak Church, the XO just shrugged. So, he'd pulled out his biggest bat, informing Xavier they had the GPS locater on *his wife's* car pinging at Chet Parson's place the night of the supposed suicide.

The XO clammed up.

Cyrus had almost hoped it'd been Will Bresnan who shot Chance, but the editor's decision to warn Lockhart that someone he thought was with the FBI had infiltrated LPS might be good for an obstruction charge.

When Cyrus announced to the XO that he'd learned Chance never saw combat in the military, that he doubted the on-site shrink recommended sending him in solo, Xavier simply said, "We're done here. I'd like to speak with my attorney now."

Blake leaned against the window with his arms folded. "So, Chance Baker panicked. Someone with Xavier's experience probably knew he would. That's why he sent him to wrap up his carry license then ordered him to the church at the last minute. The kid gave us enough for a warrant to confirm whether the doc recommended him for field work, and the XO asking for an attorney when you brought up that bit tells me what we're going find."

Misty smiled. "We're going to nail that fucker to the cross."

"Yeah, the XO is going away. But we have no emails between him and Lockhart about any of it."

She shrugged. "The compartmentalization is impressive. If Lockhart knew about the events leading to the Texas fiasco—"

"He knew," Cyrus said.

"There's no paper trail. No proof Sam even knew Michael's Bray's name. Xavier was the day-to-day guy. He ran LPS. Sam got the funding, got the building outfitted, raised the other structures, then went on a PR campaign. He's the face of it, so he wouldn't want to get bogged down in the rigmarole of actually running it, especially with a former military commander there to do it for him. Lockhart Tactical probably keeps him busy, too."

Cyrus scowled. "He knew."

"Yeah," Blake said. "Can you prove it?"

Misty sighed. "When they dragged me up to the office at LPS, I got the spiel about Sam Lockhart being the only person doing anything for veterans. They brag gun violence is down forty-percent across the whole country, not just the states where LPS has thwarted attacks. Xavier's a real fanboy of his boss."

Cyrus nodded. "When I told Xavier Lockhart was going to land him in prison, he said it was a small price to pay for all the lives saved."

Misty answered in a low tone. "I know you despise

Lockhart, but Xavier might have a point. I have nothing against the VA, but there's so much red tape, and politicians love using the system as a whipping boy come budget time. Its bloat. Maybe someone else *should* take up the slack."

Sometimes it was better to keep one's mouth shut. Cyrus hadn't served, and Misty had seen the operation from the inside. If she'd come up empty, then Lockhart had covered his bases. And his ass. If only he'd kidnapped Anastasia Clark so they had something that would stick.

The government would get warrants for Lockhart's servers, but if the operation was as walled-off as Misty'd indicated, Xavier would be taking the heat alone.

What bothered Cyrus was that he hadn't tried to whittle down the time for his murder conviction by turning on Lockhart for Texas.

Then he figured out why.

Because Sam Lockhart has the dirt on Fallujah. If Xavier goes to prison, covering for his boss means the mission continues. Maybe he actually does care about the soldiers coming home to shit deals.

But Cyrus had seen how the XO behaved. Pure entitlement. He didn't buy it.

A thought came out of left field, and Cyrus perked up. He drew out the iPhone Marsha had bought him and opened a browser.

While Cyrus searched, the SAC pressed on. "We

are where we are. Although I suspect the lawyer will come to his senses and reverse his position, right now Chance Baker will be the government's star witness. I think the case is solid enough to take to the US Attorney, and that will keep DC off my ass. Somewhat, at least."

Cyrus peered away from his cell to look down at Misty. He suspected the way she picked her cuticles reflected her disappointment with how things had gone. Once she'd known her sister was safe, she'd still gone to bat for the Bureau. But they'd come up short of the grand objective—Lockhart's ass in a cell. At least they had the XO.

He read something on his phone then did a bit of math in his head. "This is interesting."

"What's that?" Blake asked.

"Statute of limitations for war crimes."

"What?"

"The Fallujah event happened in 2004, right?"

"That's right," Misty said. "Which puts the statute's limit at 2024. Months from now."

"Exactly. Let's say Sam Lockhart has the dirt on Xavier's Iraq cover-up."

"Right," Misty replied. "I'd wondered about the same. If the XO might flip if it weren't for the potential blackmail with the military. His whole unit could be prosecuted."

"So?" Blake asked. "What am I missing?"

"It'll be a while before the XO's case comes up on

the court docket. If we're outside the statute by that point, he might roll over on Sam."

Misty's head swiveled from side-to-side. "That doesn't work. There's no statute of limitations in the Uniformed Code of Military Justice when a death is involved. Lots of civilians were killed. And now that we have Xavier for the Parsons murder, he doesn't care what the military charges or doesn't charge. It's not likely they would, anyway. It's old news, and it was fucking Fallujah. And as far as Texas goes, assuming we can prove he set the whole thing up to a jury? You're just tacking on another life sentence."

"Texas has the death penalty," Blake said.

Misty shrugged. "Yeah, that's true. But I remind you, I found nothing connecting Lockhart to Xavier on that one. Even if they spoke about it *mano e mano*, it'll be his word against Sam's."

Cyrus scowled. "He's not rolling."

Blake paced the room. "Does anything point at Lockhart?"

"You could have the IRS audit him." Misty turned over one wrist to check her smart watch then stood. "Well, it seems I have to be on a plane tomorrow morning, so I'm going to have to leave it to you guys from here."

Cyrus cocked an eyebrow. "Plane? Where the hell—?"

Blake waved him off. "We'll talk about it on our own. Misty, go get packed."

She patted his shoulder. "See you around."

What the utter fuck?

He watched her back as she turned the knob on the door, and the idea she wouldn't be around to help him wrap things up jolted Cyrus. And from that sudden adrenal surge, an idea came to him.

"Think you can do one last thing for me when you go back to your place?"

She turned. "I guess that's up to Blake."

Cyrus headed his boss off at the pass. "You don't want to know, but if I can't charge him, we might at least ruin Lockhart's day. Hell, his whole year. Probably won't lead to court, so no chain of evidence to concern yourself with."

Blake frowned. "Fine. I despise him as much as you. And you're right, I don't want to fucking know."

Raising his phone and tilting it from side to side, Cyrus said, "I'll text you in a few."

Misty forged an unconvincing smile then closed the door behind her.

Cyrus wheeled. "Where is she going?"

"Sit." Blake gestured toward the chair Misty had been occupying then settled onto the corner of his desk. He swiped up a single sheet of paper with heavy bonding but kept it in his lap. Cyrus caught a peek at the FBI logo. "She's spinning her wheels here, and I can't have someone who isn't even technically a Bureau employee risking our cases. This whole operation has clarified it for me. When she went to LPS on her own, she jeopardized everything. Sure, I can fiddle with the timeline, tell little white lies to cover for her, but she intentionally bypassed my command, and I can't have judges considering throwing out evidence because she's a contractor.

"With a judge I have to report to on one side of the equation and DC ready to light my chair on fire if anything she gathers as evidence doesn't stand up, I've been racking my brain trying to figure it out. I don't want her in jail, and I don't want her wasting away in the basement when she boasts skills the Bureau could really leverage."

He flipped the page toward Cyrus.

"So I pulled some strings. A new class is starting at Quantico in January. I made a deal with my boss, and he got her in. The badge equals accountability."

Cyrus's jaw dropped. "You're sending her to Quantico? Misty's joining the FBI?"

Blake grinned from ear to ear. "You're always lording over her how she doesn't have a badge, right?"

"I'm not sure I'd use *lording*."

"Well, she'll have one soon enough, and you'll finally have a bona fide partner. With her background, I'm thinking she's a shoe in for top five in her class."

"She'll finish at the top, trust me."

"Which only makes it better for the Denver Field Office. This way, the judge is out of the picture. I can get her to drop the five-year order because Misty will officially work for the Bureau. If anything, the judge will think her order was a stroke of genius. A success story.

"On top of that, aside from her technical prowess, she's a trained operator. An infiltrator. A spy. I could use someone like that for undercover work. Quantico will teach her limits. Make her responsibilities clear."

"And she went for all this? Did you threaten to take her to the judge or something?"

Blake snorted. "Didn't have to. You would've been shocked. Daniels actually smiled. You know, with actual enthusiasm. Not something I often see from her. No, she was all-in, happy to get the judge off her ass."

"But you understand you're giving her power back, right?"

Blake shrugged. "It crossed my mind. When the order is rescinded, she can just resign. But I'm confident in one thing."

"What's that?"

"Misty Daniels loves working with you. If we can make her love the Bureau, too, and if we can empower her to use her myriad skills to catch bad guys, everybody wins. Why would she walk away from that?"

Cyrus could think of a few reasons. Her side business was lucrative. She didn't need a Bureau paycheck. But then he thought of her friendship with Byron. The pair of white hat hackers who administered justice to dirt bags the legal system missed, and the idea of her carrying a badge seemed natural.

"Stroke of genius, Sean."

"Thanks. I'm glad you're on board. I would've hated to assign her to someone else."

"I'd resign the next day."

"You know, Cyrus, I believe that. Now I need a favor from you."

"What's that?"

"Stay away from Misty until she starts class. Since the next one isn't until January, I suspended her. Nothing formal. After all, she's not Bureau, and I don't have to file anything. But there had to be some kind of punishment and, unfortunately, you still have to obey orders. She's flying to DC for some administrative shit. When she comes back, don't use her in any capacity."

"Well, I'm not going to ignore her if she calls."

"I don't care what you do with your *personal* life, Cy. Just don't use her for *Bureau* business until she's official in March or so.

"Now, go ruin Sam Lockhart's year, and try to keep it from bouncing back on me. As a matter of fact, you've accumulated too much vacation time. Do with it as you will."

CHAPTER 39

For the second time in as many weeks, Tiffany Brooks met Cyrus at the airport. Shauna Edenborough had been relocated for a new case, but he decided they could get along without the ATF. But that wasn't to say they hadn't supplied some valuable intel. It'd been Shauna who informed Cyrus the serial numbers had been filed off Michael Bray's weapons. Reflecting on that filled out the big picture, and a new search term in the PST file revealed the XO had asked Bray to bring his own gear until LPS could get someone down there to outfit him properly.

The final nail in Xavier's coffin.

That Michael bought guns with filed-off serials was Shauna Edenborough's problem.

Tiffany eased her rental into a parking lot across from the sheriff's office around eleven, then they discussed strategy while they waited.

Like clockwork, Newsome's rotund figure waddled out the front door at quarter to noon. Tiffany dropped the car into gear, pulled up to the exit, then waited for the sheriff's cruiser to pass. Easing into traffic, they followed.

"I've got fifty that says he goes for a donut shop," Cyrus guessed.

"I'll take that bet. He'll go to a cafe a couple blocks down and take a table in the back corner."

"It's unsporting to accept a wager when you've scouted the subject."

"And it's stupid to offer one without considering the likelihood that I would."

The cruiser pulled into the parking lot of a place called *Henry's* two minutes later, and Cyrus rolled up some cash then handed it over.

"Figures you still carry paper around." Tiffany swiped it. "Don't worry. I'll use it to pay for lunch."

"Your generosity knows no bounds. Hell, it's Texas. They've probably got a decent steak on the menu."

"You know," Tiffany mused, "we should offer to pay for his."

"Might as well."

She pulled in right next to Newsome's cruiser. Cyrus snatched his attaché then slipped out of the ride before the sheriff exited his.

"Sheriff, you remember me?"

Newsome eyed the offered hand like plague would rub off, but he surprised Cyrus when he grasped it.

"Last time we spoke, I think you called me... a Lockhart puppet or something of the kind. Was it Jennings?"

"Yup, Cyrus Jennings."

The sheriff spied Tiffany walking around the car. "And Miss Brooks. You two are like peas in a pod, except the pod is a clown car."

Tiffany chuckled. "Funny, Sheriff. Mind if we buy you lunch?"

The wound up, confused expression was predictable. "After our last meeting, I can't imagine why you would want to."

Cyrus pressed a hand to his chest. "We're both law enforcement, and I have some information to share. I promise, when we're done with lunch, we'll skedaddle back to the airport and you won't see me in your town again without an invitation. How's that?"

The cop mulled it over for a few ticks before dipping his double chin then making for the door. "Little company never hurt, and I never turn down a free meal when I know who's making it. C'mon then."

The sheriff ambled to a table in the back. There was a booth on one side, two seats with red vinyl on the other. Tiffany and Cyrus took the chairs. The thick scent of eggs and red meat filled the air.

"So, what brings you back to my neck?"

Tiffany met Cyrus's gaze then said, "After you, by all means."

"Like I said, I thought we'd do a little information sharing. We wanted to fill you in on some details related to the shooting, in case you hadn't come across them yet."

A waitress appeared, and Johnny Local ordered a steak.

Go figure.

Cyrus ordered the same. Tiffany went for a breakfast platter. All three opted for sweet tea.

"So," the sheriff said. "What you got?"

"I've got the president of Lockhart Public Security in custody for murder and conspiracy to commit murder."

Newsome gaped. "For the Bray thing? But LPS kept him from shooting up that church."

Cyrus raised an index finger. "Before I go into detail, I want to ask if we can keep this between us, Sheriff. I have an idea that will benefit all involved."

"Mum's the word, assuming you fill in the blanks."

"Thanks. I have proof Edward Xavier sent Michael Bray and Chet Parsons to the same job."

Newsome's expression morphed into confusion then revelation. "Like, a setup?"

Cyrus nodded. "The day you showed up at Rayford Clemmons's house and ran us off, something he said stuck with me."

"What was that?"

"He didn't believe what the press was saying about Bray. About the documents found at his place. But when I called my friend at the ATF, she said it hadn't been her outfit who'd cordoned off his place. Was it your guys who checked out Michael Bray's apartment?"

"Yeah. Once I had the scene cordoned, I posted deputies via my radio then headed straight for it. Small town. We all know where each other lives."

It wasn't that small, but Cyrus maintained a stony expression. "Right. What did you find when you got there?"

The sheriff raised both hands, displaying his meaty palms. "Now, forgive me, but I thought you were here to share information with me, not prod me for it."

"How about a little quid pro quo? Like I said, we have Edward Xavier in custody, but I think you could fill in some details while putting the case to rest for yourself. Hell, if we play our cards right, we could get those reporters camped outside of Lockhart Public Security instead of Live Oak."

"So, you don't think I'm a Lockhart puppet, after all."

"I don't. And I apologize."

"Tempers get the best of all of us, I suppose. I was... territorial about it."

"So, the apartment?"

The sheriff's attention meandered to Tiffany, his gaze dipped for just a short glance, then he eyed his tea glass.

"Okay, fair enough, Jennings. We were the first on the scene."

"And you found White supremacy documentation there?"

"Printouts of a manifesto. The worst kind of stuff. N-word this, N-word that. One paper had a swastika."

"Worst kind, indeed," Tiffany said.

"Right. Did you collect that as evidence?"

Newsome chuckled. "The lot of it. ATF wanted it, but they didn't want to fight me for it. I thought they gave up a bit too easily, considering the nature of the crime. But like I said," he gave an apologetic shrug and accentuating head tilt, "I can be territorial."

Tiffany smiled.

Cyrus shrugged it off, almost like their conflict hadn't happened. "Anyway, Rayford said he didn't believe for a second that Michael was connected to the Truth Tellers. Said the two of them went to high school with some of those guys and, no matter how pissed Bray was, he wouldn't fall in with that crowd. That's why I asked about the documents you found in his house."

"Oh." Newsome drummed his fingers on the table. "Well, people change, right? Get mad? I've seen some unlikely pairings on my streets, people with different background who find common cause and commit common crimes."

"Well put. But tell me, were the pamphlets wrinkled?"

The sheriff sat back in the booth. "Wrinkled..." He

muttered the word like he'd only intended it for his own ears. "Well, no."

"And the manifesto sheets you mentioned. Were they strewn about?"

This time, Newsome nodded without hesitating. "Spread out on a table. But now that I picture 'em in my head, I think I know where you're going. They were clean. Like they'd never been handled. You thinking someone planted that stuff?"

Cyrus nodded. "I think one of Lockhart's lawyers planted it. A guy named Fox."

"Fox!" The sheriff thumped the table with the side of his fist. "That guy was a pain in my ass. Was at the church before I arrived that day. Really limited my ability to question Chance Baker." Newsome drummed the table with the fingers of both hands. "I don't like that guy. I'm thinking we could run prints on that Truth Tellers stuff. See if Fox ever actually touched it. But do you really believe Sam Lockhart would send a lawyer in there? Set the place up to look like something it wasn't?"

"I wouldn't put it past him."

"Nah." The sheriff frowned and swiveled his head in slow twists. "Too risky. These rich guys don't build castles by being stupid."

Tiffany snorted. "But once they have money, you'd be surprised what someone will do when ego trumps logic."

The waitress appeared holding two plates and

balancing the third on a forearm. She slid them to the correct parties without asking. "Get y'all anything else?"

Newsome smiled. "No thanks, Moira. Appreciate it." It came out *pre-she-ate*.

Cyrus cut his steak, Tiffany shoved a fork under her eggs then left it there. The sheriff dug in with gusto.

After swallowing a hunk of cow, he dabbed a corner of his mouth with a paper napkin, set his fork and knife down, then sipped from his tea. "Now, I appreciate the information sharing, especially in light of last time we spoke but, like I said, I don't think someone as rich and connected as Sam Lockhart would be so stupid as to get up to this kind of mess."

"How about Ethan Pierce?"

"Pierce?" The sheriff's eyeballs swelled.

Tiffany leaned over her eggs. "I know a PAC Ethan Pierce contributes to sent your re-election campaign fifty-thousand bucks a couple months ago."

The woman knew how to turn a conversation. More like drop a bomb.

The sheriff froze. "What?"

Tiffany raised her hands so her palms faced the ceiling. "Lord, Jesus. We're past the self-righteous shit, Sheriff. I have it all right here on my phone."

"You accusin' me of something, Brooks?"

"Call it curiosity."

"Well, it's like you said, I got money from a PAC. So what?"

Cyrus focused hard on Newsome's face, his body language, and he didn't care if he was squinting. But what he found in the lawman's expression, to his own bafflement, was surprise.

"Pierce funds Lockhart Public Security," Cyrus said. "Formed LLCs through his wife to build up the outfit. You didn't know?"

"Hell no!" The sheriff's face pinkened all the way to the folds beneath his chin. He leaned forward and lowered his voice. "Hell no. Mrs. Pierce's guy told me she was trying to keep my party in office. Donating money to campaigns across the state. All on the up-and-up."

Tiffany cocked an eyebrow. "Mrs. Pierce's guy?"

"Yeah. Pierce is in prison. I'm not taking money from him. How would that look."

Cyrus's spirit swelled. "Did Mrs. Pierce's guy ask for anything in return for the donation?"

The sheriff hesitated, leaned back again, then shoved his plate away. The nodes in his jaw worked as he chewed on his cheek.

"I'm not after you," Cyrus said.

Tiffany raised one hand. "And I didn't mean to drop it like that. Sorry. We want the same thing as you. Truth."

"Truth is subjective, Miss Brooks. It's all about perspective, ain't it?"

A long silence ensued, and everyone's food was forgotten.

"You two can assure me this isn't going to come back and bite my behind, right? I share, you keep me out of it." His steady gaze landed on Tiffany, and it turned into a hard stare boring into the political operative like he was trying to burn holes with his laser vision.

She tilted her head to one side and shrugged the nearest shoulder. "If you're on the level, and you have nothing to hide, I have no reason to make the PAC donation public."

"A threat veiled as an offer, but I guess I'll have to take your word for it. But I didn't do anything illegal. So, Tim, that's Mrs. Pierce's assistant—or whatever they call them these days—called me within minutes after Live Oak. Said he heard that Michael Bray was a racist. Suggested I check out the apartment."

Cyrus chewed the inside of his cheek. "And it was Pierce's guy? Not the lawyer, Fox?"

"Mrs. Pierce, actually."

Tiffany shook her head. "No, it wasn't her guy. It was Ethan's guy. I have intel on Tim."

"Well, the only time I ever talked to Fox or anyone else from Lockhart was during the Chance Baker interview, abbreviated as it was."

Cyrus fell back then ran his hand over his face. "And you didn't think Tim sending you to the apartment where you found that literature was suspicious?"

"I didn't know about any connection between Pierce and Lockhart where LPS was concerned, or that Tim was working for Ethan Pierce. Like I said, he was in prison."

"A Lockhart prison," Tiffany added.

Newsome pressed his temples with the finger and thumb of one hand then ran his palm down his face. "I must look like an incompetent." He sighed.

Tiffany planted an elbow on the table. "Without all the information, you wouldn't have any reason to suspect all this."

"That's kind of you. Now that you've filled me in, hell yes, it's suspicious. Truth is, I'd expected the feds to take over the scene as soon as they learned the shooter's identity. That's what they do, if they're faster than us. And they often are. "So, when he called and said it would look real good for me if I showed some speed, I got to the house and cordoned it off, took a look inside. I thought he was trying to support the campaign more directly, but I guess I got greedy. Thought my quick wit would come off in the press. I might not *like* the press, but anyone holding an elected office needs it. Still, I wasn't some spineless hack. I even told him I knew how to do my job."

"Right before you rushed to the apartment," Tiffany replied.

Newsome sneered. "Yes."

"Hey, we can all be friends, here," Cyrus said. "I'm not judging you."

"Sounds like your friend is."

"It's not judgment, I'm seeking clarity. We all have shit to own up to, and denying our shortcomings prevents us learning from them. Like I said, I'm more than happy to keep your name out of the papers if we get the right guy."

"Okay. Brass tacks. What do you have on Lockhart, specifically?"

"Full disclosure?" Cyrus asked.

"Well, I'm not holding anything back."

"Fair enough. I have bupkis. Nada."

The sheriff smiled. "So, you came because you need my help with that."

Tiffany clasped her hands in her lap, leaned over the edge of the table, then showed him the pit bull. "I have so much shit on you those reporters will be camped outside your office until the next election." She wasn't giving the guy an inch.

Newsome sighed. "Fine." He waved both hands. "But what assurances do I have you won't use it anyway? Like I said, I don't even know Lockhart."

"You have every assurance," Tiffany said. "Ethan Pierce did things to me I won't describe, but suffice it to say I'll do anything I can to make his life miserable. And Sam Lockhart? Well, I have an axe to grind with that asshole, too. Sheriff, compared to those feelings, any animosity I have toward you is miniscule."

"That'll do, Miss Brooks. I think I have a way we could all get what we want," Newsome said. "It might not land Lockhart in prison, but after all this crap about the damned Live Oak encounter, I'm not a fan of private companies rolling in here and doing my job for me. If I'd known Ethan Pierce was tied to the whole thing, well, I probably would've returned the donation."

Cyrus felt a little hollow in his chest. Guilt, he decided, about suspecting Newsome of being part of the coverup in Live Oak the whole time. The sheriff wasn't the only one gaining perspective in that café.

"You mentioned this Tim guy. Pierce's assistant... or whatever they call it these days. How often is he in touch?"

"Funny you should ask. I haven't heard a peep from him since he suggested I search Michael Bray's apartment."

Cyrus shared a look with Tiffany. "Is it even possible Pierce doesn't know I've been down here?"

"I've been keeping an eye out, and aside from a new guy who's been watching the church for LPS, I haven't seen anyone suspicious. Reporters, ATF, and parishioners. That's about it."

Newsome nodded. "I talked with that new LPS guy. Long-time veteran. New to the enterprise. Friendly enough but focused on his job. Shows up for services then leaves. I doubt he's writing reports. And if it's like you say, I can see why they'd keep him out of the loop. Tight circles, and all."

"Treacherous fucks," Cyrus added.

Newsome nodded. "And you're sure this Xavier guy sent the pair down here? Set one up to be shot by the other?"

Cyrus nodded. "On him, I've got the goods."

"Then I think you've also got Lockhart by the balls, even if you can't charge him. We could all three benefit from this little chat in big ways."

Cyrus and Tiffany shared smiles.

She took over. "What did you have in mind?"

Newsome didn't hesitate. "A little press conference. Traffic has died down in the weeks since the shooting, but I'll bet you could fill a room, Miss Brooks."

"Filling rooms is my specialty, Sheriff."

"Great!" Newsome smacked the table.

Chills ran down Cyrus's back as revelation struck. Putting the sheriff in front of the press was a nice start, but there were other, powerful pieces to be played.

"I think I can do us one better. If we do it right, drop the dominoes in the right order, we could make Sam Lockhart want to jump out his window from his top-floor office at LPS."

Tiffany rubbed her hands together. "Ooh, I've seen that look before. Cyrus has a plan."

CHAPTER 40

After flying back to Denver the previous night, Cyrus called Misty for a map to the cabin then sped to Anastasia Clark's hideaway. He handed over the relevant emails, talked through his interviews with Chance Baker and Sheriff Newsome, and verified with Tom Rhymer that he'd been ordered to send the LPS lawyer to Texas.

As luck would have it, Rhymer still had his company laptop, and even though his credentials had been revoked, it maintained local copies of the emails in his inbox. They'd use them to give Anna what she needed to launch the grand plan.

On his drive back to Denver, Cyrus listened to a radio broadcast of Lockhart praising Fitz Banner's pending legislation in Chicago and his willingness to cross party lines to do what's best for Illinois. The governor was towing the line, promising a veto, but Sam claimed they had the votes to overturn.

The bill would likely be collateral damage if Cyrus, Tiffany, and Newsome achieved their goal.

He and Tiffany spent the rest of the evening conspiring at her townhouse. The place was exactly how he remembered it. Clean. Sparsely but elegantly decorated. They sipped coffee as they'd laid out the rest of the plan.

The next morning was go-time.

Cyrus refreshed *Buzzfeed's* website while Tiffany sat before a giant mirror surrounded by lights having her makeup touched up by the staffer of the *Morning Nation* broadcast. That she'd been able to finagle her way onto the country's most popular morning show on such short notice only left Cyrus more determined to learn who she worked for.

"Is it George Soros?"

"Get real, Cyrus."

"The DNC? An anti-gun organization with deep pockets?"

"Not yet, dude. Shut up."

The possibilities were many. But in the way he hadn't looked into Misty's background, he lent Tiffany the same courtesy. Even though he fell in the center of the political road and they had their differences, the two had not only become friends, but allies.

As the makeup artist swept a brush over Tiffany's

cheeks in short, speedy strokes, his ally peered at him through the mirror's reflection.

"Did it drop yet?"

Cyrus shook his head. "Any minute."

"Don't think the Buzz backed out, do you?"

"You read the draft. No way in hell they pass on this."

A guy in a shirt and tie leaned into the doorway. "Five minutes, Miss Brooks."

She flashed her soul-melting smile and thanked him. Good thing Cyrus was immune. Once the guy departed, Tiff inspected herself in the mirror while she spoke. "I committed the draft to memory. I can work with it if she—"

"Bam!"

The headline on Cyrus's screen read: LOCK-HART PUBLIC SECURITY UNDER SCRUTINY AS POSSIBLE MURDER PLOT EXPOSED by Anastasia Clark

Cyrus handed her the phone. "Skim it."

Instead, Tiffany read aloud. "Politicians on the Hill are up in arms as Edward Xavier, President of Lock-hart Public Security, has been arrested in connection with murders in Hope Mills, Texas, and Colorado Springs, Colorado. While the CEO of Lockhart Industries makes the rounds on morning cable shows, a cloud of suspicion is forming over his company as a conspiracy to send Michael Bray to Live Oak Church..."

Tiffany waved off the makeup woman then spun her chair. "She's good."

"Got what you need?"

"I'm going to annihilate him."

Cyrus tapped a contact on his phone.

The call was answered immediately. "Yo! How's my favorite fed this morning?"

Funny how Newsome's tone had changed since the day they met. Funnier how the threat of losing his career in law enforcement could change his whole disposition.

"You're on."

"And ready. By the way, thanks Cyrus. You could've burned me."

"If I thought you were actually crooked, I would've." He hung up.

A moment later, the TV monitor in the corner of the dressing area switched over from the studio hosts to a shot of small-town Texas as Sheriff Newsome waddled up to the podium. Rodney Hinson, the pastor of Live Oak Church, stood back and to one side. Cyrus grabbed the remote to unmute.

"Good morning. Considering recent revelations and new evidence surrounding the shooting of Michael Bray, I'm announcing my office's partnership with the FBI in bringing charges against Lockhart Public Security attorney, Edmund Fox. We believe—"

By the time the sheriff finished, Tiffany would be seated in the studio and ready to use Anastasia's article about Edward Xavier and Newsome's charges against Edmund Fox to shred LPS. It was like the trio had decided in the small cafe the day before. If they couldn't charge Lockhart, they'd shut him down.

For once, Cyrus felt like he was feeding the political machine instead of having it crash down onto him. If the two sides of the aisle followed predictable narratives, the fiasco could fill the news cycle for a week.

Tiffany stood and pulled her jacket taut, facing the studio.

Cyrus tapped her shoulder. "Before you go, I have a request."

She raised a pencil thin eyebrow. "Anything."

"You might be sorry you said that."

She clutched his hand then, to his surprise, placed a gentle kiss on his cheek. "After today? I seriously doubt it. You probably just doubled my pay. Name it."

He did.

CHAPTER 41

Cyrus needed a little time off the grid and some luck. As far as luck went, Marsha had planned a trip to Orange County, California to visit her son. Saying he wanted to touch base with Misty and help her get prepped for her trip to Quantico, he promised to meet her out in Cali a week later.

Which left him with a week carved out of his own vacation to plan.

Although Blake hadn't wanted to know what his agent was up to, his tone was more cheery than usual when Cyrus called following Tiffany's interview three days before. Even if they couldn't put Lockhart in a cell, they'd gut-punched his new enterprise, and that sat well with the SAC.

Maybe Cyrus's decision to let Anastasia Clark, Sheriff Newsome, and Tiffany Brooks bring down the house of cards so Cyrus wasn't directly involved—as far as anyone knew—had bought him some good will. Either way, the SAC was beyond happy Agent Jennings was on vacation.

Taking a page out of his parents' playbooks, Cyrus spread subtle word around that he'd be renting an RV and driving west to California. That would give him the cover he needed to get the work done. He didn't like omitting any of the truth with Marsha, but at least he hadn't lied. Even if he'd told her the whole story, she would've just worried, but he didn't think she'd have shut him down. Still, he couldn't have been sure.

First, he needed some corroboration.

Although she wasn't occupying it, Anastasia Clark lived in a high-rise apartment building downtown, and when he gazed upon its posh lobby, it dawned on Cyrus that Misty's side-gigs funded more than server racks.

Despite the premium she must have been paying for her sister's abode, there were no hallway cams, and the lobby footage was erased on the regular. No backups.

Although the guard had been willing enough to help a guy with a badge, it'd been too long since the intruder broke into Anastasia's apartment for him to get any footage.

But the guy told Cyrus there'd been a string of robberies in the area a couple years earlier and, although the mini crime wave never touched the apartment building, vendors in the shops across the street had installed cameras up and down the block.

So Cyrus bought himself an ice cream cone.

The owner of the shop told him her camera was a fake, but the ones at the pawn shop next door were real as they came. That place had been hit twice, and the owner put up bars behind his new windows along with two cameras. When he fibbed about investigating the robberies, she walked Cyrus over to introduce him to the pawn shop's proprietor.

The owner went by Natty, and he had a .45 holstered on his left hip as he stood behind the counter with his beefy arms folded across his torso. Cyrus had no idea what Natty was short for, nor did he give a rat's ass. In lieu of flashing the badge this time, he bought some guitar picks and a set of acoustic strings. Of course, his guitar had burned down with his cabin in the mountains, but he planned to replace it at some point.

After his purchase, Natty proved happy to share. He was the law abiding, community-oriented type who looked out for his neighbors. He had *three* cameras, and he backed them up to the cloud. The idea of some weirdo stalker sniffing peoples' laundry rendered him more than willing to help. As he wound the video to the date in question, Cyrus held up a photo, then settled in as the tape scanned forward.

"Paydirt!" Natty's cry broke Cyrus's focus. The video was paused on a figure matching the build and haircut of the guy in the picture strolling right by the pawn shop. Natty tapped the button and they watched the figure crossing to the apartments across the street, then he backed it up and captured the best screen shot they could find.

Cyrus snatched it, then raced south to Colorado Springs to show Anastasia the two pictures and have her confirm her father's identity.

"So, it was him who broke in."

Cyrus's parting words to her were, "We never spoke of this. I was never here."

Although her confused expression left him expecting questions, Anastasia simply nodded and said, "I have no idea what you mean. Do I know you?"

CHAPTER 42

Snow had fallen in West Virginia each of the two previous nights, and Cyrus's thin, white nylon shells blended with the frosty terrain. Finally making use of the outdoor gear he'd stashed in storage, he was wrapped in a North Face ThermoBall Eco Jacket, a pair of Patagonia Quandary pants, and Icebreaker thermals. His EcoFlow Delta Pro solar generator was nested behind the wide trunk of a high pine to keep his camera, cell phone, and tablet charged during long periods of surveillance. Powering the generator via solar wasn't an option with the tree cover and cloudy skies, but he could hike back to his truck at night and plug it in while the heater warmed his body.

It hadn't taken long to establish the deputy's schedule. Patrol. Bar. Home. Rinse and repeat. All Cyrus had to do was follow. So he followed.

For the life of Cyrus, he hadn't been able to locate the tree-mounted camera Misty placed to keep an eye on her father's house, but his vantage was perfect, nonetheless. He had a direct line to the two-story structure and a view of its snow-covered gravel lot while maintaining cover in the trees.

It was a hell of a way to spend a vacation, but Misty had told him she'd be getting her security clients in order for a couple weeks before her plane took off for the military base in Quantico that houses the FBI training facilities. Everything she did for those clients would be time-stamped on her system because she kept it all for audits, to track her time investments in their organizations, which meant she couldn't be tied to his activities if shit went sideways, and that was crucial. If she'd known he sat on the hillside, even less where he planned to be soon, she might have chained him to her cage.

But justice couldn't be delayed forever. The statute of limitations shouldn't protect assholes from accountability, especially drunkard assholes who drooled over the bodies of their teenage daughters then tracked them down years later and broke into their apartments to sniff their fucking laundry.

His thoughts vanished as the front door swung open, and a woman with medium-length brown hair and a pale complexion stepped out onto the stoop in her robe. This was Nora Aiken, the woman Misty'd told him about who'd shacked up with her father.

A pair of leather boots reaching up to her bare knees left deep imprints in the snow as she crossed the gravel. She'd exited each of the last three days, made the journey through a winding path down the dirt road to the mailbox, then returned a few minutes later. One appearance per day, but on an unpredictable schedule.

Cyrus's burner buzzed in his pocket.

"The fuck?" he muttered, struggling with his padding to free it.

"Yeah?"

"Hello, Cyrus."

"Who is this?"

"We haven't spoken much, have we? Don't worry I'm not offended. This is Sam Lockhart."

Cyrus watched as the woman in the robe started her ascent toward the bend leading out to the mailbox on the mountain road. The round trip would only take a few minutes.

"I'm impressed you managed to get my burner number, Sam. How many guys do you have watching me? Did they break into my truck?" He'd stowed the burner in the F-150 to avoid Marsha's questions. Although he'd taken to the iPhone she'd bought him, old habits die hard.

It occurred to him that he hadn't checked the street outside Anastasia Clark's high-rise for the Lockhart Tactical spies. He'd assumed they would've been recalled, and he wanted to curse himself for his shortsightedness.

"You really shouldn't leave your possessions in that old thing. Too easy to get into."

"You know you just confessed to a crime, right?"

"I was hoping we could cut through the bullshit."

"I've seen your interviews, Sam. You shouldn't chastise others for bullshit."

Lockhart chuckled. "So, my guys saw you outside Anastasia Clark's apartment."

"Surprised you didn't pull those fellas once the article went viral."

"Which is why I'm calling. Truth is, I couldn't resist. I just had to ask why you have a hair up your ass for me?"

"Did you call to confess?"

"I have nothing to confess."

"Bullshit like that is why I have a hair up my ass for you, Sam. People like you think they can operate with abandon, do whatever they like. But, hey, this is America, and capitalism is the best thing we've got. I'm good with that."

"Then what's your problem?"

"I don't like it when people like Ethan Pierce buy up political seats. It's a flaw in the system."

"That's Ethan."

"And you're going to pretend you weren't part of it."

"That's Ethan," he repeated. "He has his own ideas."

"And he funded your new company through his wife's LLC."

"Okay, so you've done some homework."

The snide humor in his tone made Cyrus wish he could reach through the phone. "Why don't you get to the point, I'm kind of in the middle of something."

"The past is in the past. Bygones. It's time for everyone to be practical. Your antics of late have caused me some trouble. I'm not such a small man I can't admit that. But LPS is going to succeed anyway. It's inevitable. Do you know why?"

"Oh, please enlighten me."

"Because the government has failed. It can't do the job. How many people have died in mass shootings this year, Jennings? How many last year? Someone must fill in the gap. But the bottom line? The big reason it's going to work is because my son is rotting in the fucking ground, too, and I won't have it be for nothing! You put your fucking nose in the wrong goddamned business!"

"Are you finished?" Cyrus cast his gaze up the road just in time to see Nora appear.

"You know Cyrus, I think I am. I just have one parting question for you."

"What's that?"

"How's the coroner doing?"

Rage. Cyrus growled through his teeth. "Did you just threaten my lady, motherfucker? You seem to have forgotten what happened the night I arrested Ethan Pierce. How I marched up that mountain in two feet of snow and took out everything between me and him. So, let me tell you something, you half-wit piece of shit, you go anywhere near anyone I care about, and you'll end up in a plot beside Jake Ramon. I dare you to ask me another fucking question."

The call disconnected. Cyrus eyed the burner, considered snapping it in half. But Nora had reappeared and, if he was going to get his work done, he needed to move.

Lockhart wouldn't go near Marsha, he'd just wanted the rise. Just another entitled rich guy who couldn't keep his peace, and Cyrus wasn't about to let him fuck this up. He drew a few deep breaths then moved.

The last three days' worth of surveillance left him confident Misty's father wouldn't return before the end of his shift. So he laid his gear at the foot of the tree then stomped down the hill. Making his way to the center of the gravel lot, he faced her.

Nora's attention was trained on a stack of envelopes as she flipped from one to the other. It wasn't until she was fifteen feet away that her head came up.

She flinched, lumbered backward, then fell onto her duff in the snow.

"Sorry," Cyrus said, throwing out his hands. "I didn't mean to scare you."

She spider crawled in reverse, dragging her backside and leaving a trail on the powder. The purple and red swelling he'd noticed beneath her right eye through his binoculars two days before had receded, leaving a blackened surface with purple, webbed veins.

He'd played out the encounter in his mind too many times to count, but if Cyrus knew anything, plans were facades human beings used to delude themselves into a sense of control that almost never panned out. After all, here was this big black guy standing in her drive who couldn't have driven past her while she was en route to the mailbox. Intimidating. But at least he had her unwavering attention, as planned.

Holding position, he held up his badge, a move he'd debated with himself, over and over. But the shield didn't have his name on it, and if he played his cards right, she wouldn't care.

"I'm with the FBI."

Her ghostly face stretched into confusion. She struggled to her feet then reached for the dropped letters.

Moments passed as the pair stared at each other. Nora Aiken cast a glance over one shoulder and down the drive.

"I've seen fake badges just like that. My boyfriend is a cop."

"I know who he is. That's why I'm here."

"What do you want?"

"To give you this." He reached into his jacket pocket to retrieve the one item he'd left there. A business card. He held it out, but stayed put, leaving the decision to take it up to her.

Nora eyed him for a long time before she finally ambled forward, snatched the card, then scanned it.

"You don't look like a Tiffany Brooks."

When he'd asked Tiffany for permission to hand the card over, just before she stepped onto the stage of Morning Nation, she hadn't hesitated.

He chuckled. "No, I suppose I don't. And I promise you, she's much easier to look at."

Nora tilted her head to one side, and Cyrus wondered if the joviality of his tone had been a bit much, but Marsha had always said he had a warm disposition, so he hoped that came across.

"What do you and Tiffany Brooks want?"

"I want you to be safe. She wants to put you in a guest room in a nice townhouse in Denver."

"Who am I to you? What do you know about my safety?"

And here was the hard part. Cyrus didn't want to implicate Misty in any of this. If the plan went sideways and Nora sided with her abuser—as sufferers of domestic abuse often did—he didn't want her father knowing her new identity. He'd found Anastasia, but she was in the process of relocating, and Tom Rhymer's brother-in-law would be signing her lease to ensure her confidentiality.

Of course, her latest article revealed a murder plot at one of the most controversial companies in the country, and her star would inevitably rise. But if things went according to plan, her father would steer clear.

He tapped beneath his own eye, reflecting what covered the flesh under hers. "When's the last time you looked in the mirror? That's what I know about your safety."

"What's it to you?"

"Call me a guardian angel. Add to that shiner how you've been limping to your mailbox for the last couple days, and I think you could use one."

Her forehead wrinkled, but Cyrus noticed she didn't have many. She might not have been thirty, yet. Another long moment passed between them, and neither moved as a frigid wind rippled their clothes.

"You've been watching me?"

He nodded. "I have."

"This have something to do with his daughters?"

The question caught Cyrus off guard. Despite imagining at length how the encounter would go, he hadn't accounted for that one.

"Let's just say there are interested parties with enough connections to ensure he never touches you again. We can move you, change your identity, and even find you employment. None of it will cost you a cent and, by the time we're done, the deputy won't be able to find you."

She took a few steps toward him then leaned in, as if she didn't want the trees to hear. "He'll kill me."

"If you stay here, he may do that anyway. It might not even be intentional, but that's why we have different classifications of murder. Do you want to take that risk, or do you want to pack your stuff right now, come with me, and change your life for the better? Once I have you tucked away, I'll give you my card, and you'll have an FBI agent at your beck and call should you ever run into trouble."

"Shit." She walked around him toward the front door.

He wheeled. "Is that a no?"

She mounted the porch, turned, then swept her arms out to her sides, one hand still grasping the envelopes.

"I got no family. He doesn't let me have friends. If I had money, I'd have been out of here a long time ago. You promising me I'll never see him again? That I won't end up in one of those shelters for battered women?"

"That's exactly what I'm promising you."

"Then you must be my guardian angel, after all. I don't have much to pack. You want to come inside?"

"If it's all the same, I'll watch the driveway."

Nora's gaze flicked toward the snowy drive and back, her cold-pinkened cheeks whitened. "Good idea."

.   .   .

Phase two. With Nora Aiken tucked into a hotel room thirty minutes away in a neighboring county with instructions to call Tiffany's number if Cyrus wasn't back the next morning, he drove to the deputy's favorite watering hole. The Harty Hog's parking lot was flat in contrast to the surrounding hills. Aside from the filthy places where tires sloshed mud around, the pavement was covered in snow.

It might've surprised non-drinkers how regimented alcoholics could be. How they'd carve out their drinking time, keep a clock on it so they could squeeze by in life after the blur of inebriation passed and the clouds of suffering moved in. It took practice, dedication to their chosen demon, and although he understood the lengths people would go to, Cyrus didn't delude himself into believing he understood the depths of addiction.

He just didn't get on with the booze, and he thanked his lucky stars for that.

Many heavy drinkers were still social creatures. The movie theater images of stumbling addicts alone in their filthy homes were a cliché that often didn't apply. These socialites would stop in for a few with the boys or girls just to get their social fix, to get the ball rolling on the work they'd finish at home.

The deputy was one of these.

It was the same story every night. He'd pull his cruiser around the far side of the building to back it into the last spot butting up against the thick trees behind the place. Always in his cruiser, because who was gonna pull over a cop if he swerved a little? And he probably changed at the station because he never wore his uniform.

This night, he rolled in at seven-forty-five, like clockwork.

Having peeled off his white nylon and replaced it with black outer shells, Cyrus pulled on a matching ski mask with the tiniest eye slits he could find. When the sheriff's deputy backed in, Cyrus could see the emblem of the badge emblazoned in the driver's side door from the tree he lurked behind. Like usual, there were no other vehicles on that side of the building.

Although Lockhart's call earlier in the day had amped him up to 11, it'd also given him an idea during the drive across the mountain roads. A new strategy for this encounter. So he'd revised his lines, practiced them over and over as he stood in the frigid darkness waiting for the deputy to pull up.

His heart ticked up a notch when the sound of the door handle echoed in the quiet cold, and Cyrus drew short, deep breaths, careful to release them over one shoulder to keep the steam from catching the deputy's attention.

The cop cast a quick glance at the trees where Cyrus stood. His heart double-timed it, but when Misty's father turned toward the rear of his car, Cyrus burst from the trees. During his planning, he'd considered taking him down after he was inebriated, but he wanted this son of a bitch to *remember* the event with clarity. Fearing his boots crunching on the snow would alert his prey, Cyrus hauled ass.

The deputy never turned. Cyrus planted the stunner in his back and pulled the trigger.

Misty's father cried out, and Cyrus checked the perimeter as he tumbled to the ground. The next few seconds lasted an eternity, as he waited for someone to come around the corner to investigate the noise. But no one appeared. Doubling over, Cyrus grabbed the collar of the fucker's jacket then dragged him to the edge of the pock-marked pavement he'd cleared before hiding in the trees.

"Put your cheek on the concrete."

"Wha—? Do you know who—?"

"That's why we're here. Because of who you are." He dropped the stunner into the snowpack, whipped his 9mm from its holster, then pressed it to the deputy's temple. "Put your cheek on the damned concrete."

Eyes wide and focused on the gun, the deputy opened his mouth a few inches then closed it. Cyrus pressed the barrel harder against his temple, really baring down.

"Do it or I'll just pop you right here."

His prisoner complied. Cyrus yanked a rag from his shell's pocket then shoved it in the deputy's mouth. Then he stood and planted his boot on the back of the guy's neck. The cop flinched, howled something inde-cipherable.

"I'm going to talk. You're going to listen. Fuck with me, and you're gonna be sucking chicken noodle through a straw the rest of your miserable fucking life because I'm gonna smash your face into the sidewalk. Hum two syllables if you understand."

"Mm hmm."

"I have video of you breaking into the reporter's apartment," he lied. "Dead to rights. I should just turn it over to the Denver cops, but my boss thinks a warning would do the job. I wanted a third option. To curb stomp you, put one in your gut, and let you bleed out. But I'm biased. I don't like cops.

"Lucky for you, I don't make the calls, and the boss is more deliberative. You see, if anything were to happen to Anastasia Clark, people might think he had some-thing to do with whatever untimely fate befell her."

"Mm mmm?"

"Yeah, my boss. She wrote an unflattering article about him recently, and if any harm came to her, well, who do you think they'd blame—or, as pigs like you are apt to do, frame? So, listen up, dickweed.

"Your daughter's dead to you. If we see you anywhere within one hundred miles of her, you decompose. No warnings. And you won't even get the soup. Instead, it'll be an unmarked concrete grave at a construction site. Gimme two syllables."

"Mm hmm. Mm hmm."

Funny how quickly bullies complied when they encountered someone with ability and a spine.

"In case you have any doubt about what I'm saying, I want you to go home tonight and Google something for me. Can you remember?"

"Mm hmm."

"Lockhart Tactical."

"Hmm?"

"Oh, you've heard of us. Then you know our pockets are deep, and we have enough guys like me to track you. Hell, we've had a camera in the woods by your house. Fuck with us, and you die. Go to the media, you fucking die. Go anywhere near your daughter, and we'll take your fingernails first.

"Roll away from me and face your bumper." Cyrus raised his boot.

The deputy rolled onto his side.

"Stay right there and count to one-hundred. If I look back and you're on your feet, I'm willing to bet I can put two rounds in you before you reach the corner. You up for a foot race?"

"Hmph," he muttered.

Cyrus yanked the rag from his mouth. "I couldn't quite make that out."

"No!"

Cyrus backed away and into the woods. "Oh, and if I still haven't proven we mean business, we know about your other daughter, too. Stay away from both, asshole."

When he was sure the deputy couldn't see him anymore, he hauled ass across the half-mile jaunt to his GPS-free F-150 in an abandoned strip mall.

He thought of Misty and smiled.

EPILOGUE

Ethan Pierce sat in the gen-pop communal area watching a replay of Tiffany Brooks's interview with *Morning Nation*. On the tablet in his lap, the headline LOCKHART PUBLIC SECURITY UNDER SCRUTINY AS POSSIBLE MURDER PLOT EXPOSED glared back at him. He waved Bubba over.

"Give me the fucking phone."

The prison cop acquiesced without comment then strolled away. The line buzzed.

"Yes, sir. This is Tim."

"What'd Lockhart say?"

"Country Bank decided not to sign. He's still got a few customers on the hook, but they're holding off to see how it plays out. What do you want to do, shut it down?"

"No. What about Xavier?"

"Mum's the word. He's not cooperating. His

attorney count is up to ten, and we got Milo Masters for first chair."

Masters was famous for getting an acquittal for a Hollywood Director who'd fled the country after murdering his assistant. Sloppiness got him extradited back to the states then Masters got him off the rap.

"Good thing he owed me a favor. What're the odds of Xavier walking out of there?"

"McDaniel might be able to hang the dumbest jurors about the Texas setup..."

Ethan finished the thought. "But not Parson's suicide."

"Even a miracle worker couldn't get him out of that one. His GPS puts him at the scene. Tom Rhymer is telling a story about an interaction between Chet Parsons and the XO the day of the crime that shines a nasty light. Xavier's going in for life."

"Anyone know where Rhymer is?"

"Negative."

"And the Fitz Banner legislation?"

"Dead on the house floor."

Ethan growled.

"Any more on this Daniels bitch?"

"Yeah. Turns out she showed up at the *Denver Post* with an FBI agent. Talked to one of the Silver Stars who works as an editor there. That's how they figured out she was a spy."

"And you're absolutely sure there's no way to get the emails she stole tossed?"

"Judge seems sympathetic to the prosecution. But like I said, if the Live Oak thing doesn't get him, the GPS and crime scene evidence will. They didn't need the emails to figure out Chet's murder, so that fruit doesn't hang from a poisoned vine. He didn't even make bail."

"Well, a soldier can be brave in the face of death, but death comes absent suffering. Iron bars and a six-by-nine cell for the rest of one's life add a different equation altogether. I think you're going to need to handle Xavier."

There was a long pause on the line.

"Tim, the call is secure." Pierce eyed the guard standing in a distant corner. "Trust me."

"It'll be handled, but we'll want to wait a bit, give him some time to make enemies on the inside."

"Fair enough. Trial won't happen for months. Tell Sam to lay low on the PR shit. Let congress fight over the fiasco while he tries to sign more clients. At the end of the day, the service is real, and a rogue exec trying to protect himself from war crime prosecution isn't sinking our ship. Until Xavier is out of the picture, I don't want to hear Sam saying anything stupid, like how LPS is glad they found out about Xavier before he caused more trouble. That could get him to flip, then he'll have marshals to watch his ass."

"Smart, sir."

"Don't sound so surprised, Tim. Anything else?"

Another long pause.

"Tim. Talk, dammit."

"Well, it's about the agent who accompanied Misty Daniels to the *Post*. Turns out he's also been snooping around at Live Oak and was seen at Anastasia Clark's apartment building. Again, Lockhart hasn't been telling us the whole story."

"He and I are going to have a come-to-Jesus, real soon. Now, why do I care about an FBI agent?"

The answer came in a flash before Tim could answer.

"It was Cyrus Jennings."

"Yes, sir."

He ruminated, his temples throbbing. His favorite Mozart track accompanied the images in his mind. With the Clark article, a low percussion. Then the swelling rise of violins. Cellos enter the fray when sheriff Newsome steps up to his podium for a press conference to announce his partnership with the FBI. Finally, the orchestra's full-on attack—the crescendo as Tiffany Brooks ties the ends together in an interview on the highest-rated morning show on network TV. Then the camera pans to the conductor, his little stick bouncing vibrantly in the air as he bends and dips towards the instrument sections in perfect time. After the abrupt, staccato ending, Cyrus Jennings turns to the crowd of two in an otherwise empty auditorium to take his bow. When he rises, a wide smile expands his features in the eye of Ethan Pierce's mind.

"Vendetta." The perfect title for the piece.

The fucking fed. Cyrus Jennings, who hadn't been able to lock Sam and Ethan in neighboring cells, had instead written a little tune.

Sam's selective information sharing was rending their fabric. If he wanted to partner with Ethan, he needed to dispense with delusions that he held all the pieces—that what Ethan knew should be contingent upon Lockhart's benevolence.

But that was the rub, wasn't it? Ethan sat in a Lockhart prison and, despite the niceties for all he'd sacrificed—the cell usage, the putting green, the Internet access—the giant guard whose kid Ethan was putting through private school could be bought just as easily by Sam Lockhart if Ethan became a headache.

But Lockhart also knew he only walked around free because Ethan's silence kept him out of confinement. He'd shrouded Sam's part in Gabby Sutton's murder, kept the mention out of his mouth instead of cutting a deal because he had bigger plans. Important measures needed to save a nation from itself. If he reversed that course and implicated Lockhart, it would be him moving into federal protection for the duration of Sam's trial.

However, Lockhart's government connections almost rivaled his own, and Ethan could never keep such a move quiet.

A stalemate, at best, and maybe a heart-to-heart with Lockhart while he was at his weakest would help them bury hatchets so they could focus on the real problem.

It was time to focus. Now that he had the mental image of Cyrus Jennings waving his baton, Ethan knew he'd been playing the wrong game—one where Cyrus Jennings had left the law behind for his vendetta. Where he'd crossed the line from federal cop to judge and jury.

From a simple spade to a trump card.

To his credit, Tim had remained silent while Ethan deliberated. "Where is Misty Daniels?"

"Locked down in a place on the river. High security. But the more interesting question is, where *will* she be."

"Really? Why's that, Tim?"

"They're sending her to the FBI academy. Turns out, she isn't even an agent. She's been serving under a court order to keep her out of prison."

"You get that from Sam?"

"No. I made a few calls."

"I'm impressed. You're really expanding your network."

"Thank you, Mr. Pierce."

Ethan sighed. "I fear my ego has stunted me, Tim."

"What's that, sir?"

"Despite that federal son of a bitch getting the drop on me in my own house and sending me to this shit hole to rot, I've underestimated him."

"What would you like to do, sir?"

"What would I like to do?" He chuckled then snorted. "He's playing my game now, Tim. I'm going to *welcome* him to it."

He hung up the cell, then dropped it on the floor, where he stomped it into oblivion.

"Then I'm going right for his queen before I systematically wipe the rest of his pieces off the board."

THANK YOU

Thank you for reading *GUARDIAN PROTOCOL*.

What lines Cyrus did cross to force his exile from DC?

Be sure to read *Conflict Of Interest*, a Cyrus Jennings novella available exclusively to our VIP readers.

You'll also get news, pre-release reading opportunities, deal alerts, and book reviews and recommendations — because we read faster than we write!

Get it all at AlexParman.com

ALSO BY ALEX PARMAN

Get them all at AlexParman.com

ABOUT THE AUTHOR

Alex Parman is the *nom de plume* for the writing team of Ric Beard and Chris Niles.

This collaboration is a long time coming. Friends for nearly a decade, Chris and Ric first started talking about this series in 2018. They drafted the first book and outlined the second. But after Ric cut his teeth writing sci-fi, his game-lit series took off and demanded his full attention. He developed into a drafting demon in the highly detail-oriented game-lit genre, but despite twenty successful gaming sagas, he couldn't shake the pull back to thrillers.

Chris cut her teeth on international thriller, then settled into a double life writing sea adventure (think Jimmy Buffett meets Indiana Jones) and plotting cozy mysteries. But she's always looking for new places to hide a body and get away with it. So she can't stay away from thriller for very long either. So here we are.

Its a match made for the ticking clock, and we'll be doing this as long as you're willing to keep reading them!

ACKNOWLEDGMENTS

Writing a novel is never a solitary act. But when it's a team doing the writing, the list doubles of folks who deserve our heartfelt thanks. (Thankfully, we know a lot of the same people and they've encouraged us as a team, so just bear with us, okay?)

First, our eternal thanks go to Emily and Mark, who stand behind us, cheer us on, and make sure we eat. (They also keep the businesses running and the lights on, so we appreciate everything they do for us!)

We also are grateful to our editor Staci Troilo, who makes our words worth reading.

We are indebted to Becca, who talks Chris off the ledge regularly and back to Emily again, who does the same for Ric.

But most importantly, it's you, our readers, who make this dream possible for both of us. We know that you could choose to read anything you want, and we're grateful you chose us.

Thank you.